Anywhere But Here

THE TRADIE LADY SERIES

BOOK THREE

RIAN BIRCH

www.rianbirchauthor.com

Edited by Kathryn Harris

Proofread by Booklyst Editing Services

First Edition: March 2026

eBook ISBN: 9781763884076

Paperback ISBN: 9781763884052

To all of you who tried ***so hard*** *to colour within the lines while growing up. I see you.*

Australian Language and Slang

Anywhere But Here is set in Australia, and has Australian English throughout.

This book features a road trip into the outback, so there's going to be some Aussie slang to keep an eye out for:

Akubra - A wide-brimmed Australian-style hat, often worn by rural farmers.

Biscuits - Similar to crackers (if savoury) or cookies (if sweet).

Bloody Hell - God damn it! *technically British, but Aussies use it a lot!

Bloody Woop Woop - Middle of nowhere.

Brekkie Roll - A breakfast damper roll with bacon and egg.

Damper - An Australian yeast-free bread, often cooked over a campfire.

Doughies - Short for doughnut, and used when steering in fast circles, usually in a car or on a jet ski / boat.

KI - Kangaroo Island. Pronounced as "Kay-Eye", which is how refer to it in South Australia.

Long Drop - An outback toilet. Usually an enclosed stall with a wooden bench and a hole cut out of it... with a long drop. ;)

My Shout - The drinks or food are on me.

Quilt - A doona.

Road Train - Long freight trucks also known as doubles or triples, depending on how many trailers they're pulling.

Servo - A gas / petrol station.

Sook - Someone who is a complainer or whinger.

Station - A cattle or sheep farm, usually found in parts of outback / regional Australia.

Stuffed - Exhausted.

ONE
Brooke

Fuck this place.

Long strides carried Brooke to the end of the street. The itch inside her grew, mind racing. *Where is it?*

She picked up the pace and jogged faster. Running. Sprinting.

Everything blurred past her under the dim streetlights, familiar and different all at once. There was the bike path. The river. Brooke's chest burned, her messenger bag thumping against her hip with every stride.

The opening came into view.

It was still there.

She exhaled, the sound loud and rough.

Her legs wobbled as she ran down the slope to the tall reeds. The angular, stacked rocks sat beyond them, barely lit by the pathway lights. She clambered onto the first rock and hopped across.

One. Two. Three—Four.

Made it.

Brooke bent over and gulped in a lungful of air. The effort to get here was absurd.

Probably because she wasn't nineteen anymore.

No. Brooke Mayfield was twenty-nine and back here in this shithole.

Home.

It didn't feel like home anymore.

She straightened and took in the space around her. The old gums towered along the riverbank, closing out the dark sky above.

Ten years.

The family house had been sold, three streets down from where Hayley and Marie had settled down—where Brooke had landed on their doorstep and into their guest bedroom five weeks ago, her chest growing tighter with each passing day. At least it wasn't Steven's house, wedged in the kid's bedroom between her nieces. No, thank you.

Staying with her sister, Hayley, was bad enough.

Always with the questions, as though she cared. Hayley's face pinched as she tried to solve Brooke like a puzzle—a problem to be fixed.

Why are you back, Brooke?

What's wrong, Brooke?

This was never her plan. Travelling was her life. Living and working overseas was all she knew. Not being back in this bottomless hole of nothing.

Yet here she was.

Adelaide.

She'd shoved this place so far back into the recesses of her mind that being here felt like a dream.

No, a nightmare.

Brooke dropped onto her favourite rock, worn smooth from years of use. Her fingers traced the long gash in the stone. While she liked to think this was her spot to get away, many others must have come here too. If only the rock could talk, revealing the stories and secrets it held.

Brooke exhaled, finally away from piercing eyes, smiling faces, and so many questions. She picked up a pebble and flicked it into the water with a *plink*.

Of course Hayley still had her game nights, where everyone had so much fun, living their perfect little lives with their perfect partners. *Ugh*. Brooke couldn't be surrounded by that. Not tonight. She had no answers to give.

Her frown etched deeper and her temple throbbed.

The ripples spread across the surface of the water. She scuffed in another rock with her foot, new rings chasing the old until they faded into nothing. Just like the life she'd left behind—the expectations she never lived up to, that she strove to achieve but never quite grasped. Always a step behind her siblings. In the shadows.

Life was better on her own anyway.

Travel had given her that freedom. Freedom to discover who she was when she was just Brooke, without the expectation of being a Mayfield.

She pulled her legs up, chin resting on her knees. The water trickled around the stones, a balm trying to slow her heartbeat. Frogs played their soothing cadence alongside crickets in the reeds. She closed her eyes, willing her frown to ease and allowing herself this moment with no one around. To just... be.

Sorting out her next steps was a top priority if she

didn't want to be stuck here forever. She'd spent the morning applying for every job she had the slimmest chance of getting: admin roles, bartending, even local hostels in the city. While overseas, she'd flitted from job to job depending on the location. A Jill of all trades, her last role was a kitchen hand for a yoga retreat in the heart of Canggu in Bali's south. But even the cheap living in Bali had risen in cost. Travelling full time now was a different world from when she'd first left for Paris at nineteen.

Jumping back to Australia, back to family, was the one viable option. She was tired of trying to make it work. She needed time to regroup, re-energise and replan. Her dwindled savings only added to the pressure—the pitiful amount stretching even less now she'd left Indonesia. Dollar breakfasts at the morning markets in Bali were a thing of the past. Now, it was a choice between eating Hayley's fancy granola that cost a week's worth of meals back in Bali or paying thirty dollars for a latte and avocado toast if she headed to a cafe. It was like being a teenager again, back to relying on others. Though, now she had no low paying job and no parents to fall back on. Technically asking her parents was an option, but hell could freeze over before she uttered those words aloud. She had no intention of speaking to them now she was back. They were probably too busy anyway.

Her phone vibrated in her bag. Was Hayley wondering where she went? Slipping into that parental role again and checking if Brooke was behaving herself?

Another vibration broke her solitude. Her eyes snapped open as she yanked the phone out.

Brett has swiped right, say hi!

Why not? Nothing better to do tonight.

Fifteen minutes later, a Jeep careened around the corner, pulling up to Brooke's dropped pin. The passenger window wound down and the driver leaned over. He flashed her a brilliant white smile, matching his profile picture exactly.

"Brett?" she asked.

His eyes dipped, roving over her low-cut top. The guys were always the same—too much money and not enough sense. No strings at least.

"Hi," he replied, his confidence wafting out like his French cologne. He leaned across and pushed open the door.

She smiled, slipping into the car. His hand landed on her thigh before she'd even clicked on her seatbelt.

Might as well have some fun in Boredom Town.

"Hey," Hayley said as Brooke snuck through the lounge room.

She hadn't expected her sister to still be awake, reading alone on the sofa. Hayley sat in her long-sleeved PJs, a matching set in plum satin, of course, with a blanket pulled over her lap. Her long blonde hair—the same dead-straight type as Brooke's—brushed her shoulders. Hayley's gaze swept over Brooke. Yet another moment to be judged.

Brooke swallowed, hoping to suppress her blush. She raised her chin, gripping her shoes tighter in her hand as she continued through the room with purpose, Brett's acrid cologne no doubt betraying her with every step.

"Night," Brooke mumbled as she made it to the bottom of the stairs.

"Um..."

Brooke glanced over her shoulder. Hayley's self-development book was now closed in her lap. The room's single lamp cast a soft golden glow that shadowed most of her features, but Brooke could just make out the slight frown.

"What?" Brooke snapped, turning to face her. *Argh, that's not*—midnight was not the time to start a conversation. Especially when she reeked like this, a shower calling her to wash away her decisions, the touch she thought she'd wanted. Needed.

Hayley stared for a moment, opening her mouth then closing it. She swung her legs off the stupid blue velvet couch and let out a sigh. "I just..." She avoided Brooke's eyes, hand tracing the spine of her book. "How long are you planning on staying?"

Brooke had been waiting for that question. She wasn't good enough to stay with her sister. Hiding in her room, staying out to give them space—it hadn't made a difference. The itch to run returned, her heel pivoting back to the front door.

She remained frozen on the spot, squeezing the shoes in her hand. "I don't know."

God. Could people give her some time to catch her breath and figure her shit out?

"Have you still been applying to those jobs?"

"Yes, Hayley. I haven't been sitting around doing nothing."

"Clearly." Hayley looked at her then. Brooke wished she hadn't. Not now.

Her face flamed.

"I'm going to bed. Good night." Brooke spoke through her teeth, unable to keep the edge out of her voice. At least her voice hadn't wavered.

"Sure. Night." Hayley sighed and tossed her book on the coffee table with a thud.

Brooke tensed. The pressure was back at her temples, blocking the right words to say, to explain, or be able to answer with something—anything. Why did she get like this every damn time she was in the same room as her sister?

Brooke turned, hand gripped on the balustrade and strode upstairs.

Hayley used to be Brooke's favourite family member. Technically, she still was. She just didn't know who Hayley was anymore. Her sister lived the dream—perfect wife, perfect house, perfect friends. Every aspect of her sister's life was a constant reminder of how little Brooke had to her name. It was easy to forget what a failure she was when on the road, where nobody knew her.

While she'd kept in touch over the years, it wasn't as much as she should have. A Happy Birthday here or a Merry Christmas there. At this point, Brooke didn't know how to "sister" anymore. There was *before* Brooke and Hayley. And there was *now* Brooke and Hayley. Two strangers trying to tip-toe around each other, the friction growing stronger each day, and Brooke had no idea how to fix it.

She entered the bathroom, sighing as Hayley's questions rattled around on repeat. For the first time in her life, Brooke didn't know what was next. It felt like being in a car at night without the headlights on—life was still moving, but Brooke had no idea where she would end up.

She needed time. Time and a little space to figure things out.

Brooke slipped into the shower, allowing the water to cascade down her back as she stared at her hands. She rubbed at her skin, desperate to feel clean, to feel *something*. Usually, she loved a random one-night stand. A drink here, a bit of fun there. Yet tonight, it didn't hit the same. No matter how much she'd tried to relax in the moment, her mind wouldn't shut up. Every random thought wanted to step up on stage and be heard. She'd been counting down the minutes, questioning why what was usually a fun time now felt... empty and... almost dirty.

Was it because she wasn't travelling anymore? Living overseas, hooked on the vibrancy of life and bouncing with the same energy as all the other backpackers and people passing through?

Tears joined the streams of water trailing down her body.

If only showering could clean up her life too.

TWO

JJ

The woman across from JJ droned on, blending into the chit-chat from the over-crowded restaurant.

"...still haven't got the ignition fixed. It runs enough to get me where I need to go..."

JJ shifted in her seat. Yeah, this wasn't working.

"...I don't have the money anyway. Oh! Last night I was out with friends, and you've *got* to try this new Greek restaurant that's just opened in the city..."

Red flag. Red flag. Red flag.

This was the cost of dating these days. Spending an hour with a stranger, attempting to look empathetic instead of cringing at their lifestyle choices. JJ tried to keep eye contact with the woman. How was it this hard to find someone who had their shit together in their thirties?

Surely.

Surely there was someone out there who'd worked their life out, no longer living paycheck to paycheck. Then they could banter over home loan rates and business overheads rather than run down cars. JJ held her barely touched beer, the crisp IPA the only thing keeping her cool. The label was wet, peeling easily as she picked at the corner. It tore right off, a satisfied smile blooming on her lips.

Eyes snagging on the woman's furrowed brows, JJ eased the corners of her mouth into a solid line. Right, empathy time. The woman continued on about her lack of finances, all while downing the most expensive glass of shiraz on the wine list. JJ's mind began a list of *Ways To Get Out of A Doomed Date*.

Phone a friend?

Her phone was in her jacket pocket on the back of the chair. Damn. She didn't want to make it obvious.

Head to the toilet, then bolt?

Nope—she'd taken Remi's advice to try Korean, and this place was so tiny, there was no bathroom.

She just had to say it. *Thanks for your time, but this isn't a good fit, yadda yadda*. She'd wait for the next gap in their conversation and get out of here.

This was her seventh failed date in the last month. What was the definition of crazy? Doing the same thing, expecting different results?

Yep. That was JJ's dating life.

Crazy.

Jess and Remi made dating look so easy. It was a pity JJ wasn't hiring any apprentices anytime soon, as that seemed to work out well for Remi. No, JJ was just fine painting houses on her own.

With the constant questions from her family and seeing Remi paired up with so much love, JJ had jumped onto dating apps full steam ahead. It was time. Putting so much focus into her home and business over the years, she'd be the first to confess she'd swept her dating life under a rug. A chance connection had never come along, not like her friends and parents had experienced.

Watching Remi and Jess together was a stark reminder of what she could have if she put herself out there. Her hypothesis was: the faster she dated, the quicker she could find The One—her perfect person. Though, at the moment, all she was doing was burning herself out. Her upcoming holiday couldn't get here quick enough, just to give her a break from the dating pool.

Plates clattered on the next table over where a noisy family shared food, shoving the dishes between them.

JJ blinked. Her date's glass of shiraz sat empty in front of her while the woman leaned over, gathering her handbag. "So sorry, I've got to rush off."

JJ blinked again as the woman pulled at her dress, smoothing it down as she stood.

"It was lovely to meet you. I'll be in touch." She pressed herself between the tiny tables and fled out the door.

JJ blinked a third time.

Thanks for your time, but this isn't a good fit. She hadn't even given JJ a chance to spit it out.

So, that was how the woman saved her money. Touché.

After finishing the last of her beer, JJ paid their tab and left alone.

The moon was too bright overhead as JJ drove home, taunting her with its clarity as she plunged further into the murky dating pool. Another one to strike off the list.

JJ stepped inside her house and let out a long sigh. Jess looked up from her study notes at the kitchen bench, a hand threaded into her blonde hair. A failed date was at least more entertaining than TAFE study. JJ didn't miss those days.

Eyes tracked JJ's movement across the room. "You're back early. No luck?"

JJ avoided Jess's eyes and beelined for the fridge.

Roommate shame was a real thing.

Living alone, she could get away with everything. Living with Jess? Not one failed date or bad hair day went unnoticed.

She was always there, ready to ask the big questions and grill JJ in a way that made her feel seen and heard, but also wanting to run for the hills. It was a pity she wasn't attracted to Jess. Actually, no, that was a good thing. Her best friend, Remi, would be growling at the mere thought of someone being interested in her girl.

JJ grabbed a beer, twisted the cap with her arm, and leaned against the benchtop. "No luck," she replied to Jess, who was still watching JJ, arms now resting on her stack of notes.

Jess was the perfect roommate, exactly the kind of person JJ had been looking for. She had Remi to thank for putting them in touch and couldn't believe that was over a month ago now. Jess and Remi had been dating for around the same time, but were taking things slow, so she couldn't see Jess moving out anytime soon.

Jess frowned and pushed out her bottom lip. "Bugger. What was wrong with this one?"

JJ scoffed and took a swig of beer.

Jess stared.

"You don't even know how the night went. She might not have liked *me*."

Jess raised a single eyebrow.

JJ mumbled into her beer.

"What was that?" Jess tilted her head, eyes zeroed in. She waited with slow, unwavering blinks.

"She *clearly* wasn't my type," JJ burst out, arms flinging and almost spilling her beer. She should've known. "She arrived late, droned on and on about having no money while rattling off all the fancy restaurants she'd dined at lately, all while batting her stupid false eyelashes at me. Then, to top it all off, she left me with the bill!"

"You poor thing. That must've been terrible." Jess mock-consoled her.

"It was torture," JJ persisted. "I wanted to point out all the ways she could save her money rather than whinging about it. Instead, I took an extra swig of my beer to make my big mouth shut up."

"I commend you on holding back from trying to solve this woman's life problems on your *first date*." Jess's face told her she did not, in fact, commend her. As kind as Jess could be, she also wasn't afraid to call JJ out. "First dates are like a job interview, a get-to-know-you gig. Do you get along with the person or are you attracted to them?"

"No and no." JJ scrunched up her nose. "Not after meeting her in person anyway."

"You gotta give 'em a bit of a chance, JJ." Jess sat up straight, a piece of notepaper sticking to her arm. She pulled it off and continued, "While I agree she doesn't sound like the best fit, I'm not sure judging your dates' everyday flaws straight off the bat is gonna get you far. They're only human."

JJ folded her arms. "I can't help that I know what I want."

"Just be careful you're not making up this ideal woman who doesn't exist." Jess mimed doing the robot.

A smile tugged at JJ's lips as she chuckled at her roommate's antics.

"I don't see them as perfect machines, I just want someone perfect for me. Same values, interesting personality, have their life together..."

Jess's blue eyes were unwavering, pressing JJ to dig deeper.

"Well, it's important," JJ said.

Everyone had standards, and for good reason. The only problem was, the more dates JJ went on, the longer her list had become. Still, when she met the right woman, she wouldn't hesitate.

Jess's features relaxed. "I get that. I don't mean lower your standards or settle for less. Knowing what you want is half the battle. Just make sure you're seeing them for who they really are. Holding people up to high expectations—especially if they need to meet every standard you've set—could be holding you back. Just think about it, okay?"

JJ shifted, leaning an arm on the bench and looking away.

"Maybe, you just need a break for a bit?" Jess continued. "From dating, and maybe even everything else for a few days."

JJ looked back at Jess, lips pressing together. "I'm trying. The time's booked off and everything."

"I've heard that once or twice before. Gotta watch you

tradie ladies and your skewed work-life balance. You saw where that got Remi."

"You're a tradie lady now too, remember." JJ eyed the study notes Jess had been working on. "And, as I heard it, you patched Remi up *real* good."

Jess threw a pen at her, narrowly missing her head.

"Hey!" JJ lifted her beer in the air to protect her face. "Missed me."

She launched a kitchen sponge next, clocking JJ on the chin.

"Gotcha. And I don't want you changing the subject on me," Jess said with a wide grin. "Why haven't I heard about this time off? Haven't seen you planning anything."

JJ's stomach churned. She had two whole weeks cleared in her work calendar. But whenever she sat in front of her laptop or looked something up online, she froze. She'd open a million tabs, only to close them all before actually looking through them. Now, she didn't even like checking her socials because the algorithm had latched on to her plans, showing her videos of the beautiful South Australian outback, pink lakes, cliffside hikes and dozens of other picturesque places, all within her home state.

"I have no idea where to start." JJ walked around the kitchen bench and plopped herself onto the stool next to Jess.

"Well, they say honesty is the first step," Jess replied.

JJ's face contorted. "I'm not an alcoholic." She glanced at the beer in her hand, rolled her eyes and set it down on the bench, turning to Jess. "But I know I'm procrastinating. I just can't make a decision."

Exactly like the time she'd had to choose which shade of

white for the interior of this house. She'd spent weeks going back and forth to the paint shop, getting samples, painting patches on different walls in different rooms to see the light contrast. Then more samples and showing the options to almost everyone she knew, until finally, she chose the first colour she'd picked out. As a professional painter by trade, looking back, she didn't know why she hadn't just listened to her gut—it was the same white she recommended to her clients all the time.

"You know what you want in a woman, but not where you want to holiday?" Jess prodded, breaking JJ from her thoughts.

JJ picked up one of Jess's highlighters, twirling it between her fingers. "This is different. There's so many choices and everything sounds so good, I can't pick!"

She'd even resorted to asking her family to help at last Sunday night's dinner. Instead, her parents went on a tangent about their own holiday memories, and her gran—who doesn't travel anywhere—merely shrugged.

"Is this a 'too-high-expectation' thing again? Or are you afraid of making the wrong decision?"

JJ pulled in her lips, picking her beer back up and tapping the neck against her chin.

"Hmm. Both, maybe?" She took another sip. "I want this to feel like a holiday, a complete break from my day-to-day." JJ shifted, making her back twinge. She winced and rolled her arms, trying to crack her shoulders. Her muscles remained tight.

Jess eyed the movement. "I'm all for you stepping away from the tools."

"I know," JJ replied.

Jess had made that very clear after Remi's recent work accident and recovery. JJ's conversation with Remi had been the catalyst she needed to book the time off. Seeing Remi's arm in that sling wasn't where she wanted to end up. It was time to get away from nights on the couch watching TV after slinging paint rollers all day.

"So." Jess pulled a hair tie off her wrist and threw her blonde strands up in a messy bun. "Why don't you just look up a top ten list and go to each place in order. Cut out the thinking and go with a pre-planned route. Or just pick a destination and drive?"

"Nah, I want to look into it."

Or maybe she should cancel the whole thing. It was too bloody hard. She could stay home instead, make it a staycation—get some new plants for the garden, spend extra time with her family. But... no. She had to do it, get out and actually live her life a little. Time to get her act together and just organise the thing!

But then there was work.

JJ's business, *Precision Painting*, wasn't slowing down anytime soon. She had clients booked back-to-back for the next few weeks, starting with Jess's friends—Marie and Hayley's place—which kicked off bright and early on Monday morning. It was a monster of a job: she needed to paint the entire internals of their two-storey home and patch up a few wall cracks. Her shoulders ached just thinking about it. With all that, when would she have time to sit down and look at everything? She should've pushed through the overwhelm and organised it sooner.

Well, there was no choice now: she'd have to figure it out, otherwise she'd be off in less than a month with nowhere to go.

THREE

Brooke

Brooke clicked "send" on her latest job application—a customer service officer at the airport. She sat back on the bed, snapping her laptop shut. That was enough for this morning. If she did get the airport job, maybe it could lead to cheaper travel? Oh! Maybe she should apply to be an air hostess?

She yawned, took off her headphones and stretched her arms overhead. Shower time. She slipped out of her room and across the hall, trudging to the bathroom door and swinging it open—

SMACK!

It stopped a quarter of the way.

Weird. Was it stuck on something? She shoved harder, trying to stick her head around to see the obstruction.

"What the hell?" she said, hitting the door with her shoulder. No luck.

"Hey!" a voice shouted. That wasn't Hayley. Or Marie.

Oh shit.

The person grunted, shuffling on the other side. Brooke

slammed the door shut before they got any closer. She gripped the handle with both hands, knuckles white, heart hammering. In all her time overseas, she'd never experienced an intruder in her accommodation. Less than a month back in Adelaide and now this!

Fuck. *Okay, breathe, Brooke.* Should she yell or stay quiet? She glanced around. Should she run? Wait, Hayley should still be downstairs.

"Help!" she yelled. "Hayley!"

The door wrenched from her grip. A woman stood on the other side with wide eyes, big headphones on and one arm in the air in surrender.

"Hey, hey," the woman said. "Hang on." She held up a finger and took her phone out, jabbing at the screen then slipping her headphones off. "I'm the painter—for Marie and Hayley? Is everything okay?"

Brooke could now see the woman wasn't an armed burglar. She was about the same height, with a similar shade of blonde to her own, but where Brooke's hair was over halfway down her back, the painter rocked a side fade and a pixie cut. Painters didn't usually look this cool. Or muscular. Those were some very toned arms. Curious brown eyes waited for Brooke to respond. Her overalls were extremely clean for a painter.

Brooke's eyes narrowed. Just as she opened her mouth to question her, Hayley made it to the top of the stairs, out of breath, head swinging between them.

"What's going on?" Hayley asked.

The painter's face burned crimson. "I'm so sorry, I didn't know you had anyone else in the house. My ladder was against the door." She pointed to the ladder, now moved out of the way and propped up against the wall of the bathroom.

Hayley faced Brooke, eyes imploring. "Bee, I told you *Precision Painting* was starting this week."

Brooke had no recollection of that. At all. And she'd continue to spend the rest of the week avoiding those conversations. Anything to keep away from more sisterly chats where she just froze like a fool. The sooner she got a job, the better. Especially with Hayley's recent line of questioning, it was becoming obvious they didn't like her staying with them any more than Brooke did. She was just another annoyance in their busy lives.

"I forgot." Brooke shrugged and moved past Hayley to the top of the stairs, heading to the kitchen. Her face heated with each step, flashes of her overreaction fuelling the flush until she was steaming by the time she turned on the coffee machine, her attempt to have a shower long forgotten.

She scoffed. "So embarrassing," she mouthed. Travelling alone for so long, Brooke was used to being on guard in hostels, BnB's, and the occasional seedy locations. She really needed to work on her fight or flight response now she wasn't travelling.

"Are you okay?"

Brooke jumped, then bristled as she grabbed her mug and shoved it into the coffee machine. Hayley checking on her was the last thing she wanted. It was bad enough Brooke had called out to her for help. She shouldn't be relying on her family like that. Shouldn't need to.

"Fine," she responded, eyes on the machine as it whirred loudly and sputtered an intense espresso into her mug. Hayley's footsteps faded behind her. She grabbed the cup and held it to her nose. Fuel of the gods. She took a sip, and her shoulders dropped.

The bitterness mirrored her mood as Brooke sat on the perfect couples' disdainful velvet couch. Leaving home at nineteen, she'd felt real freedom, finally away from her parents' expectations. The places she'd been, the things she'd done—ten years worth of memories. Yet sitting here and seeing everything Hayley had built with her life, it felt like Brooke's own life meant nothing. They weren't real achievements in her family's eyes. You couldn't invest memories or buy a house with travel experience.

Why had she resorted to coming back here?

She took out her phone. Maybe a few minutes mindlessly scrolling social media would help her forget this moment? Unfortunately, it was filled with friends and acquaintances; on boats, tuk-tuks, skis and even husky-pulled snow sleds. Her heart ached to be in any one of those places. She pictured being back in one of her favourite spots—Thailand. Memories rushed back to her. The amazing small islands, being on her motorbike exploring lush rain-forest-like winding roads, sailing past pristine beaches, breeze whipping in her hair. Oh, and the food. The local street stalls with their plates of pad thai and khao pad piled high.

"You look a little happier now," the painter said as she walked through the lounge carrying two very large paint tins.

Brooke's smile pulled tight. "Just wishing I was anywhere but here." She waved her phone screen at the woman, showing her current newsfeed: a sunset photo of palm trees framing an ocean so still, it looked like a mirror.

The painter paused mid-stride, changing her grip on the paint as she took a closer look at the screen.

"Oh? Me too." She placed the heavy tins on the floor. "Any travel plans?"

The painter's smile tweaked the smallest of guilt in Brooke at the earlier shrug off.

Brooke assessed the professionally-presented painter. She didn't know anything about this woman, but she didn't look like a traveller. She was probably one of those people who, if they did travel, went to a resort and had the same buffet food that they ate at home and called it a *cultural experience*.

Brooke toyed with how to answer the question that brought an ache to her gut. When *would* she travel again?

"I wish. You?" Might as well make polite conversation.

"I wish," the painter parroted with another grin, then she grimaced. "Got some time booked off but haven't done anything about it yet. All I know is I want to see South Australia."

"But you live here." Brooke scrunched up her nose. Of anywhere in the entire world, why would anyone choose Adelaide? Not even Melbourne, or Sydney? They were such vibrant cities with a lot more to see and do.

"There isn't a better place to start than right at home."

Brooke swallowed down a scoff and swung her feet onto the couch. "Hard disagree."

The painter's eyebrows shot up, and Hayley chose that moment to re-enter the lounge.

"My sister is the queen of travel. She's been everywhere. I'm sure she has a tip or two—"

"Not about Adelaide I don't."

Hayley's expression flattened as she turned away and headed into the kitchen.

The painter looked between them. "I'm sure you know a thing about travelling well though, right? Making itineraries, how to pack..."

"I guess." Brooke pulled her legs to her chest and gulped her coffee. Travelling was her life. *Was* her life. Past tense. But Brooke could book a flight to Thailand and know what river boat she needed to get on to head to Cambodia—no problem. Back here, she felt like she didn't know how to "life" stuck in the one place. Talking about someone else's travel was a kick in the teeth.

"Maybe I could pick your brain later?" the painter asked, eyes wide, pleading.

Brooke twisted her bracelets. Not likely. Her entire body ached to be away again. Could she even stomach talking about travel? This moment right now was hard enough. She tried to run a hand through her hair, getting stuck halfway. She shook her hand loose, hair flying everywhere.

Brooke sighed.

"Maybe," her traitorous mouth said.

Ugh. She couldn't just leave someone in the lurch like that.

Well, going out could be better than sitting around applying to more jobs all night, and god damn it, she always ended up helping others anyway.

"Thanks," the painter said, muscles flexing as she hefted the paint tins back up and moved to the stairs.

Cocky thing. Brooke hadn't technically agreed yet.

Brooke hopped off the couch, her limit reached for sitting on the velvet monstrosity, and returned to her room. She spent the day applying for more jobs than she could count. Two had already emailed back asking for an interview: one with a local hostel and the other for a nightshift pick packer. Not the most exciting jobs, but they at least had earning potential.

There was a knock on Brooke's bedroom door. Her eyes flicked to the time on her laptop—how was it four o'clock already?

Brooke opened her door to the painter pulling off her big headphones again.

"Hi, sorry. Um—is it possible to still pick your brains about travel? My shout. That is, if you want to go for a drink?"

Her hair, face and once-clean overalls were now dusted in a fine white powder; her right arm almost completely white. The woman noticed Brooke looking. "Oh, don't mind me. I've just finished sanding the first couple of rooms."

"Right. Looks like a messy job." Brooke smirked.

The painter grinned back. "Being dirty comes with the industry."

Brooke liked the sass with this one. As for helping her though... it really wasn't—oh jeez, the woman was giving her puppy dog eyes now. She sighed. "Fine. I suppose I could do drinks this once."

"Yes!" The painter fist pumped, sending a white cloud into the air. "*The Wharf* at five? I just need to pack up and grab a shower—clearly."

"Clearly," Brooke replied, a slight pull at the edge of her

mouth. "And..." She hoped she wouldn't regret this. "I'll come, I just need to borrow my sister's car."

"Oh. I can drive you if that's easier?"

"Um—sure. That'd be great."

The painter nodded once, picked up a few bits and pieces and headed for the stairs.

"What's your name?" Brooke called out to the incessant blonde, realising she'd never asked.

"JJ." The woman flashed a grin over her shoulder. "And you're... Bee?"

"Brooke." The last thing she wanted was anyone else referencing her childhood nickname.

"Got it." JJ disappeared down the steps.

Brooke shut her door with a click. She stopped. On the other side, a loud British woman's voice rang out. Was that a moan? "*—she dipped her finger in once, twice, before filling her. 'So greedy,' Celine purred, undoing Loretta as each thrust hit her harder than the last.*"

Brooke opened her door. Another moan. The source coming from a mobile phone left on top of a paint tin.

Thumping to Brooke's right ripped her gaze away from the sexual story playing out to the entire house. JJ leapt the stairs three at a time. She dived for the phone and silenced it, her harsh breaths like a continuation of the explicit scene. Wide brown eyes met her blues as Brooke pulled in her lips. And waited.

JJ shoved the phone in her back pocket and visibly swallowed. A laugh caught in her throat. "Sorry—that was—audiobooks. And I..." Her mouth clamped shut as she looked back to the stairs. She cleared her throat. Red bloomed up the woman's chest in real time, so deep, no amount of white dust could hide it. "Umm, they're Bluetooth. Short range. So... short." She lifted the wireless headphones around her neck by way of explanation and nodded once. "Anyway, uh..."

Brooke's grin widened, eyebrow twitching as she watched JJ squirm.

"See you at five?" JJ asked, an octave higher than usual. She backed away to the stairs.

"Can't wait for you to *come* and pick me up."

Brooke laughed as reddened ears disappeared down the stairs.

Maybe helping the painter with her travel plans wouldn't be so bad.

FOUR

JJ

"Is this really *The Wharf*?" Brooke asked as they walked through to the outdoor area.

People milled about on the real wharf nearby, fishing and crabbing off the side. The tide was out, and the white sand dunes gleamed under the setting sun. The pub was already pumping for five o'clock. Groups of tradies sat around in their hi-vis, happy hour beers in hand.

Thank god Brooke hadn't brought up the mortifying moment from earlier. JJ had sworn her book was paused. As soon as the sultry female tones blared down the stairs, she'd almost left the house then and there—job be damned. Sapphic romance was her kryptonite, and audiobooks kept her sane. Listening to those stories made it feel like watching a movie while she painted.

"Uh, yeah?" JJ slid onto one of the chairs, back still aching from patching and sanding all day.

"I haven't been here for over ten years."

"Oh, right."

Brooke took a seat opposite, still looking around with

interest. It was nothing special—tired wooden tables dotted the outdoor area, varnish peeling. The "new" outdoor space was now years old, worn down by the coastal beating of constant wind and sea air. A warm breeze played at the nape of JJ's neck, a gentle reminder to soak up every last hour of these balmy nights while autumn still masqueraded as summer.

"What are you having to drink?" JJ asked. "Beer?"

"Do you usually ask someone a question then answer for them?"

Brooke's response was like a whip. JJ would've taken offence had she not seen the hint of curve at the edge of the woman's mouth.

"My apologies. What would you like?" She mimed zipping her mouth shut.

"A beer, thanks. Whatever they have on tap." Brooke batted her eyelashes.

JJ scoffed with a shake of her head and went to the bar.

Brooke was an intriguing woman, abrasive in her mannerisms yet somehow she still drew JJ in. Her bristliness towards Hayley was slightly jarring to witness, and while JJ was now somewhat cautious, she still wanted to know more. Who was this traveller extraordinaire? And why did she seem hesitant to even want to come out tonight? Hopefully JJ could persuade her to at least help figure out where to go on this holiday. Surely all that knowledge could be put to good use?

JJ placed an ice-cold glass of beer down in front of Brooke, taking a large and necessary gulp from her own pint.

"So, do you always listen to porn while you work?"

Beer sprayed all over the table and down her arm. A few futile dribbles caught at the last minute when JJ finally clamped her mouth shut. The couple at the next table turned to stare. Just great. She snatched up a napkin, mopping at her chin. Brooke waited, the ghost of a smile that said she was enjoying this way too much. So much for getting away with not talking about it...

"It's not—" JJ looked around, still dabbing at a few wet spots on the table. She folded the napkin and met Brooke's eyes. "It's not *porn*." She whispered the last word. "It's romance. And the stories are calming while I work."

"Calming. Right. Interesting way to describe it." Brooke's eyes danced as she sipped her beer. She placed the glass down. "So, travel."

JJ let out a breath. A much better topic. Though something told her it wouldn't be the last she'd hear about the humiliating incident.

"When Hayley says you've been everywhere, she means...?" JJ enquired.

"Over a hundred countries and counting." Brooke sat back in her seat. She wore the lightest of makeup, a dusting of freckles still showing over her nose and her skin was so gloriously tanned. Her whole look screamed world traveller the more JJ took it in.

JJ's eyes widened. "Wow, she wasn't kidding, you've been around the block."

"A few times. So how can I talk you out of travelling around SA?"

"What do you mean?" JJ frowned and brushed some wind-blown sand off their table.

"It's so boring. There's literally nothing to do here. If

you want to travel—travel! Get out and see the world. What about exploring the Colosseum in Rome or hiking up to Machu Picchu in Peru? Surely that's more intriguing."

A waiter brought out a bowl of wedges.

"Here," JJ said. "Got us something to nibble on with our drinks." She offered them to Brooke, then took one and dipped it into the sour cream, followed by the sweet chilli sauce.

"And I have to disagree about going overseas." She pointed the loaded chip at Brooke then took a bite.

Brooke arched a brow and picked up a wedge. A small collection of bracelets coloured her left wrist, braided in blues and greens.

JJ sipped her beer and continued, "I love Adelaide and I love South Australia. It's such a beautiful state, but I've hardly seen any of it. Sure, I can see those other places, but they're just another bucket list item, probably filled with thousands of tourists cramming into each other with selfie sticks and BO. Anyway, I'd feel safer staying local to start. But that's my problem, I don't *know* exactly where to start. I don't know how to plan a good itinerary. I just know I want it to be perfect."

"And no interest in going interstate?"

"Nup." JJ sat back in her chair and folded her arms. The location was non-negotiable. Hopefully Brooke would actually help her, because right now? All she seemed to be doing was arguing. If this was a date, JJ would be out of here as soon as she'd finished her last sip. Why was Brooke so against her plans? And how could she not like Adelaide —her hometown? Especially as someone so well-travelled. Surely JJ could twist her arm on that opinion.

"Fine, what places do you want to see? If you make a list, you can then plot out the spots on a map and see if it's easiest to see a bunch at the same time." Brooke licked sour cream off her fingers.

JJ was momentarily distracted. She passed Brooke a napkin. "I don't really have any particular places in mind. My housemate suggested going with a top ten list."

Brooke reeled back. "You can't do that."

"Please, by all means, tell me how I should do it then." This was like hitting a dead end with every idea she had. Read: nowhere. A kestrel hovered in the air nearby, ready to swoop down on its prey.

"Firstly, how do you want to travel? Are you looking to stay in hotels or resorts?" Brooke asked.

"I want to take the Subie—"

"The what?"

"My Subaru Forester. And I wouldn't mind camping or whatever. I'm not there for the accommodation."

"More like a road trip?"

"Yeah," JJ replied, scooping another wedge with sauce.

Brooke nodded along. Finally, something they saw eye-to-eye on.

"Okay, and what sort of things do you think you'd be interested in? Wineries, food, history, nature, activities?"

"Nature would be my number one. History is interesting but in small doses, and I'm always up for good food. Activities-wise, it depends. I'm not interested in diving with the sharks, I know that much."

"No diving out of planes either?"

JJ shook her head.

"Noted. No extreme sports."

Brooke gazed out at the view, her long blonde hair fluttering gently in the breeze. The tips were bleached lighter than the rest, which seemed more from the sun than an intentional effect. Beaded earrings hung long on each side, the bright colours popping against her golden hair. African maybe? JJ was still fixated on her face when Brooke started talking.

"Let's try a simpler question: How long do you want to go for and when? Late this year, or early next?"

"I've got two weeks off work, and I'm leaving in three weeks."

Brooke's eyebrows shot up. "Three *weeks*!? And you've booked nothing?"

JJ held her glass in front of her face. "No?" she squeaked. Surely she still had enough time to work everything out? She dropped her head and groaned. "This is too hard. Maybe I should just pay someone to organise it for me. Do you have any travel agent friends?"

"You're not using a travel agent."

"Of course not." JJ swatted at a couple of sticky flies hovering over their wedges.

"What do you mean?"

"Every single idea I've suggested for my trip tonight has apparently been 'the wrong thing' or 'a bad idea'."

A fly landed on her eye next. Swat. Then the corner of her mouth. Swat. *Bloody, stupid—argh.* Maybe she should just cancel the trip.

"I never said that," Brooke said.

JJ levelled her with a stare.

"I don't mean it in, like, a negative way. I'm just passionate. Travel can be such a life-changing experience—

if you do it the right way. Get away from those tourist traps, get off the beaten path and find your own way. That's when the magic happens." Brooke fiddled with her bracelets.

"Why don't you do it then?"

Brooke's eyes narrowed. "Do what?"

"Plan my trip for me. I'll pay you." It was genius. JJ had no idea what she was doing. Brooke on the other hand...

Brooke chewed at her lip, eyes dropping to her beer. "I'll think about it."

It was a start. And that was more than JJ had before. "Can I give you my number? You can let me know when you've made a decision."

"Sure," Brooke replied, pulling out her phone and entering JJ's number.

If JJ could get a world traveller to plan her trip, she'd be set. Just the idea had the tension easing between her shoulders. She'd be happy to hand over the reins to Brooke. No more staring at a million options in front of her, trying to decide where to start and worrying about every single decision.

If the trip was organised by a pro, it wouldn't just be a getaway from the monotony of her life, but maybe an epic holiday.

So long as Brooke decided to help.

If she didn't, JJ had no idea what she was going to do.

FIVE
Brooke

Brooke let herself into the house a little after six. The drink with JJ had been interesting. She'd never planned someone else's trip before, only ever looking after herself. There were times she'd travel with friends or in groups, but that was different, a shared experience.

She passed the kitchen. Marie was stirring a pot on the stove while Hayley prepped vegetables on the kitchen island.

"Hi," she murmured.

Hayley stopped chopping her onion and looked up. "Are you having dinner with us tonight?"

"Probably." Brooke still couldn't speak in full sentences around her sister. She scratched at her arm and kept moving to the stairs.

"Can we not do this?" Hayley waved her hand between them.

Brooke stopped walking, jaw stiff. "Do what?"

"Whatever—*this*—is. Ignoring us, treating us like you couldn't care less. Each time we try to instigate a conversation with you, it's either a brush off or a one-word response. I don't know what happened overseas. I didn't force you to tell me. I just let you in. Let you stay. I know we aren't close, but that doesn't mean you get to treat us like shit."

Brooke's stomach dropped. Staying out of their way was meant to make things easier for them. Apparently it was only fucking things up worse.

Hayley's hand was visibly shaking on the counter as she tried to press her palms down.

"It's okay." Marie stepped next to her, a hand slipping over Hayley's and squeezing.

"I'm not..." Brooke's lips pressed together, jaw quivering as she tried to set it. Tried to keep her head held high. She blinked rapidly, taking in the scene before her and trying to come up with the words. It was all too big. Too much.

The bright downlights overhead were like a spotlight, beating down on her and burning her eyes.

Suddenly she was seven again, trailing home with Steven and Hayley from their school sports day. She couldn't contain her grin, so wide and so proud. Pinned to her shirt were a rainbow of ribbons that shimmered as the breeze caught them with every step she took. Her parents had greeted them at the door, her mum twirling Hayley on the spot, her dad clapping Steven on back—a row of solid blues pinned to each of them. When they'd stopped celebrating their wins, her mum had bent down to Brooke with a small smile and said, "Better luck next year, Sweet Bee." That night, those colourful ribbons had laid flat on her bedside table, stripped to a dull grey in the darkness.

Brooke stared at her sister now, her tongue dry, unmoving. She dropped her gaze, turned on her heel and left the house. The itch was back, gnawing at her. Grating on her. She couldn't stay any longer and burden them further. She couldn't be around Hayley without hurting herself, but she couldn't keep out of the way without hurting Hayley.

So she ran down the street again, travelling the well-worn path and found herself at the riverbank once more. With the reeds. The rocks.

One. Two. Three—Four.

She smoothed her hand over the large rock's gash as she sat down.

How could Brooke explain to Hayley the weight since being back?

It had been building ever since she'd stepped off the plane. Old baggage she'd long thought had disappeared, but those memories kept resurfacing. And so did the emotions, making her tear up one moment and grind her teeth the next; reliving them like they'd only happened yesterday—not years ago. She hadn't experienced anything like it overseas. It had all been left behind, but clearly, it hadn't left her.

Coming back was a mistake. She couldn't stay.

Her phone stared back at her, JJ's number on the screen.

She hit call.

"That was quick," JJ answered after the first ring.

"I've thought about what you said, and I have a different idea."

"Go on."

"What if, instead of being your travel agent, we took it one step further and I was your tour guide? I've just got back from overseas, so I don't have a job and I'd much prefer to be on the road than under my sister's roof. I'd take care of the lot. The itinerary, the accommodation, the food... everything from the packing list to the driving. You'd just sit back and relax. I wouldn't charge anything, you'd just cover the trip."

JJ laughed. "What? I don't even know you."

Brooke shrugged, forgetting JJ couldn't see her. Well, that wasn't a no. She needed to take a leaf out of JJ's book and keep pushing. "So? I've known people for a lot less time and ended up on all sorts of trips with them. I met one guy on a train and we ended up travelling and meeting up through three different countries. You and I have already shared a beer; we're practically best friends at this stage."

"What happened to 'I hate South Australia'?"

Brooke sighed and flicked in a rock. "I don't hate it—I just think it's boring. However, before you say what I think you'll say, I'd still rather be on a boring road trip than stuck back ho—at Hayley's house."

She could plan the shit out of this holiday, no matter how crap the destination. It would buy her time to decide her next steps, get her out of the house to clear her head without spending more money *and* she'd make sure it was a memorable trip for JJ. Even if it was forgettable for her.

"Fine. You should come then."

Brooke shot to her feet. "What? That was a quick turn-around. Why?" She scuffed at the rock with her foot.

"Because I'd love nothing more than to prove you wrong."

Brooke scoffed. "I *highly* doubt that." It was fine. JJ would enjoy the trip if Brooke was planning it. But her?

No. She'd play the perfect tour guide and come along for the ride, but this wasn't her holiday. This was her escape.

"Aside from making sure you *love* this trip just as much as I do," JJ continued, "I actually wouldn't mind the company and making a new friend. Working for yourself gets kinda lonely. Plus, my friend Remi made us watch *Wolf Creek* the other night, so if you're along for the trip, I can sacrifice you first if we get taken."

"How kind of you."

JJ chuckled, the sound causing a small smile to form on Brooke's lips.

"Okay..." JJ said. "Just so I have this straight—you want to join me on a two-week road trip to travel places you don't want to go, and you'd organise the entire thing from start to finish if I pay?"

"That about sums it up."

She picked up a gum leaf, crunching it in her hand. It fell in brittle pieces onto the ground. Was this the right decision? Was leaving again really the best option to solve her problems?

Brooke wiped her hands on her pants. "So, is that a yes?"

"Looks like you've got a road trip to organise, tour guide," JJ replied.

Brooke grinned.

And just like that, she'd found herself the time she needed.

SIX

JJ

"Oh come here and give me another hug."

JJ found herself smushed into her mum. It was like being hugged by a cupcake.

She ate with her family every Sunday and popped in at least a few times during the week. Being away from them was going to be weird, so she squeezed her mum a little harder than usual, basking in the overabundance of love.

"Have you packed your sunscreen?" her mum asked before pulling out of the hug.

"Yes, Mum." JJ tried not to roll her eyes. They stood in the foyer of her family home. Cheese and garlic wafted down the hallway from the kitchen.

"Your dad's out the back with Gran picking tomatoes for the salad."

"Still?" JJ headed down the hall. It was early April, though in Adelaide it might as well still be summer. The heat had been as prolific as the tomatoes.

In the kitchen, there wasn't an inch of bench space left. Dishes littered every surface, either in line to be cleaned at the sink or filled to the brim to be taken outside for their lunch. Once again, her mum had cooked for an army. An army of four.

"Give me a hand with those, love." Her mum passed her the salad and a bowl of huge SA king prawns on a bed of ice. JJ's mouth watered as she eyed off which one to eat first. She slid open the glass door with her foot and stepped outside. The sun beamed into the backyard, making her squint. She hurried over to the table, setting down the plates so she could flick her sunglasses down on her face.

A large straw hat poked out amongst the tomato vines, and JJ made her way over to the veggie patch.

"Happy Easter, Dad!"

Her dad was bent over the raised garden bed trimming up the bottom of the plant and picking off the odd tomato at the same time.

"JJ! Happy Easter." He squinted up at her with a big grin from beneath his hat. He stood, groaning as he straightened up and stretched his back. "That's enough of that for today." He brushed the dirt off his knees and opened his arms for a hug.

JJ was crushed again for the second time that day. She inhaled the distinct earthy aroma of the tomato leaves clinging to her dad's shirt—the smell of summer and dirt and family.

"Still off tomorrow?" Her dad grabbed the bowl of tomatoes, and they wandered back to the table for lunch.

"Nah, Brooke wants to leave Tuesday to avoid the holiday traffic. So we're heading off at lunch."

"Sensible. You don't muck around with peak hour traffic. And you'll avoid the roos too." He nodded, taking off his hat and hanging it on his chair.

"I thought I heard my Bugaboo!" Gran appeared from the other side of the garden carrying a couple of lemons. "Excited for the trip?" She slipped into a chair at the end of the table and began slicing the lemons.

"That's an understatement." JJ leaned over and gave her gran a side-armed hug, then took a seat next to her dad. "Brooke's made it so easy. Everything's organised, and I've barely had to do a thing. The biggest workout has been my bank balance." Every item was emailed across to be booked, all with clear instructions from Brooke, so JJ could keep her focus on wrapping up work.

Her mum brought out the potato bake and sat down across from JJ. "Right, tuck in everyone before it gets cold." She smiled, then frowned, clicking her tongue. "JJ, that's not enough on your plate. Here."

A mountain of creamy, cheesy potato landed next to her prawns before JJ could object. "Thanks, Mum." She ignored the potato and picked up a prawn.

"You sure it's a good idea to be travelling with this random woman?" her dad asked, serving himself a healthy slab of tuna mornay. JJ, in the midst of peeling the prawn and eyeing off the homemade cocktail sauce, paused. This "random woman" was the only reason this holiday was going ahead.

"She's not random. She's a friend of Jess's." A friend of Jess was probably a stretch. Speaking with her housemate, Jess had filled her in on the Brooke she knew before she'd become a world traveller. She didn't have much to say about her now; only that she seemed more reserved and aloof.

"Not to mention, she's a client's sister, so I know where she lives."

The joke fell flat, her parents exchanging glances.

"Is this your latest girlfriend?" Gran asked over her glasses, cracking a shell off her prawn like it was nobody's business. JJ's cheeks heated as all eyes turned to her. Gran was no stranger to JJ's dating struggles, her eyes alight as she waited for a response.

Brooke would be the last person JJ would date, they were complete opposites. Thankfully Brooke's bickering banter and expertise kept their interactions fun enough for JJ to want to travel together. JJ didn't mind differences of opinion, especially short term. Two weeks was nothing. If she had to consider spending the rest of her life with Brooke, that would be a different story.

"No," she replied. "Just my tour guide."

Around her, shoulders sagged and faces fell as everyone went back to their meal.

JJ plucked up another prawn. She would worry about all of that when she was back. Right now she needed to put all thoughts of dating into the recesses of her mind.

JJ paced around the dining and lounge, checking off her list. Everything was done and running on time.

It was D-Day.

That sounded ominous.

It was holiday time!

Much better.

Only one last paint job and she'd be out of here! Her stomach roiled.

She passed Jess, who was finishing the last of her coffee. She popped the mug in the dishwasher and grabbed her lunch bag from the fridge.

"Soak the peace lilies every other week," JJ reminded Jess. "And water all the seedlings every second morning. Unless this hot streak continues, then every day."

"I know. The schedule is on the fridge." Jess made a show of pointing to JJ's neatly handwritten notes plastered on the front. "I'll do my best to green up that black thumb of mine and keep your plants alive."

"Thanks, Jess. If you could also—"

"Check the mail, pay any bills. Swipe your credit card details and go on a shopping spree."

JJ narrowed her eyes.

Jess cracked a grin. "I promise I'll look after the house while you're gone."

"And no sex on the couch!" JJ shook her finger at Jess.

"Hey! I told you that in confidence, not so you could use it against me."

JJ walked to the kitchen cupboard and grabbed a glass. "I don't trust you or Remi around my furniture." Bloody rabbits in their honeymoon stage.

"That's fair. I wouldn't either." She cackled. "Especially without you around cockblocking us."

"That was *one* time. Plus, I didn't know you two were together and I *know*—"

"—we weren't actually together," Jess finished for her.

"Not sure who you were fooling."

Jess ignored her, pulling on her pink safety boots and

heading off to work with a friendly wave and a cheshire cat smile.

Alone again, JJ stared at the completed checklist for a third time. She put a hand on her chest, heart thudding against it. She couldn't seem to slow it down, even though everything was set. Her suitcases were packed; she was ready to go. She poured herself a water, almost hyperventilating as she watched the glass fill. Gulping it down, she braced her hands on the sink to give herself a moment. *You're only nervous because this is new and out of your comfort zone.* Brooke would be with her, and she was a travel expert no less.

Everything would be fine.

Now to get this last-minute paint job out the way for the morning. Her back ached at the thought of cracking out the paint roller again. Nerves aside, the open road was calling. Keeping busy until it was time for tools down would be good. Plus, it was only a single bedroom—nice and quick.

Two hours in, there was nothing simple about the job, and JJ was still struggling with the prep work. It turned out, the homeowner had rented out the spare bedroom, and the last occupant was very fond of wall posters. There were Blu Tack marks everywhere, and not only were they a pain to remove, but time-consuming. The residue wasn't something you could just paint over. She texted Brooke an update, but hopefully she'd still be ready to hit the road just after lunch.

Rolling on the final coat, JJ downed her tools and stretched out her back. Regret seeped into her bones as her legs ached from standing all day. She pulled her headphones off and took her phone off focus mode.

3:30pm. Five missed calls. Three text messages from Brooke.

Fuck.

"I'm so sorry!" JJ cried as soon as Brooke answered the phone. She raced around the room, tidying up one-handed and pulling off the last of the masking tape. "I can't believe the time. I could've sworn I'd only been painting an hour. I was completely in the zone. We can leave now. I'm just finishing up here." She stopped to take a breath.

"Honestly, there's no point in leaving now," Brooke said, then sighed.

JJ paused, a sticky ball of wadded tape in hand. "What!? What are you talking about?"

"Relax, I mean no point leaving right now. It'd be rush hour by the time you picked me up. So don't stress. I'll call the accommodation, then how about you come get me when you're ready. We can have dinner and leave after the mad rush."

The suggestion sounded good, but with the amount of driving they had ahead of them...

"Wait... that means we wouldn't get there til like... midnight." JJ walked outside and put the leftover paint in the car.

"I mean, it's not the best-case scenario, but I've arrived at midnight in plenty of places. I once had a bus that dumped me on the outskirts of Venice at one in the morning. Come on, what would you rather: sleep in and wake up in the Flinders tomorrow? Or lose a night and have to leave at lunch tomorrow?"

"Ugh." JJ scratched at her arm, the itch travelling right up to her shoulder.

This was not ideal. She closed her eyes and breathed out her nose, leaning on the side of her car. Why had she taken on the extra work? She could've said no. She didn't need the money. Now, waiting around for another morning sounded like torture. She'd been antsy enough today. Plus, the plan was to leave today. The thought of everything switching around—

"Well, what do you want to do?"

Right. She hadn't answered Brooke.

"I'll pick you up for dinner," she replied, walking back inside.

It was going to be a long, dark night.

SEVEN

Brooke

JJ's car looked like it had been driven straight out of a showroom instead of the ten-year plus daily driver it seemed to be. There wasn't a speck of dust on the dashboard. No food wrappers or random crap in the foot well. A single rainbow pendant dangled from the rearview mirror, the only personalised item in the front.

A gnawing ache started in Brooke's lower belly. Yes, she was using JJ to get away—*run away*—but JJ had been so excited at her idea to be a tour guide, surely it wasn't technically using her by that standard? JJ had wanted this as much as she had.

They'd pulled into *The Wharf* for dinner. The delay wasn't great, but Brooke would take night driving over rush hour any day. She'd learned long ago not to hold tight to schedules and plans. Going with the flow was key to successful travel. Plus, travelling in the dark felt more adventurous, more alive. Like most of her bus trips in Southeast Asia and Europe, overnight travel was what all the cool kids did to get from place to place.

They ended up at the same table where they'd had drinks three weeks ago. Tonight was schnitzel night, and if there was one thing Brooke had missed from her hometown, it was the schnitties. Not that she'd admit that to JJ. So, doing her best to hide her eagerness, Brooke sat with JJ as they waited for their meals.

It was nice to see her out of overalls and in casual clothes. Though her outfit was still as polished as her personality—squeaky clean Vans with fitted dark pants and a long-sleeved white shirt. JJ's fingers drummed on the table. She straightened the salt and pepper shakers next.

"Sorry again for making us late." JJ set out her cutlery, nudging the knife until it was just so.

"You already apologised on the phone *and* when you picked me up. No big deal, we're on our way."

"The food's taking a while." JJ's knee bounced against the table, making it vibrate.

"We ordered like, five minutes ago." Jeez. This probably wasn't going to be the first thing to go wrong. Was JJ going to be like this every time things went slightly off-track? "It's not a race to get there. If we're half an hour late, we're half an hour late."

Brooke never understood why people lived their lives in such a rush. Always keen to get to the next thing or they'd fail some big imaginary goal in the sky. It was a painful way to live. Much easier to accept things as they were and adjust as needed.

Their meals were out no less than five minutes later.

Almost no words were exchanged during their dinner. JJ was focused on her food. Neat cuts. One mouthful after the other.

Brooke took one huge decadent bite. Okay, that was way too much to fit in her mouth, but it had been *so* long since she'd had a good Aussie style schnitzel. She chewed, cheeks filled to the brim. The chicken had the perfect crispy coating, and the pepper sauce had her mouth zinging. She darted her tongue out to try and catch the errant drip on her chin. Missed it. She wiped it off with her hand instead.

JJ's eyes were on her mouth. She passed her a napkin, nose upturned. "Hate it when I get the gravy everywhere."

Brooke had no feeling on the matter. The succulent chicken and crunchy coating held all her attention. It went down one way or the other. She took the napkin though and wiped at the mess.

Even with JJ's mess-free eating, she still finished before Brooke and bounced out of her chair before Brooke had even swallowed her last mouthful.

"Let's get this show on the road," JJ said, keys swinging in her hand as they returned to the car.

The further out of Adelaide they drove, the more the pressure eased in Brooke's chest, lungs lighter. Being at Hayley's, Brooke was like a caged animal, lashing out at anything that came near. Here, on the road again, she was free. *Just Brooke.* It was the most human she'd felt since stepping off that plane onto home soil. It may not be far, but it was better than being holed up in her room avoiding her sister and her past.

She stretched back in her seat and glanced at JJ. Both hands were at ten and two on the steering wheel, face tight as they zoomed along the expressway. Whenever they were wedged between a couple of road trains, JJ sat up straighter and gripped the steering wheel. Compared to some of the situations Brooke had been in, Australian roads were bliss. She tried to imagine JJ driving along some of the single-lane-wide cliffside roads she'd been on through parts of Asia and even in Scotland. She smiled.

Yeah, nah.

"I can't believe we're actually doing this," JJ said on a clear stretch with no cars around them. Giant powerlines whipped past overhead. "Feels surreal."

"Feels like we're just on the outskirts of Adelaide to me," Brooke said.

They passed a home centre and a row of fast-food restaurants.

"Oh shut up. You'll be begging to see more of SA by the end of this."

"There's nothing you can do that'll change my mind. We're like oil and water—I'm not meant to mix with this place."

"Mhmm." JJ grinned anyway, brown eyes flashing to Brooke.

That smile. JJ's cockiness was as grating as it was charming. Like she knew with all confidence that she'd win this argument.

Game on painter girl. Game. On.

Her dislike for this place had been decades in the making. Some random trip wasn't going to change that. This state just wasn't for her. Adelaide was a rest stop.

Brooke adjusted her seat back a little. Buildings gave way to flat plains of what looked like dirt. Rows and rows of dirt. Some had rows of seedlings, but otherwise the fields were brown vacant fields of earth. How thrilling.

Brooke propped her elbow up on the door. "So, painting, hey? How'd you get into that?"

"Originally, I wanted to get into woodwork back in high school. I never liked science or maths. Hands-on stuff was more interesting. Doing things." JJ checked her mirrors and changed lanes. "My first work experience place fell through, and I ended up scrambling until I landed a job with a renovating mob instead. They did a bit of everything, and I found myself up scaffolding, learning to fill and sand cracks on this old 1900s place. By the time I got around to handling a paint roller and finishing those first walls, I was hooked. The transformation was"—she let out a low whistle. "After that, I signed up for TAFE, did my apprenticeship, and went out on my own as soon as I could."

Brooke couldn't imagine jumping into a career and business so whole-heartedly. She'd never found that drive or nudge toward a particular occupation.

"Sounds like it was meant to be."

She played with the bracelets on her arm, twisting the charms between her fingers. More barren land whizzed past. Her eyes slid to JJ who pulled up her sleeves, one at a time, highlighting those painter muscles again.

"Do you go to the gym?" Brooke blurted out. *That was meant to be an inside question, Brooke!* She shrunk in her seat and focused back on her bracelets.

JJ frowned and let out a chuckle. "No?"

"Ah, perks of the job then."

"What do you mean?"

"Your arms. They're all, you know, beefy. Not beefy. Strong." She needed to shut up. What was wrong with her?

She usually excelled at chit-chat with new people. "I mean I wish I had those kinds of arms from hefting my backpack around everywhere, but these are pretty sad." She waved her sad arm in the air for effect.

JJ laughed. "There's nothing wrong with your arms. They're just normal. And trust me, the pain you go through to get these muscles isn't fun. Painting can be pretty hard on the body. That's one thing I'm looking forward to with the trip—a complete break from all that."

They lapsed into comfortable silence. JJ's music played on low, a pleasant hum in the background. It was nice to just sit, watching the world flash by, even if it was just another row of dirt. Rumination had become such a large part of Brooke's day-to-day since being back, but constantly replaying all that old crap on a loop only ramped up her stress. Maybe Hayley had picked up on that energy too with how spiky they'd grown around each other? This space away was good. Necessary. Not that Brooke would actually enjoy travelling around South Australia—she looked forward to proving JJ wrong on that front. With any hope, JJ would be so bored after a few days, she'd be begging Brooke to revise their plans. Brooke could shoot them off to Indonesia instead.

"I've never been glamping," JJ commented out of the blue.

"Figured. You said you hadn't travelled much since you were a kid, and glamping wasn't really a thing when we were young."

Brooke's nose wrinkled. "You make us sound so old."

"Well, I mean we're not twenty-one anymore."

"How old are you?" JJ asked.

"Rude." Brooke folded her arms, lips curving into a small smile.

JJ shot a quick look her way.

Brooke caved. "I'm twenty-nine."

"Jeez. Still in your twenties."

"Yep. You? Thirty-seven?" She had to be a little older.

JJ scoffed. "All right, now I'm offended. I'm only thirty-five."

Brooke shrugged. "Close enough."

A large flock of corellas flew overhead, their screeching cutting into the car's interior. They'd hardly talked about themselves in the lead up to the trip, all their focus on planning and holiday discussions. It wasn't necessary information at the time. But with another four hours' drive ahead, Brooke found herself curious about the painter she was travelling with.

"Is JJ your real name? Or short for..."

"Jade." She spoke her name like that of a villain and scrunched up her face. "Full name Jade Johnson—hence, JJ."

"Got it." Not a fan of her first name.

"What about you, 'Brooke not Bee'?"

Damn curiosity. She couldn't keep her mouth shut. It was fun to ask the questions—not have them lobbed back.

"I prefer leaving old nicknames in the past." There. Boundaries established. "What's the weirdest thing that's ever happened to you?" she asked next. Anything to get them away from personal topics.

"Dunno." JJ drummed her fingers on the wheel. "Going on this trip with the random woman sitting next to me is pretty up there."

Brooke just shook her head, biting down on a smile.

From Adelaide to Hawker, they ended up chatting non-stop, pegging each other with questions the entire time. Childhood or family topics were avoided, and for that, Brooke was thankful. With so many travel tales, there were plenty of stories to keep JJ entertained.

"Are you serious?" JJ asked after the latest re-telling. "They're not going to put you on a bus like that."

Brooke laughed. "I'm serious! I was squished up the front, sitting in the aisle for six hours straight by the driver with another ten people on the floor behind me. So enjoy the room in this car."

"Now I can never travel to Vietnam," JJ replied, pulling into the Hawker servo so they could get out and stretch their legs. This stop was on the main turn off to get to their accommodation for the night.

"Then I won't tell you about the time we had so many cockroaches on the bus, I lost count at thirty."

JJ jerked the handbrake on. "That"—JJ turned off the car with a shudder—"is disgusting."

Brooke released her seatbelt. "Nah, it's amazing. Those kinds of stories just make the trip even more memorable."

Every tale had her yearning to step back on a plane and get back overseas. One day.

For now, Adelaide would have to do.

EIGHT
Brooke

Brooke's nose knew she was in the middle of nowhere. Dirt. Fresh air. More dirt. More air. She stood beside the car at the service station. Insects swarmed two spotlights which emitted a low-level buzz, like they were so old they wheezed from the need to keep themselves aglow.

Brooke checked the time on her phone.

11:30pm.

They were still on track to get to their destination just after midnight. That wasn't too bad really. Barely a late night.

"Far out, this is a long drive," JJ said, stretching out her back next to Brooke.

They gazed at the horizon, the faintest outline of ranges standing off in the distance.

Brooke let her head fall back. "Wow."

JJ leaned against the car and followed suit. "Man. You forget how bad the light pollution is back home until you come out here."

"It's pretty magical."

The milky way always took Brooke's breath away, making her feel small and everything else so big at the same time.

JJ nudged her shoulder with a smirk.

"What was that for?" Brooke asked.

"Thought South Australia was boring," she teased.

You could look at the night sky anywhere in the world. Brooke just appreciated the stars, that was all.

"The universe isn't in SA, *Jade*. It doesn't count." She said it with a smile.

"Ooh burn, bringing out my real name already, *Bee*? Touchy subject?"

JJ's teeth were so white in this light, eyes sparkling.

Brooke shot her daggers, lips still upturned and returned to the night sky.

A soft chuckle next to her had Brooke elbowing JJ in the ribs. Playfully, of course.

"Ow, okay, truce," JJ said, her arm flinging out to defend herself.

JJ settled back next to her, their arms now touching.

They stood like that, taking in the stars for a couple more minutes, but after JJ's fifth yawn, Brooke offered to drive the last stretch.

"It's only another forty minutes," JJ said, keys clasped against her chest.

Driving while tired was no joke, and there was no way Brooke wanted JJ micro-sleeping at the wheel doing 110km.

"C'mon, gimme your keys. You look stuffed."

"I shouldn't have taken on that job this morning. I'm wrecked." JJ turned to face Brooke, still leaning against the side of the car, eyes now watering from yawning so much.

"Fine." She slapped the keys into Brooke's waiting hand. "I gotta get in the car anyway, it's freezing. Be nice to the ol' girl, yeah?"

"I'll drive it like it's my own."

Brooke adjusted the mirrors. In the driver's seat, everything looked extra clean and shiny, like JJ had just detailed it. Must be nice to have it all so neat and orderly. Fancy possessions to preen over and care for. Brooke's parents would approve. She'd never owned a car, but she'd operated plenty of vehicles. Motorbikes, jet skis, sail boats... though, it'd been a while since she'd driven, and on a highway doing one-ten no less. She eyed the gear stick.

"You do know how to drive manual, right?"

Brooke had successfully got her driver's license in a manual when she was sixteen. Hadn't driven one since.

"Pfft. Yeah, 'course."

She stuck it in first and stalled it with one giant bunny hop. JJ was clutching the oh-shit bar and glaring. Brooke waved it off.

"Just learning the sweet spot." Fuck. What was it Hayley had taught her? *Be smooth, more revs as soon as you feel the clutch grab.*

It jumped again and conked out.

Oh, come on!

JJ's hand landed on hers over the gearstick. Brooke sucked in a breath.

"Relax," JJ said, removing her hand. "This clutch grabs quickly. Try again."

Brooke blew her hair out of her face and restarted the car. This time she got it into second gear successfully. She over-revved it but at least it didn't stall this time. The warmth remained from JJ's touch.

They made it out of the petrol station and onto the new road. It was incredibly dark out here, even with high beams on. Now they were off the highway, it was eerily quiet, though she was thankful not to have any traffic to contend with at this hour while she brushed up on her stick shift.

JJ's head was tipped back, eyes closed within ten minutes. Brooke would do the same as a teenager whenever Hayley had driven her places, feeling completely at ease. Though Hayley was only a couple of years older than Brooke, Hayley had felt more like a parent in those times than her own. If their parents were working, which was more often than not, it was usually Hayley who'd pick up the slack and drop her places or cook dinner. Those memories hadn't surfaced in a very long time.

Two towering ghost gums came into view. No wonder they got that name; they were like giant wraiths looming over the road as the headlights hit them. Watching them fade into the rearview mirror made it look like there was mist swirling around them.

Wait. The mist wasn't going away.

Plumes of white billowed behind them.

Brooke swept her eyes to the bonnet. Smoke escaped from the edges and whipped away from the high speed. A lookout sign flashed before her. That'd do. Brooke slowed and pulled onto the dirt driveway. The car bounced over potholes, bumping left and right until it opened out onto a dusty, dry expanse—presumably the lookout's carpark. JJ came to, swivelling around at the disruption as Brooke cut the engine.

JJ turned to Brooke. "What's going on? Are we there already?"

Brooke sucked in a lip and chewed. "Um, no. I've just pulled us off the road because of"—she pointed—"that."

Now that the car was stationary, smoke poured out of the bonnet, swirling up towards the sky. The headlights made the scene look sinister.

"Oh. Fuck."

"Yeah."

JJ was out of the car before Brooke had unclipped her seat belt. Her door was wrenched open as JJ leaned inside, one hand landing on Brooke's leg as she leaned down. *What is she doing?!* The bonnet popped open. *Oh. Right.*

JJ disappeared again, the frigid air and oddly sweet stench of the smoke making its way into the car. Brooke scrambled after her. JJ lifted the bonnet, releasing heat like an oven. Brooke felt like it almost singed her eyebrows.

They coughed, waving to clear the air and get a closer look. Brooke held up her phone with the torch on. That was going to be the best use of her time, as her knowledge of cars went as far as knowing the car was now broken. End of story.

"Coolant's gone everywhere," JJ said. "That explains the sweet smell. It's steam, not smoke. It's sprayed all over the engine. Ah shit, I see it. Here." JJ pointed as she leaned in to inspect the damage. Even Brooke could see the very obvious crack.

"I don't understand," JJ said. "I keep it serviced—I've never had an issue." JJ walked off, muttering to herself. "I checked everything this morning, and I even topped off the coolant."

"We'll sort it. It might be easy enough to fix," Brooke said. "Do you have a tool or something?"

JJ was shaking her head. "No way. If that's blown, no amount of tools is going to fix that. Pretty sure it's the radiator, and that's a big crack. I can't tape it up or anything. I'll —I'll... call the RAA. I can't believe this. I've never had an issue with the car. Never. And now tonight of all nights. This isn't off to a great start."

JJ grabbed her phone, pacing back and forth.

Brooke stayed quiet, hopeful the mechanics would sort it. The steam had started to dissipate at least. She hugged her arms around herself and waited.

"Well, shit." JJ dropped her head with a rough exhale. "No coverage." She shook her screen at Brooke. "You?"

Brooke pulled hers out.

Empty bars stared back.

"Okay. Okay. It's fine. Umm." JJ paced again. She clapped her hands, stopping mid-stride and whirled on Brooke. "We can walk to get help! Get back to Hawker. Or —or a place nearby. One of the stations. Yeah."

JJ was back on her phone in an instant. "Damn it. Of course, no GPS either."

"Here." Brooke came up alongside her. "I've got offline maps on my phone. With travelling and all... it's kind of necessary."

She entered the directions and hesitated.

"You're not gonna like it."

"What?" JJ's eyes flicked between her phone and her face.

"It's a five hour walk back to Hawker, or two hours to

the closest sheep station. It's way too cold and dark to walk that far, and too dangerous."

"Shit." JJ stood in thought, hands on her hips. Her eyes widened. "Oh my god, this is just like *Wolf Creek*."

JJ paced again in front of the car, ironically looking like a crazed psycho under the dim of the headlights.

Brooke suppressed a smile.

Time to try and calm down the control freak travel newbie.

NINE

JJ

Being stuck out in the middle of the outback at midnight was not the plan.

This was exactly like the movie. Broken down car. Trapped in bloody woop woop. No moonlight. Nothing to see past the shining headlights, the very definition of pitch black. Trust Remi to make her watch that movie right before she went away. She'd be hearing from JJ as soon as they had reception!

JJ took a breath, the cold seeping in.

It was just a movie. It's fake. It's not even real.

No—it *was* based on a true story.

A shiver ran up her spine.

She stopped pacing. There were no sounds of life, only the scuffing of her shoes against gravel, the car clicking and groaning as the engine cooled and the steam from the radiator dissipated.

Brooke grabbed JJ's arms, a freakishly big smile on full display. "Come on JJ. We're not in a horror movie. We're not going to be abducted."

Brooke held firm, forcing JJ to hold eye contact with her.

Blue eyes, glinting off the headlights. Such bright blue, like the head of her favourite fairywrens.

JJ cleared her throat. "Says you who thought I was an intruder in your own home."

Brooke glared and dropped her arms. "That's not the same thing. We'll be fine. I have a plan, so no need to stress." She put her hands on her hips. "Here's what's going to happen: we're gonna pull out the camping mattress, and our sleeping bags, and make a bed in the back of the car. We'll sleep here tonight, and first thing in the morning, we'll catch a ride back to town and get ourselves sorted. All right?"

JJ gave a small nod. What choice did she have?

The staycation idea was looking mighty fine right now... but she had a point to prove. She had to see this through. South Australia was worth it.

"It's really not a big deal." Brooke shrugged and moved to the boot.

JJ laughed. It bubbled out of nowhere. *No big deal?* She laughed harder. This was not the start to the trip she'd imagined, not the trip she'd planned for.

JJ took a deep breath. "How are you so okay with this?"

"This is travelling. It's just a hiccup." She opened up the boot and started shuffling their gear around. "We'll get it fixed and we're both fine. Sometimes things don't go to plan, so you pivot." She shoved JJ's suitcase and grunted. "We're pivoting. We're going to sleep in the car and sort this out in the morning. So, come on. It's sleepover time!" Brooke strode back to JJ, took her by the hand and pulled her down the side of the car. "Open up your rooftop cargo."

JJ responded on autopilot. Within ten minutes, the back seats were folded down and they had makeshift beds for each of them stretching from the boot to the front seats. They currently sat crosslegged on their sleeping bags. Both were still dressed, having opted to not crank out the PJs in case they needed to get up for any reason. JJ had switched off the car's headlights and turned on a battery-powered camping lamp instead. It gave them some light and was able to charge their phones at the same time.

The usual fresh, clean car scent had been replaced with the strong aroma of things that had been in storage for a long time—aka the mattress.

Brooke was right, it did feel like a sleepover with a friend. All they needed were some fairy lights strung up on the roof, and it'd look like a post from one of those van influencers JJ followed online. They were basically just free camping for the night. No big deal. Her knee bounced as she checked her phone for coverage for the tenth time.

Brooke snatched the device and tossed it aside.

"Hey!" JJ reached for it.

Brooke blocked her, leaning in front of JJ. "You're not going to magically get reception tonight. Let it go. Distract yourself. I'd play I Spy with you, but we can't see shit out there."

When JJ relented, Brooke leaned against a suitcase with a soft smile.

JJ needed to absorb some of Brooke's chill energy. To sit back, relax, and try to enjoy this night instead. Because right now? JJ wanted to be anywhere but here. Take her back home to her comfy couch or set her up on a tropical beach somewhere. She didn't care.

No... she did care. She wanted to explore SA and give the holiday a chance. Anyway, Brooke was right. They'd be fine. They'd get back on track in no time.

JJ let out a slow exhale. "Feels like I've got one hand tied behind my back with no phone. Makes you realise how much we've come to rely on them." Such tiny things that had become an addictive part of their lives. To help with so many situations... until they couldn't. Maybe no reception was a good thing, forcing them to enjoy the moment. No need to message anyone, or reply to all of Mum's check ins —of which there'd already been several on the drive up alone.

"I get that. It's weird to think we didn't grow up with them." Brooke nudged her own phone with her toe.

JJ shuffled back and leaned against the window. "I say we're lucky."

"Agreed." Brooke met her eyes.

"So, world traveller, ever found yourself in this situation before?" JJ asked.

Brooke spun the bracelets on her arm. "This specific one? No. But travel as long as I have and this is nothing. I've found myself in more than a few bad situations. It's just the nature of doing what I do. Travelling is fun, but it can be unpredictable and you can definitely end up in crazy situations very quickly."

Brooke shifted to lay down, propping herself up on an elbow, her golden hair falling over her shoulder in waves.

"Tonight? This is just unlucky. But at least we don't have to worry about watching our backs like I had to in

Cambodia. One night I tried to get a ride home in a tuk tuk from a restaurant, and two men on a scooter zoomed past, ripping my bag straight off me. Luckily, it snapped against my neck or I would've been dragged along the street."

JJ gasped. "What! Were you okay?"

"I was lucky. I walked away with only a bruise and a stiff neck. But with no phone, no cash and a driver who didn't speak English, I ended up walking back to my accommodation alone in the middle of the night. That was one of my scariest moments—coming home along the streets and alleyways feeling so defenceless. Thank god my key had been in my pocket at the time."

"Wow. Look at this. I have goosebumps on my arm from that story!" JJ shivered and held out her arm, hairs standing on end. She hugged her knees to her chest. "I can't even imagine. That does put things in perspective."

Brooke's life sounded so colourful. In comparison, JJ's was so black and white. Go to work, come home, repeat. It was truly inspiring just how much Brooke must've seen and done in her time overseas—the good, the bad and the ugly. Her stomach settled knowing she had this person with her as a travelling companion.

"Sorry I freaked out earlier." JJ interlaced her hands, fiddling with her thumbs.

"You don't need to apologise for getting in your feels. Feel your emotions, it's only natural. But you can trust me when I say we can just have fun tonight and it'll be sorted in the morning."

"I like the sound of that." JJ smiled and rested her chin on her knees. "Did you ever get lonely travelling?"

Even though they'd spent the last five hours talking,

apparently JJ had more questions. It had nothing to do with the fact she was avoiding going to sleep.

"Not really," Brooke said. "I like the space from others, doing my own thing. And I'm usually around people one way or another. Like this." She waved her hand between them.

"That's true. Oh my god, if I hadn't brought you along, I'd be in this situation by myself." JJ shuddered. "How could you feel safe being alone?"

"You get used to it."

"I don't think I could do it."

Tonight was bad enough, even with Brooke.

"Sure you could." Brooke flicked at the zip on JJ's suitcase. "If you want something badly enough, you make it happen. Like running your business."

"I guess," JJ said through a yawn, her eyes starting to water. "If I want the morning to come badly enough, can I make it happen?"

"Depends, how fast can you fall asleep?"

At Brooke's word, JJ's bladder made itself known.

Her gaze slid outside. Complete darkness.

TEN

JJ

Brooke peered out the black windows. "You locked the car?"

JJ nodded, swallowing. She squirmed on the spot as her bladder screamed louder.

"What's wrong?" Brooke asked.

JJ closed her eyes, face heating. "I need to pee."

"Off you go then." Brooke gestured outside.

JJ didn't move. She played with the sleeping bag material instead. How could she ask... her eyes flicked to the ceiling and back to Brooke. She felt like a child.

Brooke rolled her eyes, biting down on a smile. "Would you like some company? Still scared of psychos out there?"

"Not funny." JJ flattened the sleeping bag. "Do you mind? Just to keep an eye out."

"In the pitch black. No problem." She smirked. "Got any paper?"

JJ leaned down, sliding an arm under the driver's seat and pulling out a fresh roll of toilet paper. "Dad always taught me to keep a roll in the car. For emergencies."

"He's not wrong," Brooke said. "You learn very quickly that toilet paper is a precious commodity while travelling. Never go anywhere without a spare!"

JJ unlocked the car, opened the boot and hopped out. Brooke followed suit, the portable lamp swinging at her side and making all sorts of shadows that JJ avoided looking at. They puffed white with each breath as they stepped over rocks and scraggly shrubs. She should've put a hoodie on to come out here.

They came across a waist-high bush. "This'll do," JJ said and walked around the other side. "You can shut off the torch and turn around while I... go."

Darkness enveloped them, the only sound a quiet snigger and gravel crunching under foot as Brooke turned on her heel as requested.

"Bloody hell it's dark, I can't even see the toilet paper next to me." JJ had propped it carefully onto the bush. She blinked a few times, willing her eyes to adjust. Nothing. It was so disorienting. Then she became aware of the stillness. It was like all sound had been sucked away except for the two of them. Their breaths, rustling clothes and her too-loud heartbeat.

You know what? Maybe she didn't have to pee after all. She could hold it until they got back into town.

Pain clenched in her bladder. She winced.

Shit.

She shuffled on the spot, face heating. "Um, can you like, hum something?"

This was mortifying.

"Got pee fright?" Brooke chuckled.

JJ swallowed and pulled down her pants and hoped to god she could go.

At first, it sounded like Brooke had started talking to herself. Then JJ realised Brooke was singing. Well, talk-singing—the entirety of *One Week* by Barenaked Ladies.

It was all fine, entertaining even. Brooke crescendoed into the chorus. It blasted out across the ranges as JJ stood to pull up her pants. Her foot twisted on a loose rock and she skidded, flailing to try to grab onto the bush. She missed, tripping backwards into the thick brush instead.

Her screech echoed into the night. Brooke's singing cut off.

The lamp clicked back on, light crossing JJ's vision as her backside throbbed.

"Fuck! Something's bit me on the bloody arse!" JJ cried. She flung an arm out for Brooke to help pull her up. JJ yelped, the pain searing as she stood. She twisted around, scrambling at her backside. What had bitten her?

Please don't be a snake. Please don't be a—

"Will you just stop a second and let me look!" Brooke grabbed JJ by the hips, steadying her. JJ was trying to be strong, she really was. But this was... this was—argh. Why had she talked Brooke into travelling through SA again?

The lamp lowered to her backside. JJ's face burned like a Christmas cracker. She would not think about the fact her pants were only up to her knees right now and Brooke was currently looking right at her—

"Found the culprits."

There were multiple? JJ squeezed her eyes shut.

This wasn't happening.

"What is it—*fucking*, OW!"

It felt like Brooke had stabbed her in the butt cheek. Twice.

Brooke straightened, holding up two thick spikes in front of the light.

"Yeah, so it turns out this bush is spiky as hell. Hang on." She turned away again before JJ had a chance to respond. "Here." She'd torn off a few sheets of toilet paper. "Your, um, butt is bleeding a bit." She bit her lip, handing JJ the sheets.

Of course. Just when this night had started to turn around.

"Hold those on there. I'll run to the car and grab some Band-Aids. Where are they? Glovebox?"

"I can come with you," she said, already knowing Brooke's answer.

"And let you trip over again? Just wait there and give me your keys."

"Fine. Yes, they're in the glovebox." Her butt ached as she did what she was told and held the paper there.

Bloody hell. JJ had not expected her first night on holiday to win awards for Most Horrifying and Most Embarrassing. She awkwardly wrangled her pants up as far as she could to give herself a little more modesty.

She gave the bush daggers while she waited. This holiday plan was going down the toilet, fast.

Brooke was back in minutes, plasters in hand.

"I can do it," JJ said, hand outstretched.

"Don't be stupid. It'll take me two seconds, and it's not like I haven't seen your butt already."

JJ groaned. Still not thinking about *that* fact.

"Here, hold the lamp a sec."

JJ took the light and held her breath.

Brooke was gentle, one warm hand on her hip, the other brushing her backside as she stuck on the Band-Aids. Once again, JJ was thankful to have Brooke with her.

"There. All patched up."

Face still on fire, JJ inched her pants over her behind. "Thanks," she said, avoiding Brooke's eyes. Did she always have to embarrass herself in front of the pretty blonde?

"Need a hand getting back?" Brooke asked.

"No, I should be fine."

Brooke eyed JJ up and down with furrowed brows.

"I'm fine. Really. Thank you, though."

Shuffling back, they made it to the car. JJ could barely keep her eyes open now the adrenaline had worn off. She wriggled into her sleeping bag and settled on her side to avoid any pressure on her backside.

What a start. JJ had pictured a slow beginning, easing into the holiday with a well-deserved break from work. Hopefully JJ had made the right decision bringing them out here. Surely tomorrow they'd get things back on track. It was too tiring to think about it anymore.

She shifted, hip bone digging straight through the thin mattress and onto the hard floor of the car. She shuffled again. It was only slightly better.

Brooke reached an arm out of her own sleeping bag. "You okay if I switch off the light?"

"Please." JJ yawned. "Good night. Thanks for your help today."

"Night. We'll have a better day tomorrow, yeah?"

"We better," JJ mumbled through another yawn.

She curled up on her side—just comfortable enough—and began to drift...

Her eyes fluttered open, back aching and butt smarting.

There was crunching on the gravel outside.

She stilled, holding her breath, heart picking up speed.

More shuffling. More crunching. Footsteps?

Please, no.

BANG.

Thump.

BANG!

JJ bolted upright, straight onto her tender backside and winced. "Ow."

Brooke moved beside her. "What was that?"

"I don't know. Grab the lamp."

It was still dark, the dawn only just beginning to outline the horizon. She fumbled around, grabbing her phone and keys. Not that they'd help much. JJ clutched Brooke's arm as Brooke's hand gripped her knee. JJ squinted and rubbed at her eyes, searching outside. Nothing. She leaned over to look out the window. Something dark loomed up—BANG! It hit the car, disappearing like a ghost.

"The fuck was that?" JJ screeched, fumbling back into Brooke.

"Wait, I see something." Brooke flicked on the light, holding it up to the window.

JJ's head swivelled to the other side of the car, then to the back. She couldn't see shit.

Thump. Thump. THUMP.

Something jumped onto the roof. If JJ's heart beat any

faster, it was going to leap right out of her chest. A shadow moved to the left.

Brooke held the lamp higher.

Two sets of eyes glowed back.

ELEVEN
Brooke

Goats.

There were actual goats headbutting the car and jumping on it like a god damn playground. Brooke had never seen anything like it and the relief had her bursting out with laughter. JJ began to shake next to her, still grasping Brooke's arm as she joined in on the giggles.

"At this rate, I don't even care if the goats are damaging the car," JJ said. "I'm just happy they're not serial killers. *And* it's morning." She let out a long sigh, ending on a little chuckle. "C'mon we might as well herd these guys away from the car. I think I've got the rest of those BBQ Shapes around here somewhere..." JJ grunted as she reached into the footwell and felt around. "Got 'em." She held up the box and unlocked the door.

Brooke threw a jumper on and scrambled after her. She stepped out into the morning air and hissed, rubbing her arms. She reached back inside the car and pulled everything out of her bag until she found her beanie. Necessary. Back outside, it was getting lighter, and Brooke could now see all six goats surrounding the car. The one closest to them, with a black and white mixed coat, bleated and beelined for the green box. JJ held it up high, the other goats taking a step back at the sudden movement.

"Right you lot, away from the car." JJ shook the box to get their attention as Brooke waved her arms around behind them in an effort to get them to move and warm herself up. Success! They started following JJ like the pied piper into the bush. Brooke brought up the rear, treading carefully over the rocky soil, avoiding any remotely spiky shrubs.

JJ stopped once they'd gained some distance.

"I'm gonna call you Nancy," she said to the black and white goat who trotted straight up to her. "I bet you were the one tap dancing on my roof like a bloody menace. Don't you have a farm you should be on?"

Brooke chuckled at the display. JJ met her eyes, grin widening.

While this wasn't the start she'd envisioned for JJ, it was nice to see her pivoting this morning—accepting their bizarre situation with the wild goats and running with it. Even with everything that had happened, they hadn't missed out on much in terms of their itinerary. Brooke only had them checking into their accommodation and relaxing for the night. With any luck, they'd still be on schedule for today.

Nancy courteously ate the two biscuits out of JJ's hand then headbutted her for more. "You cheeky devil. Where're your manners?"

The biscuit box was wrenched from JJ, Nancy taking full advantage of the moment's distraction. Brooke couldn't do anything but watch on, laughter spilling from her lips.

"Oi! Come here." JJ chased after Nancy, who was currently—and very effectively—evading her lunges. It was quite the show.

"You could help you know?" JJ threw over her shoulder.

"And ruin this entertainment? Never." Brooke hugged herself tighter and watched on. The other goats had lost interest in the antics and began trotting deeper into the scrub.

JJ feinted to the left and launched to the right, hand clamping down on the corner of the box as Nancy tried to jump out of the way. She bleated, indignant the biscuits had been removed from her possession.

"No more," JJ scolded the goat and hid the box behind her back. "Go on. Off with your friends. That way." She motioned with her free hand at the disappearing group of four-legged firecrackers, off to cause mischief and destruction somewhere else. Nancy cried out one final time, then turned to see the rest of the group had already left. She took off, kicking up rocks and dust as she went.

Brooke waltzed up to JJ and wrapped an arm around her. JJ's eyes blew wide at the sudden proximity, and Brooke had to bite down on a smile. She rustled around and withdrew her hand, now filled with a handful of BBQ Shapes.

"I'm starving. Didn't want all our snacks to go to the goats." She playfully tossed a couple into her mouth.

"Right," JJ said, a little breathlessly.

The sun was bursting over the ridge now, lighting up lush green hills and an old, red-stained dirt road, overgrown with shrubs and grass. It looked more used by the local wildlife than vehicles. A small sign stood out near where they'd pulled in the night before.

"Walk with me," Brooke said. She shoved the last biscuits in her mouth and wiped her hands on her pants. JJ fell in step beside her as they strolled over to the sign and a weathered bench, the wood barely holding itself together.

"I guess this is the 'lookout'," Brooke said. "Riveting."

"My butt hurts just thinking about the splinters we'd get if we attempted to sit on that." JJ ran her hand over her behind, drawing Brooke's eye.

That was one glimpse of JJ she hadn't expected last night.

Then they saw the sign.

No camping. No access.

Oops. Well, breaking down and camping were two completely different things.

But now they'd sorted the goats, it was time to sort the car.

Brooke had an idea.

"I swear I saw a mechanic shop as we drove through Hawker last night, so we can—oh, hear that?" Brooke jogged down the dirt path to the edge of the road just as a farm truck bumbled over the slight hill. Brooke waved her arms wildly with a grin. The truck slowed at the very last minute, brakes squeaking as it pulled off to the side.

A man wound down the window. It was a very normal-looking young guy in an old flannel shirt and battered Akubra. Phew.

"Morning," she said. "Any chance of a lift to Hawker?"

With a quick explanation of everything that'd

happened, minus the goats, Harvey—a chicken farmer it turned out—was more than happy to take them to town. With a skip and a hop, she settled into a jog back to JJ, grinning from ear to ear.

"Quick, grab your bag. He'll take us. And no, he's not a serial killer; he's a chicken farmer."

"That's what they all say." JJ squinted. "Chickens could be a ploy to make you *think* he's a regular guy."

Brooke ignored her, lips still curving up. She wasn't about to play into the woman's irrational horror movie fears.

Harvey was fine, just as Brooke promised. Though JJ was pushed up against Brooke's side so hard the whole ride, it was as if she thought the truck was going to bite her. The painter only eased up once Harvey spoke about his farm work in such detail, there was no way he could be anything more sinister.

Twenty minutes later, they were in town. And not only did Harvey drop them off in Hawker, but he also offered them a dozen eggs fresh from his farm. Bless. With a polite decline and a wave goodbye, they dashed across the road to the mechanic. Brooke pushed the door. It didn't budge.

"It's closed," JJ said. She pointed to the now very obvious sign.

"Well, shit."

JJ checked the time. "It'll be open in an hour. Maybe there's somewhere around here that does coffee."

Brooke did a quick search of the area on her phone. "Right around the corner."

"Convenient when the entire town is only two streets wide."

An old bell dinged as they entered the cafe. The scent of roasted coffee beans and grilled bacon were thick in the air. They'd come to the right place to wait. Her stomach gurgled, not happy with only the few biscuits she'd fed it this morning.

They sat in two armchairs by the front window. A small coffee table was wedged between them, topped off with a couple of *Women's Weekly* magazines. They looked at least five years old. Hopefully the food was fresher than the decor.

"So," JJ said while they waited for their order. "You mentioned you were job hunting. What do you do?"

Brooke leaned back in the chair. She hadn't thought about the work situation once in the last twelve hours. It was the last thing she wanted to think about. A job was just a necessary thing she had to do in order to have money to travel. The particulars weren't important.

"What haven't I done would be a shorter list. Bar work, hostel manager, kitchen assistant—you name it, I've probably done it." She glanced out the window, dusty with red dirt. A road train rumbled down the highway

"Oh. But you've never worked *in* travel? More a traveller who worked as you roamed?"

"Bingo. I go where the money flows. Or, at least, I used to. The scene has changed over the years. Prices have doubled or tripled in some places with increased tourism."

"I had no idea."

Brooke pulled her lips tight. "Hence, why I'm here. I needed a break for a bit. To give myself some time to reevaluate if I could do things differently."

"But Australia is expensive. I mean you said you came

from, what—Indonesia, right? Why not just stay there and live on the cheap?"

"I wasn't making more than I was spending." It was so tiring constantly making it work.

JJ's eyebrows furrowed, so briefly Brooke almost missed it. Brooke crossed her legs. She didn't need to be judged, especially by someone who didn't know her.

"I also had family to come back to here." Even if she'd stayed with them as a last resort and had come to question that decision.

JJ cocked her head to the side, gaze boring into Brooke. "Listen, it's probably not my place, but Hayl—"

"It's not," Brooke snapped. This conversation was shutting down *right* now.

JJ shifted in her seat. Thankfully, the waitress chose that moment to bring out their coffees. Brooke worked to relax her jaw, reminding herself that JJ wasn't the enemy.

"So, looking forward to getting things back on track today?" Brooke asked.

If JJ was thrown by the jump, she didn't show it. "Please. I'm looking forward to seeing what amazing things you've planned. The unplanned ones, I'm happy to leave in the past."

"Life is full of unplanned surprises. That's just living. I don't think it's something you can avoid."

JJ blew on her coffee and took a sip. "Not when you're around."

"What's that supposed to mean?" Brooke folded her arms.

"Well, it's only the start of the trip and it's already been way off the rails."

"You can't blame me. It's not my fault your car broke down. I also didn't push you into a spiky bush with your pants down, nor did I gather a bunch of hellbent feral goats to trample your car."

JJ looked sheepish, a small smile appearing behind her mug as she took another sip of coffee, attempting to appear nonchalant. "Well, when you put it that way..."

They stared at each other a beat, then dissolved into silent giggles just as the waitress brought over their breakfast.

"Looks delicious, thanks," Brooke said to the older woman, trying to compose herself.

Once they were alone again, she asked JJ, "How's your, uh, backside?"

JJ slid her cutlery out of the packet. "Fine, a little tender. Like a bruise. I won't be doing that again anytime soon."

"No, I'd imagine it'd be pretty hard to recreate those specific circumstances."

Brooke smiled, happy to be back on lighter topics and away from anything to do with family or finding a job.

The rest of the hour flew by. JJ left to meet with the mechanic, while Brooke contacted their accommodation with an update on their arrival. When JJ returned with a wide grin in place, Brooke was just finishing the last sip of her second coffee.

JJ dropped back into the seat opposite. "Mechanic said it sounded like the radiator, and if so, the car should be towed, then fixed within a couple of hours."

Brooke placed her mug on the coffee table. Must be nice to have the kind of stable income to throw at an issue like that. If it were Brooke, she would be scrounging for odd jobs to cover the cost.

"Not bad at all," Brooke said, focusing back on the trip. "Really, we've only lost half a day, and look at the adventure it's been!"

JJ didn't indulge her with a response.

TWELVE

JJ

JJ had never been so thankful to have her car fixed and be finally—*finally*—pulling up to their accommodation. They were glamping and she had no idea what to expect.

Brooke came out of the station's front office, keys and booklet in hand. "Okay, I've got the park map and the lady highlighted our site along with what roads to get us there. The tents are near the edge of the park and apparently have some of the best views."

JJ followed her directions, coming up on a row of tents with enough space between each to not feel overcrowded.

Tent wasn't the right word. "Now I know why they call it glamping—this is the size of a cabin!" It towered next to the car with a 360-degree verandah and built on solid metal stilts. Theirs was right on the end and overlooked dense scrubland set before red cliffs which climbed up to the very edge of one of the ranges.

"Wait till you see inside." Brooke jumped out of the car, dashing around the side of the tent and out of view.

JJ would usually unpack first and take a couple of bags

with her—less trips that way—but FOMO won out as she leaped from the car. She jogged to catch up with Brooke, who was unlocking the doors—because apparently their "tent" had full glass sliding doors across the entire frontage. The latch unlocked with a loud click and Brooke pulled it open.

"After you." She waved one hand between herself and the entryway.

JJ stepped over the threshold. It was stuffy, already warmed from the morning sun and smelled like canvas with a hint of hotel soap. The khaki green walls had expansive zip-open windows and fly screens. The ceiling was held up by a tall, pitched roof with the thickest poles she'd ever seen. With circus vibes, this tent was no instant thirty-second pack-down. A king-sized bed took up most of the room.

"Oh." Brooke walked in behind her and stopped short, turning to JJ. "Didn't you book the twin tent?"

"I don't know. I just clicked on the link you sent and paid. You were organising the itinerary."

"Well, surprise!" Brooke joked. "Pretty sure you could choose from the drop-down menu."

JJ turned to leave. "I'll go and get it fixed."

"I doubt there'd be any available tents to switch to. They're usually fully booked." Brooke sighed and tucked her hair behind her ear. "It's fine. I guess you and I already slept in the back of your car last night. At least with a king, it'll feel like we're basically sleeping on opposite sides of the room. It's probably more space than the twin singles anyway."

Sharing a car space in sleeping bags was one thing, but

sleeping in the same bed? Well, Brooke didn't seem bothered... so she wouldn't worry either.

After everything, it was just nice to be at their accommodation and get a proper start on this relaxing holiday. No more hiccups, just following the itinerary and having fun.

"What's this basket?" Brooke asked across the room.

JJ crossed the room to a small cabinet setup with a mini fridge, kettle, and tea and coffee supplies.

"I dunno." JJ poked her head over Brooke's shoulder, spiced vanilla hitting her senses.

Brooke picked up the small card lying on top of the basket. "*Brooke and JJ*," she read out. "*We were sorry to hear of your troubles in getting here. Please enjoy this complimentary picnic basket of local produce on us.*"

JJ took the card with its neat, printed handwriting.

"Aww, that's so nice," Brooke said. "All I did was email them this morning to explain our non-arrival last night. Oh look, they've given us a local trail map. Fancy an afternoon hike and picnic?"

"Thought you'd never ask," JJ said, setting down the card, ready to get into nature on their own terms.

Rather than taking the entire basket up the hill, they packed their day packs, splitting the load between them. After changing into their hiking gear, they made their way out to Emu's Nest, a relatively short but steep hike that promised views of the ranges at the top.

Brooke led the two of them with long, confident strides as she manoeuvred her way up the path in front. JJ followed, her pulse racing.

Loose rocks and half-sunken pebbles lined themselves along the rich red earth; the ants using the trail's well-trodden paths for their routes between their colonies. There was no way JJ was stopping, those things looked mean. Every time she stepped near them, they changed direction and dashed for her shoes. The landscape was a better focus; a mishmash of greens, all blending into one another between native shrubs and tall gums humming with birdlife that echoed through the trees.

"Going okay?" Brooke asked around halfway up. She was visibly out of breath. At least JJ wasn't the only one feeling the effects of the near constant elevation.

"Yeah, good."

Brooke had checked in a few times along the way, always making sure JJ was all right. She never stormed ahead or made her feel left behind. Courteous. That's the word she'd use for Brooke. Still very incongruent with the woman seen back in Adelaide with her sister. Though JJ had a glimpse in the cafe when she'd tried to push a little. Clearly, even a little was still too much. JJ brushed away the thoughts along with the two flies ferociously buzzing around her ears and continued their upwards trajectory.

The flies were so distracting, JJ ran headfirst into Brooke's behind as she came to a halt on the steep slope. JJ stumbled, reaching out and grabbing onto Brooke's hips instead to steady herself.

"Sorry," she said, dropping her arms and straightening. She really needed to pay attention to her surroundings.

Brooke turned, but instead of asking about JJ's mishap, she brought a finger to her lips. "Shh." She gestured in front of them with her chin. A few metres up the path, JJ spotted it: a mother kangaroo and her joey, grazing to the side. The joey lounged in the pouch, one paw on the ground as it lazily nibbled at a clump of wild grass. They slowed their steps, making sure the mother knew they were coming. She hopped a few metres away, then stopped, not seeming fussed by their passing proximity.

"How cute!" Brooke said. It took everything in JJ not to remind her travel companion she wasn't meant to be enjoying this destination, but she didn't have it in her to ruin the moment.

After another hour, they reached the peak. The trail broke out of the trees and onto a flat expanse of red rocks. The last section had been an absolute scramble as the rocks grew larger and harder to clamber over.

JJ took in the complete panoramic views of the ranges surrounding them. "Well, this was worth the effort."

"Not bad," Brooke admitted. "I'll agree, photos don't do this place justice. The sheer scale of the ranges is something else."

They stood side-by-side, taking in the views. They hadn't seen anyone else on the trail, and with no one else at the peak, the entire place was theirs. Brooke found a flat rock nearby that made the perfect raised platform for their picnic. JJ sat opposite Brooke as she unpacked their goodies —cheese, salami, crackers...

"Oh, my favourite," JJ commented as Brooke pulled out a small tub of quince paste.

Sitting atop the mountain, JJ's mind slowed. Work schedules, failed dates and wondering if Jess was respecting her furniture, all took a backseat in her mind. The sun poked out from the clouds, her whole body breaking out in goosebumps. She tipped her head back, soaking in the warmth.

"I needed this," JJ almost moaned.

"I can see that." A wry smile played on Brooke's face.

"I'm sure it's not as fancy as all the faraway places you've been, but how can you not like this? Sitting here in the middle of nowhere, eating fancy cheese with amazing company?"

"Mmm, debatable," Brooke said, head tilted and smile still in place, her blonde hair catching the light just so.

She was really very pretty. It suddenly struck JJ that she was going to be sharing a bed with her tonight. She swallowed.

"I'm happy to be travelling again, even if I do wish it was anywhere but here."

That was the second time Brooke had uttered those words. Why was "here" never good enough for her, never to be discussed? JJ tamped down her question. Instead, she asked, "Have you travelled much with other people over the years?"

"Mostly alone. But I'd usually end up in group trips to places, or hanging with all sorts at a hostel. Occasionally I'd end up with someone to travel with briefly."

"Travelling with them, like as a partner?"

Brooke laughed. "No. I don't do relationships. Just friends. Travel buddies. Or you know, a bit of fun here and there."

"Right." JJ took a bite of salami. She couldn't have been more opposite to Brooke if she tried. Just the thought of one-night stands sent a shudder down her spine. How could people open themselves up like that to someone they didn't know? Call her a romantic, but she wanted dates, chats—a little getting to know them first. "I don't know how you do that. I'm a relationship girl, or at least, I would be if I found the right woman." JJ shoved all her recent failed dates to the back of her mind.

"Relationships don't work for me," Brooke said, topping a biscuit with cheese. "I'm never in one spot long enough for it to mean anything anyway." Brooke gave a half-hearted shrug.

"God, we're a pair of sad sacks then," JJ replied.

"Hey, at least I've been jumping in the sack."

"Lucky you." JJ did not want to think about *that* with Brooke in all matter of—

"So women, huh?" Brooke asked as she cut off a large wedge of cheese and popped it straight in her mouth.

"Yep. You?"

Another shrug. "Usually guys, or whoever I gel with. I've had fun with a girl or two in my time."

JJ nodded along. She'd wondered if the lesbian gene ran in the family, but maybe not. It didn't sound like Brooke was necessarily into women, as much as it was experimenting. Or, well, *fun* as she'd described it. Not that JJ was interested in Brooke. This walking red flag was the epitome of the wrong woman for her, even if she was objectively beautiful. JJ was on a break from dating anyway.

The sun slipped behind the clouds again and this time the sky grew dark and ominous. JJ blinked. Where had that come from?

"Ah, Brooke? I think we need to head back down. That"—she pointed over Brooke's shoulder—"doesn't look good."

She'd barely finished her sentence when the wind picked up. Gentle at first, then a gust that swept across the top of the jagged rocks, picking up loose hairs around Brooke's face.

"Yeah, we gotta move." Brooke dove into her backpack and just as JJ went to question her, she pulled out a small fluro sack.

"What's that?"

"Waterproof bag cover. Everything you need to keep dry, stuff it in here."

"Is that really necessary?"

"I'm not waiting around to find out."

Bags packed and zipped, they had just started the mad scramble across the top of the ridge when the first drops hit.

"Ow," JJ said, a stinging sensation hitting her body. That was some hard rain.

"Oh my god. Is that hail?" Brooke's eyes rounded. "Okay, this is crazy, we need to move—now!"

JJ stumbled on a loose rock. Brooke's firm hand grabbed hold of JJ's with assuredness, helping her up and along the path. The hail fell harder, large droplets of rain joining in on the downpour.

"It's going to get slippery. Don't let go of my hand!"

JJ barely heard Brooke's shout over the roar of the wild weather. A clap of thunder bellowed overhead. Brooke was right: this was insane. They were on top of a mountain in the middle of a thundering hailstorm. JJ's family would freak if they could see what she was up to right now.

"Remember what I said about pivoting?" Brooke shouted, wiping droplets of rain from her face.

"Yeah?"

"We're pivoting!"

She understood Brooke's words. Unplanned surprises.

She might not like them, but right now, they didn't have a choice.

Brooke held on tight, fingers interlocked with JJ's as they dashed as fast as possible without risking slipping.

Reaching the top of the descent, Brooke stopped and turned to JJ. "I think running down will be our best bet. Use the edges and large rocks for grip, and step sideways where you can. I've hiked in wet terrain, but not during an active downpour!"

"Got it." She squeezed Brooke's hand back in response with a sharp nod. Gone were the moments of appreciating the view, taking in fresh air and slowing time. This was life on fast forward, like listening to an audio-book on double speed. Every step was a calculated dance. Left foot on the rock jutting out, right foot against the bank by a tree root, repeat. She wiped the rain from her eyes over and over to keep her vision clear enough to see her next steps.

Once past the steepest and rockiest section, they were able to pick up the pace. By this point they were both laughing at the sheer craziness of the situation, running full pelt down a mountain hand-in-hand. Brooke's grip never faltered, any jerk, any slip, and she was there. They may be opposites in some ways, but at this moment, they were completely in sync.

The hail had, thankfully, been replaced by rain, but the thunder still roared in the distance. The trail opened wide —they'd reached the base—but it was no place to catch their breath. Instead, they ran, and ran, and ran—all the way back to their over-the-top tent. They only stopped once they reached the alcove of the deck. Brooke released her hand. In the post-adrenaline haze, JJ missed the warmth and support.

No matter what was thrown at them, Brooke took it in her stride. If it were up to JJ, she'd probably still be up the top of the mountain planning the best way to get down. Even now, Brooke's face was bright and alive from the rush of it all. Cheeks pink and hair plastered to her face from the rain, her ponytail barely intact. JJ wanted to take a sip of that energy, to have even a taste of it for herself.

"I can't believe how quick that rolled in." Brooke bent in half, hands on knees, catching her breath.

"Right! That was one of the most dangerous but exciting things I've ever done." She had to give it to Brooke, today was no ordinary day. A far cry from painting and patching walls at home. Her body still ached, but this time from living on the wild side, a breach from routine.

JJ shook out her hair, running a hand through the top. She had to look like an absolute mess. She was about to comment on it when she caught the odd look on Brooke's face.

Almost as though her eyes were roaming over JJ's body. But that couldn't be right, could it?

THIRTEEN
Brooke

Oh.

That was the only coherent thought running through Brooke's mind.

JJ looked like she'd just stepped out of a fashion magazine with one of those wet hair looks, a soaked half-unbuttoned shirt and a half-smile that had Brooke mesmerised. Read: JJ looked hot.

Brooke dropped her eyes to the floor, realising she'd been staring. That was new. What was also new was the realisation they were wet, sweaty, muddy and in dire need of a shower.

"You can shower first," Brooke offered. "I'll hang out here until you're done."

"You sure?" JJ asked.

"Of course."

Anything to give her five minutes to work out why she'd been ogling the painter. It was probably the rush of endorphins and adrenaline that was messing with her head.

A hot shower would fix it. No need to question her reaction or picture JJ like that over and over again.

Showered and dressed, Brooke and JJ sat on the bed playing cards. The storm rolled through the trees across their tent, shaking the entire thing with a vicious roar. The canvas top whipped and clattered in a frenzy above their heads. It felt like they were about to take flight any second. Brooke hated to think how other campers in a basic tent were getting on in these conditions.

JJ was quiet. It was hard to tell if she was paying attention to the current game, so Brooke folded her cards. It took JJ a full thirty seconds to realise. Not paying attention, then.

"What's going on?" Brooke asked.

JJ picked at a bit of fluff on the quilt. "I just feel frustrated."

"With the game?" Brooke had won the last couple of rounds, but she didn't think JJ would be that much of a sore loser.

"No, this." JJ lifted her hands, gesturing to the room around them. "Being holed up in our tent. I don't want to pivot again."

The tent shook extra hard with another lashing of wind. The rain joined in on the fun, as if to make a point.

"JJ..." Brooke tempered a smile. "You can't control the weather. Getting frustrated won't make it go away, it just... is. We still got to hike—"

"That wasn't a hike. That was a race for our lives."

A little dramatic, but Brooke pushed on. "Listen. We still hiked today, despite having a broken-down car this morning. We still *got to* see the views of the ranges and enjoy a picnic, and then we *got to* experience a possibly once-in-a-lifetime event of being hailed on while running full bore down a mountain—it even made you laugh. I don't know about you, but I think that makes for a pretty cool story to tell your friends or family when you get back, don't you?"

"Yeah, but, I just wish we could be enjoying the outdoors now too, you know—the whole reason we came here."

"Focus on what you can control. If you don't want to play cards, fine. Make yourself a tea, read a book or I dunno, do something that makes you feel good."

"Maybe I'm not that into the cards to keep my mind from wandering," JJ said. She thought for a minute. "I can't think of anything else, so I guess we can chat."

"Jeez, don't sound too enthusiastic about spending time with me." Brooke smiled, then asked seriously, "I'm curious though, where do you think these expectations you put on everything come from? The holiday, the weather..."

JJ fiddled with her hands. "I'm—not sure."

Brooke packed up the cards as she waited. The box barely held them together; it'd seen her through many hours of waiting in airports and upturned plans over the years. Maybe she should've taught JJ how to play *Patience*?

"There was this one time—god, this is going to sound so stupid..." JJ covered her face with her hands.

"Back in primary school we were given these colouring books. My friend at the time was always so talented at everything they did. Halfway through the morning when I looked at her work, it was exactly as expected—a perfectly executed drawing of a seahorse. It had matching colours, all neatly shaded within the lines. I didn't think it was possible to colour that precisely as a kid. I'd chosen a shark picture and decided to colour it black. It was going to look so cool in my head."

JJ rubbed and kneaded at her hands. "Instead, it looked like it had been attacked by a toddler using markers for the first time. It looked like shit, I knew it looked like shit, and the thing was—I'd tried so bloody hard to keep within the lines, but I was just so excited to colour in and do it fast, I'd always slip outside."

"That would've been hard," Brooke said. Hearing the story, she could easily picture her brother or sister doing the same thing and placing herself in JJ's position. It was eerily similar to some of the situations she'd found herself in while growing up. Steven was particularly gifted in the drawing department. Brooke wasn't. Obviously.

"It was. I guess that's just one example, but I compared us a lot over the years. Wanting to be her or be better than her—I don't know—even though she was my friend. Who knows if that's truly why I like to control situations now and want them to be perfect, or run smoothly, but I do like trying to live life within those lines."

"Does living within those lines make you happy?" Because living that way for Brooke sure didn't bring her any happiness living with that expectation from her parents.

"Wh—yeah." JJ sat up, straightening her shoulders. "I mean, I think so? I like to think my precision has helped me achieve things in life like running my business and buying a house."

"Achievement and happiness are two different things though," Brooke said. "Do those things bring you joy?"

"Now you just sound like Marie Kondo," JJ joked.

That was a deflection as good as Brooke's own. She saw the boundary for what it was and backed off. At least she had more understanding.

They steered clear of any further personal topics as Brooke let JJ's story simmer in the back of her mind. She hadn't expected such a simple tale to hold so much weight to this day for JJ. Though, wasn't that exactly what had been happening to Brooke since she'd been back? Maybe they had more in common than she thought.

That night, Brooke's eyes flung open in the darkness.

She blinked. Something was touching her.

Her heart pounded as she tried to figure out what was happening. Was JJ touching her? Her stomach flipped at the thought with a flash of JJ standing on the deck in her dripping clothes.

The hand was pressing itself between Brooke's underside and the mattress, and it was... wriggling?

"JJ, what are you doing?" she whispered.

"Mmpphmmph," JJ grumbled, the wiggling intensifying as Brooke rolled away from it and turned to face her.

"What. Are. You. Doing?" she asked again, sitting up this time, heart beating faster.

"*Mmmove*. You're on my phone," JJ groaned.

Brooke's face burned, shoulders slumping slightly. Right. JJ wasn't actually trying to touch her.

Brooke felt around on the bed. There was no phone, only JJ's hand still flailing about. "I don't have your phone."

"Mmkay," came the mumbled response. JJ rolled over and Brooke was met with silence. No movement. Nothing. Only the dull thud of her heart.

"JJ?" she checked, fully awake now.

Soft snores were the only thing that came back. JJ was asleep.

The woman was sleep-talking. Not trying to touch her. Why would JJ have even been doing that in the first place? So stupid. Now Brooke lay awake, unable to sleep with the whirlwind of thoughts cascading through her mind. The storm had at least tamed, only a gentle patter of rain hitting the canvas.

After a while, she fell into a fitful sleep, that weird in between of not knowing when she was awake or dreaming.

Eyes fluttering open, the cacophony of birdlife outside the tent was a natural alarm Brooke didn't know she needed. She pulled up the covers around her chin. It was so much chillier in the outback.

JJ was on her side, eyes open. From the look on her face, she had no idea she'd been touching Brooke last night.

"Morning," she said through a yawn.

"You don't remember anything do you?" Brooke asked.

JJ went to roll on her back, winced, and rolled back to face Brooke, her eyebrow raised. "About the storm?" She rubbed her eyes, one still shut. Sleepy JJ was kind of cute, and clearly not a morning person.

Brooke broke into a smile. "No, not that. Any recollection of sliding your hand underneath me last night?"

"What!" JJ squeaked, head lifting off her pillow, fully awake now, her face colouring.

"Yep. Someone decided to get handsy with me last night, but according to you, you were 'looking for your phone'." Brooke's grin widened as JJ's blush deepened.

JJ groaned, head flopping back onto the pillow. "I have zero recollection of that. Are you sure? Ugh. Here I was thinking I was done with embarrassing myself in front of you. I'm so sorry." JJ's face was so absolutely stricken, for a tiny second Brooke felt bad for rubbing it in, but she was enjoying this way too much.

"And then you rolled over and..." Brooke paused.

JJ's eyes widened. "Oh no, what? No. Don't tell me." A hand covered her face, one eye peeking between her fingers.

Brooke broke out into laughter. "Nah, there was nothing else. You rolled over and snored. No more touches. Promise."

JJ closed her eyes, hand dropping. "Thank god." She opened them again. "I'll speak with the front office today and try to get that twin room." JJ got up and pulled out her clothes for the day, setting them out just so on the bed.

The pang hit Brooke out of nowhere. As disrupted as her sleep had been last night, she'd still felt comfortable sharing the bed with JJ. Their friendly companionship had Brooke at an ease she hadn't felt in a long time.

She waved JJ off. "Honestly, it's no big deal. It was funny. I've never shared a bed with someone who spoke in their sleep before."

"Yeah, well, I don't usually share my bed with anyone, full stop," JJ replied.

Neither did Brooke, but she didn't say that.

While it was a throwaway comment from JJ, it landed a little heavy between them. Maybe JJ felt safe with Brooke too?

The possibility warmed Brooke.

FOURTEEN

JJ

"Please don't tell me we're going in that?" JJ pointed at the way-too-small helicopter with its red body and thick gold-striped panel. That couldn't be safe. It was tiny.

"We certainly are."

This was JJ's first helicopter ride, but this was not what she had envisioned. Sure, Brooke had been extremely tight-lipped about the experience when JJ had paid over the phone, and all JJ knew was it was some kind of special helicopter package, but *this*? This looked pretty fancy... and terrifying.

JJ wiped her now-sweating palms on her pants. She and Brooke were still in their hiking gear after their day spent exploring a couple more trails. The sun had come out and cooperated for the entire day, a complete turnaround after yesterday. Brooke had told JJ not to get changed, and not to bring anything, so here she was with nothing but her day pack.

Brooke fit right in with the rugged red plains, like she'd been born to hike around the outback. Her hair was woven into a single plait which dropped over her shoulder and rested atop a dusty pink hiking shirt. They were both wearing cream-coloured hiking pants as though they'd tried to match. When they'd first seen each other this morning, they'd chuckled at their similar outfits, but there was no way JJ was wearing the muddied grey pair from the day before! That's why she always packed a spare—just in case.

Brooke nudged JJ's elbow and led her to the pilot halfway to the helicopter.

"Afternoon, ladies. I'm Ed, and I'll be looking after you today." Ed looked like a park ranger in a blue button up work shirt, light work shorts and chunky work boots that appeared more brown than black with the amount of red dust caked on them. He readjusted an old baseball cap on his head and gave them a brilliant smile. JJ's nerves settled just a little.

Ed ran through the safety measures and within minutes they were walking the rest of the way to the helicopter. JJ had only been on a plane once or twice and in this moment wished she had more flying experience.

"Which one of you is in the front with me?" Ed asked, looking between them as he held the door open.

Brooke grabbed JJ by the arms and pushed her forward. "This one!"

Cramped into the front passenger seat, JJ turned with a tight smile to check on Brooke, who gave her two thumbs up. JJ would've preferred to be sitting next to her in the back, but the pilot had explained proper weight distribution was necessary.

Buckled up, the noise and vibrations from the engine and rotors intensified along with her heartbeat. The pilot handed JJ a pair of noise-cancelling headphones to help deaden the sound and allow them to speak with each other.

"You good?" Brooke's now digitised voice came through the headset.

"Yep," JJ said, gripping the edges of her seat as the pilot started flicking and fiddling with the switches between them.

JJ took a deep breath. She really did have the best views in the front with almost a solid 180 degrees. Her phone burned in her pocket, screaming for her to take a video of the experience, but she was frozen on the spot. They hadn't even moved yet and her stomach was already doing somersaults. Then her stomach really did lurch as they pulled away from the ground.

"Whoa," she said. It was the strangest feeling as they lifted in a cloud of dust and dirt, leaving the scorched earth behind. They now towered over the old gums which had surrounded them moments before.

Her grip tightened as they banked a little to the left. Up they climbed, her view of the land becoming vast and breathtaking.

So breathtaking.

No, really, she needed to breathe. Her lungs were burning.

She sucked in a big gulp of air and forced her breath into a natural rhythm as the helicopter pushed forward. There was a squeeze on her shoulder. A gentle rub. A reminder that Brooke was there. The silent support had JJ's muscles relaxing.

JJ assumed they'd do a loop of the ranges and hoped they'd get to see all the main points of interest in the area. It was one thing to hike the trails up to the viewpoints, but this was something else entirely. Ed explained the landmarks and pointed out random sightings—like a line of emus beelining for a creek, their shadows making them look like tiny chickens on the ground. Ahead, Wilpena Pound stood proud from this high up, all red and white rock with swathes of dark green bushland covering it for kilometres. JJ eased forward, a soft grip still on the chair as she drank in everything she could.

"Goats!" Brooke said, her exclamation blaring in JJ's ears.

Ed growled. "Those pests are everywhere up here now, destroying all the vegetation. They're out of control."

JJ turned to face Ed. "We had a run in with some the other day."

"I'm sure it won't be your last," he muttered.

Ten minutes later, they came upon a ridgeline thick with trees. Ed lowered the helicopter, coming so close to the tree tops that JJ scooted her feet back as if to avoid them. They sank below the canopy into a small clearing, a tiny helipad coming into view.

"Oh, we're stopping?" JJ asked.

"Of course," he replied with a slight raise of his brow. "Wait till you see this view."

JJ clambered onto solid ground. Her knees almost collapsed under her like jelly, muscles aching. That was intense. She felt like running to the nearest tree and giving it a hug. What a ride!

They walked to the edge of the viewpoint. Okay, wow. Even after seeing it all from the sky, the new angle hit differently. JJ inhaled, the scent of eucalyptus thick. Brooke stood next to her, gaze soft as they took it all in.

Dozens of notifications filled the quiet, the incessant pings and buzzes sounding frenzied. JJ blinked several times, her pocket pulling at her attention. Her eyes met Brooke's. The beeps ceased and they returned to the view with small smiles. Tech couldn't compete with this outlook.

Clouds formed deep shadows on each ridge, etching into the towering red land mass and making the ranges appear even more rugged. The ancient formation seemed so untouched, like a scene straight out of *Jurassic Park*.

"Welcome to Sky Ridge," Ed declared, coming up behind them. "One of the best and most secluded sites to view the ranges from. I'll go prepare your things." Without another word, he turned on his heel and headed back to the helicopter.

"Huh?" JJ said.

Brooke bumped her shoulder. "We're staying here tonight."

"What?!" JJ rounded on her.

Brooke hooked a thumb over her shoulder. "We're swagging it, and Ed here is dropping off our supplies. Food, firewood—everything we'll need for, oh, the next fifteen hours or so." Her flash of teeth was absolutely wicked.

"No. Way." JJ beamed. "Okay, this is honestly one the coolest things I've ever done." She tamped down the urge to lunge onto Brooke. Brooke was just her tour guide. JJ had asked her to do this. Though Brooke's glowing face told JJ she was pretty chuffed at her response.

"We haven't even done it yet!" Brooke chuckled, playing with the end of her plait.

JJ shook her head. “I don’t even care. This is—wow.” Then she stopped. “So glad this wasn’t booked for yesterday. Being in a swag during a hailstorm would be the worst.”

“Um, yeah, no thanks! Though, they probably would’ve cancelled.” Brooke turned back to the view.

JJ frowned. That would’ve been worse. It was nice knowing their plan had worked out weather-wise for this section of the trip.

Ed had everything set up in five minutes, then gave them a quick rundown of everything they needed to know. “Have fun ladies. See you in the morning at ten.” With a wink and a wave, he slipped back into the chopper.

JJ’s eyes widened. “Oh, does he think we’re...”

Brooke’s head whipped around. “Oh! Gosh, surely not?” The laugh that followed sounded forced, a little awkward.

Both faced away as Ed took off, wind kicking dust at their backs.

And then they were alone.

In the middle of nowhere.

Again.

At least it was on purpose this time.

And no need to worry about serial killers, not unless they flew helicopters...

“Going to have to watch out for drop bears tonight!” Brooke said, poking JJ in the side.

JJ ducked out of reach. She didn’t need Brooke adding any more fuel to her nightmare fire!

Brooke looped an arm through JJ’s and pulled her towards their camp for the night.

They came to a flat, rocky outcrop setup with a fire pit, an esky of food, two camping chairs with folded blankets, and one very tiny, extremely cosy swag.

JJ swallowed.

"I thought we'd have individual swags," Brooke said, eyes zeroed in on their sleeping quarters. "You're really going to have to keep those hands to yourself tonight."

"Ha-ha. Well, there's no way we're changing the sleeping arrangements now." The helicopter was long gone.

For dinner, JJ offered to cook as a thank you to Brooke for organising the experience. They'd been left with hamburger supplies, which happened to be one of JJ's go-to dishes. The cheese was currently melting onto the beef patties, a little dripping off the sides and sizzling onto the cast iron pan, while the buns toasted over the open fire. It smelled like summer, camping down south with her family when she was little, her dad at the barbecue, always burning the meat. She breathed in deep and smiled. Brooke sat staring at the flames, glass of wine in hand.

"Sauce?" JJ asked, turning the squeezy bottle upside down and giving the bottom a good whack.

"Oh, definitely."

JJ brought over their two plates, handing one slowly to Brooke so it didn't fall apart.

"You didn't tell me you were a master chef," Brooke joked.

JJ shrugged and smiled. "I learned from the best—my mum and Gran. Careful, it's hot."

Brooke could only be described as a savage eater. Within seconds there was sauce running down her hands, a splotch on her pants and a dob on the end of her nose. Instead of reaching for a napkin, JJ sat still, caught off guard at the adorableness of the situation happening next to her. By all accounts she should be scrunching her nose up, not leaning back with a soft smile as Brooke completely annihilated her dinner with the enthusiasm of a wolf.

Yeah, tonight, she didn't mind it one bit.

"What?" Brooke asked, catching her stare.

"Nothing. Glad you're enjoying it is all."

JJ dabbed at the corner of her own mouth, not sure she could ever eat with such abandon. She took a clean bite of her burger without spilling a single crumb onto her plate.

Dinner a success, JJ cleaned everything as the sun began to dance on the edge of the ranges, casting the long expanse of rock in a glow of oranges and reds as vibrant as the sunset itself. She threw another log on the fire, poking it around with a stick, then handed Brooke one of the thick woollen blankets. The last of the light had clawed at the remaining warmth left from the day. The cool, crisp air snaked its way around JJ's ankles as she sunk into her own seat. She spread her blanket over every possible inch of her body.

Minutes ticked by in silence as they soaked in the fast-changing landscape of the South Australian Flinders Ranges. This is what JJ had needed: to be immersed in nature, sitting with such a deep and profound appreciation for her country—her home—and the traditional lands of the Adnyamathanha Aboriginal people. Here, there were no walls waiting to be painted, no garden that needed watering. Her senses were abuzz with the newness of her surroundings, filling her with energy that prickled under her skin. Here she was, making memories instead of sitting at home with the same repeated evening routine. And Brooke had made that happen.

She closed her eyes.

Light wind played in the gums above them. A kookaburra laughed in the distance, then another answered, fainter across the gorge. The fire spat and crackled as the new log settled in over the coals.

This was living.

She opened her eyes and turned to Brooke. "Thank you for this."

Brooke seemed far away before she met JJ's gaze, a smile blooming. "You're welcome."

It wasn't until they were settling in for the night that JJ noted the swag was even smaller up close than what it had appeared before. She stood next to it and called out to Brooke, who was checking their fire was completely out. "Are they sure this is a double swag?"

It was so narrow, her arms would touch the sides if she stretched out in the middle.

"I mean, there are two pillows, right?" Brooke called back.

"Yeah." A shiver ran through her as a gust of wind rolled over the range. She pulled her hoodie over her head. Close quarters could be a good thing with this frigid night air.

Brooke joined her, rubbing her arms up and down. "You want left or right? Actually, maybe you should have the zipper side in case you need to pee."

JJ went to protest, but Brooke wasn't wrong. "Fine by me. After you then."

Brooke pulled off her hiking boots in a haphazard pile

and slipped into the swag. "It's comfier than you'd think." She shuffled over and patted the squeezy space next to her.

JJ gave herself a second, still not used to sharing a bed with someone. The car was fine. They'd been in their own sleeping bags. And their king bed at the station really was like a small island, but this... JJ swallowed. This was small. Confined.

JJ straightened Brooke's boots, then placed hers next to them. She crawled into the space and sunk into the sleeping bag. Her butt smarted at the hard ground. She ignored it. There was no way she was rolling onto her side this close to Brooke. As it was, their bodies were now pressed together from their shoulders all the way down to their knees. Tingles bloomed wherever they touched. JJ shuffled, trying to get her shoulders to fit down flat, but bumped into Brooke.

"Sorry," she muttered. At least they were fully dressed, or this would've been even more awkward. She pulled her sleeves up, starting to overheat already.

"Shooting star!" Brooke gasped.

JJ had been so engrossed in the sleeping arrangements, she hadn't taken in the night sky above them. A few clouds hung above them, but they still had a clear view of the stars. It felt closer to the universe here, each star a little brighter, the colours of the Milky Way on show like swirls of ethereal magic.

Backside beginning to ache, and not wanting to be rude and face away, JJ gave up and rolled onto her side, scooching as far back as she could against the swag. She was so hard up against the edge, there'd be a JJ-sized imprint on the outside. All the movement had her overheating again. She sat up in a huff and pulled the hoodie off.

"Sorry, I sleep hot," JJ said, flopping back down.

"Absolute cold frog here," Brooke said, snuggling deeper into the sleeping bag and moving to the side to face JJ.

Though JJ had tried to give them space, Brooke's spiced vanilla scent still crept onto her side. The smell was like a warm chai latte—comforting, homely.

"Happy if I close up the mesh?" JJ asked. It felt weird getting ready to sleep without doing her usual routine of brushing her teeth or washing her face. Being spontaneous was hard.

"Go ahead." Brooke's wine-laced breath was warm on JJ's face, causing a knot to pull at her centre.

Okay, what was happening? The sensation settled low in her gut. Brooke was attractive, but the thought of something more? No. She'd never.

JJ sat up to zip their swag and reminded herself of everything she wanted in a woman. Brooke wasn't it. She was messy—with her life and in person, and she was argumentative, and, well, just not who JJ was looking for.

By the time she'd wrangled the mesh screen shut, Brooke had shifted onto her back again. JJ breathed easier.

With mumbled goodnights, JJ forced her eyes shut and willed her body to relax.

She needed space from this pretty woman, stat.

FIFTEEN
Brooke

Brooke's body was on fire.

She'd tossed and turned most of the night; trying to get comfortable, trying to get warm and trying to give JJ her space. At some point, she must've dozed off, only to now wake, feeling as if she'd been dropped straight into a scalding hot bath. Though, said bath currently moved, pulling her closer.

Oh.

Recognition swam to the surface. The helicopter. The swag. JJ.

She stiffened, the jerking motion making JJ's hand slip beneath her shirt, pressing onto her stomach. *Oh.* Warm breath tickled the hairs on her neck.

Brooke didn't cuddle. She'd never been cuddled, never given cuddles. She wasn't a spoon type of girl. She was the fork. Get too close and the pointy end would make sure the other person was back on the other side of the bed. Now she couldn't move, couldn't think, her brain still scrambling nonsense about warm baths and cutlery.

Allowing herself a moment, she could admit it was... nice. To be held. JJ's arm draped over her protectively like they'd lain in this position dozens of times before. Everything about it felt right. Yet this current situation was so very wrong. JJ would be horrified if she was awake. But, if Brooke woke her now, would that be more awkward? At least one of them was getting some sleep.

The sounds of the bush began to stir like a welcome chant for the sunrise. A cockatoo screeched from a tree directly above, making both women jump.

The hand, still so warm against her skin, wrenched away as JJ rolled to her back. Crisis averted, hopefully. Brooke turned over to face her. If JJ was aware she'd been spooning Brooke, she didn't show it.

"Morning," JJ yawned, stretching like a bent banana to avoid touching her. Okay, she definitely had no idea.

Brooke stretched herself, stiff and sore from a night of hard ground and confined sleeping space. Her hips had been digging into something particularly lumpy, and Brooke empathised with the *Princess and the Pea* in that moment. At least this experience was only for a night.

JJ unzipped them from the swag and insisted she make breakfast. Brooke wasn't about to turn down a chance to be wined and dined, even at six in the morning. If this were a date—not that she *did* date—JJ would be getting bonus points for this kind of behaviour. These things usually fell on Brooke to look after when travelling with other people. She was the competent one, the one who made sure things got done. Mainly because she'd been the one to look after herself for so many years, it was instinctual. Everyone else just went along with it. So sitting back like this? It was nice; a welcome change.

Brooke sunk into the fold-out chair with a sigh, wrapping a blanket around her shoulders as JJ got the fire going again. She inhaled. The scent of fresh dew, gum leaves and old smoke filled her lungs as the first rays of sun touched the earth.

Getting to see the sunrise on the other side of the ridge gave them an entirely different view from the night before. Now the plains came alive in vivid reds with veins of green running across the flat expanse of land and fading into the distance.

This was how to travel the right way: slowly, living on nature's circadian rhythm. No waking up to screens, alarms, or the usual busyness of life. Instead, this type of travel broke everyday living down to the bare minimum: food and shelter. Nothing else mattered.

For now.

Her stomach dropped. Now things had slowed, her mind ticked back into gear. The reminder that this current lifestyle wouldn't last pressed into her, closing in. Getting away like this didn't solve what she was doing next with her life, or the awkwardness waiting for her back at Hayley's. Her hand twitched, remembering the notifications and missed calls that had streamed through when they'd landed on top of the range, high enough to get reception. She'd swiped them all away. Now wasn't the time either. Adulting and responsibilities could wait, she had bacon and eggs to eat on a fresh damper roll.

"Penny for your thoughts?" JJ asked, passing her a plate before biting into her own brekkie roll.

Brooke smiled sheepishly as she balanced the plate on her lap. "Thanks. Sorry, that fire is mesmerising. Nothing profound. Just going through my to-do list for when I get back—and pretending it doesn't exist."

"Ah. Yeah, I get you. It's been nice not thinking about work or having to paint. I'm finally able to give my mind a break—not to mention my neck and shoulders." She ran a hand through her hair.

How could JJ look this good after barely touching her hair or showering? Brooke hadn't touched her own hair, still plaited. It'd be a bee's nest if she tried to wrestle it into anything else.

JJ licked a wayward dollop of sauce off her thumb. Brooke stopped mid-bite, watching.

"You don't have to answer, but have you had any more thoughts on what you'd like to do when you get back?" JJ asked.

It took Brooke a moment for the question to register. "Sorry, um. For now I've just applied to everything and anything available."

"I know you said that's what you did while travelling, but is there anything you *want* to do? Not for the money. For you."

She... hadn't considered that. The question surprised her more than it should have. Her life was a cycle of making money and travelling. That was going to be her method back here too, though it was starting to feel stale. Like a favourite jacket that didn't quite fit anymore. Rough, uncomfortable, old. A voice stirred, buried deep, trying to surface: *You could have stayed overseas. You could have made it work, you always had before. You* chose *to come home.*

Who was Brooke now if she wasn't Brooke the World Traveller? She certainly couldn't go back to being Brooke Mayfield, the imperfect, weird, black sheep of the family. But if not either of them, then who was she?

Her last bite lodged itself in her throat, forcing its way down uncomfortably.

"I... don't know," Brooke croaked out.

There weren't people in her corner to bounce life ideas off like this. No one stopped long enough to ask, too busy on their phones streaming their hashtag-travel-life. Influencers were one thing she didn't miss overseas. They were everywhere now—the new world travellers. Brooke classed herself as an OG nomad, those who still travelled for themselves, for the adventure and the culture, not for the likes and follows.

"That's fair. Sounds like it's a big change for you, a new chapter of sorts. These things take time."

"Do you think I'm a failure?"

JJ stopped chewing and stared a beat. "What? Where did that come from?"

"My family thinks so." Brooke shrugged. "What do you see? An almost thirty-year-old woman with no job, no money, no car, no house, and no idea what she's doing with her life?" She needed clarification, someone to tell her what she'd known all along.

JJ set the rest of her roll down and shuffled to face Brooke, eyes unwavering. "I see a fierce woman, unafraid to speak her mind, calm in the face of chaos and crisis, caring and courteous—when she wants to be." JJ flipped her a grin, continuing, "Also incredibly attractive but down-to-earth and—my tour guide extraordinaire. I'm sorry, but remind me, which one of those sounds anything like a failure? So, you're figuring some shit out. Who cares? No one has all the answers to life, and those who say they do are lying through their teeth."

"I..." Brooke stopped, nodding once. "Thank you."

No other words came. She'd expected—what had she expected? Not that question slipping from her lips. But also, not that response. They hardly knew each other, yet JJ's considered reply spoke directly to that little child inside, whose chin rose a little higher, sitting up just a little straighter.

JJ gave the moment space. They went back to their meal and let nature fill the silence.

Mulling over her words, there was one in particular JJ had said that didn't match the rest. One that had nothing to do with success or failure as a person.

JJ had called her attractive. Incredibly attractive.

The edges of Brooke's mouth pulled up.

SIXTEEN

JJ

Forty-eight hours and 400km later, they were sun-drenched, nature-soaked and both aching in places they didn't know muscles existed. They hobbled around like two women in their eighties. The last of the ranges had slipped into the distance as they made their way to a specific palm-lined destination: Seppeltsfield, Barossa.

Reaching Trauben Winery at noon, they pulled up to their eco tiny home plonked at the far end of the vineyard's property. JJ got out of the car, hands on hips and took in the space. It screamed serenity, seclusion and—was that a hot tub on the decking? Wow. Brooke had outdone herself on the unique accommodations so far, and this tiny house was no exception. They'd barely dragged their bags inside and changed before there was a horn outside.

The bus was here.

"Told you we should've left earlier." JJ rushed out the door while Brooke tried to figure out how to lock up.

Brooke jammed a third key into the lock and twisted

with a huff. "You're the one who made us stop three times on the way here."

The door locked.

"I needed to pee!"

"Your bladder is literally the size of a walnut," Brooke replied, stalking past her. JJ jogged to catch up; they didn't want the driver to leave without them.

Brooke nabbed a window seat and JJ fell in the chair beside her. Her butt had barely touched the seat when Brooke started educating her on all things grapes, vineyards and tastings.

Wine was not JJ's forte.

She didn't hate it; she just didn't know it, couldn't appreciate it. But as the bus took off for their tour, JJ hoped she'd have a little more knowledge by the end of the day.

Beer was her drink of choice. Something floral and hoppy, supposedly concocted in the back shed of a local surf hangout somewhere. Now, she was completely out of her depth, memorising fruit names like apricot, mulberries and peach. Brooke was currently explaining tannins, leg pressing into JJ's as they went around a particularly bendy road.

"Tannins fuck you in the mouth."

JJ recoiled. "Excuse me? That doesn't sound right."

"You've had red wine before. It's that feeling of it taking over: gripping you, pulling at you and making you feel it everywhere—your teeth, your gums, and of course, your tongue."

The visual was... oddly hot. JJ slid her tongue over her teeth reflexively. "Aren't you quite the wine connoisseur?"

Brooke pretended to sweep her hair off her shoulders

and stuck her nose in the air. "Oh yes, *darling*." She dissolved into a soft chuckle at her own silly display. "When you've been to as many wineries as I have, you start picking up the spiels and the lingo, until eventually you grow a moustache and sound like an astute arsehole."

"Ah," JJ said, nodding sagely. "Seems I have a lot to learn then."

Brooke patted her knee. "Don't worry, you'll be a certified wine-sipping wanker in no time—I've got you."

JJ let her head drop back against the seat, waiting for what Brooke would teach her next. After so many years working alone, headphones on, painting house after house after house, it was a nice change of pace to have Brooke's constant company over the last five days.

No matter what they were doing, she always had a story. Some random event that had cropped up on her travels and somehow related to where they were. Like while waiting for the helicopter to pick them up, they'd seen a line of ants. Brooke commented that while she was in Laos waiting for a bus to Vietnam, she saw a horde of ants team up and work together to lift an entire fish fin out of a trash can. The fin had looked like it was floating up the side of the bin at first, until Brooke had seen the thousands of legs staggering underneath it to keep the upwards momentum.

Those stories made JJ smile, amazing her with the sheer amount this woman had seen in her lifetime while JJ had just been painting house... after house... after house. It made her reflect. Maybe her life needed a little less work and a little more play. Was she boring? She nibbled at her lip as rows of vineyards flashed past the window. Today, she'd make sure she had some fun, let go a little.

The first winery came into view as the bus pulled off the main road. Rows of vines lined both sides as the bus crunched down the long and winding gravel driveway. With the beginning of autumn, the leaves were starting to turn, each row a mix of greens blending into yellows and reds. It reminded JJ of her gran's chopped salad. She missed her mum's cooking already, especially anything made with Gran's plump red tomatoes! She sent a quick photo to her mum, who replied with a picture of said chopped salad already in the fridge ready for their dinner. If only she could be in two places at once.

JJ put her phone away, eyes catching on Brooke's bright red lipstick. Brooke was only in the bathroom five minutes before they left, and yet, she'd emerged completely transformed. JJ hadn't had the privilege of seeing this side of Brooke yet—a little more dolled up and absolutely killing it in a floral maxi dress and sandals. It suited her. She looked ready to be the one to lead the wine tour. Instead, they had Veronica.

Veronica was a Barossa local and extremely informed about everything around the town, not just the wineries. She was also wearing red lipstick, but that's where the similarities between her and Brooke ended. Veronica had red curly hair that had so much volume she could be in a hair commercial. JJ played with the back of her own short hair. How'd the woman get it so shiny?

"...specialises in white wines and a couple of punchy reds that'll have you racing to order a bottle—or a case! As you enter, our group will be at the closest end of the bar. Keep an eye out for Curtis, he'll be our pouring assistant this morning." Veronica rattled off more winery facts as they disembarked the bus.

Brooke's arm looped through JJ's, pulling them through their group and over to the cellar door. To anyone else on the bus tour, they looked like the best of friends. How had she only known this woman for less than a month? Really, it was more like a week if she only counted the time they'd spent together.

JJ took in the radiant blonde walking next to her, each step made with such purpose and flair like she owned the place. It was a stark contrast to the Brooke who saw herself as a failure during their talk over breakfast on the ridge. JJ would never view her that way. While they might not be a dating match, the thought of them as friends was nice. She pulled Brooke's arm in close as they entered the tasting room.

It was spacious with old barn vibes, exposed wooden rafters and a stone bar that ran the length of the back wall. The bar top looked crafted out of red gum with a natural edge that gave a rustic feel. A light shiver ran through JJ as she entered, the temperature noticeably cooler as fruity notes clung to the air. Two other tour groups stood around at the far end of the room. A man, Curtis she presumed, poured the glasses for their tour group's first tasting as they all made their way to the bar.

Brooke stuck her nose into her glass, a pinot grigio, and swirled it. JJ took a gulp of hers. Whoops, too much. She pulled a face and swallowed. The wine made her jaw ache as bad as eating a lemon. Her head shook involuntarily as Brooke watched on with a wide grin.

"Copy me."

Brooke lifted her glass again, and JJ followed suit—sniff, swirly swirl, small sip. Got it. Her face pulled instantly, lip curling, nose wrinkling. Wine just wasn't her thing. She wanted to like it, but at this rate, her face would be permanently changed by the end of the day with the amount of uncontrolled wincing.

She could pretend to be refined at least.

"Pear?" she posed the question to Brooke, who was still watching JJ. See? Look at this awesome person throwing out fruit names.

"Close." Brooke smirked, taking a delicate sip and holding it in her mouth before swallowing. "Crisp. Smooth. It reads more strawberries and cream for me."

They went on like this down the list, JJ taking a stab in the dark, and Brooke illuminating her with more true-to-form tasting notes. A full-bodied Shiraz was the last in their line-up, according to Veronica as she informed the group. JJ swirled the glass, copying everyone else in the room and pretending to inspect it. Ah yes, the legs on this one were looking very leggy. Whatever that meant. She took a large sip.

"Ready to be mouth-fucked?" Brooke whispered in her ear, leaning so close JJ could feel her warm breath.

JJ did everything within her to hold onto that mouthful of wine, forcing it down with a gulp so she didn't spray the room. Her hand still flew to her mouth as she turned, glaring at the blonde who beamed, cheeks rosy and bright.

"You're trouble," JJ said, pointing a finger at Brooke.

"I'm only explaining wine basics. Now, how does your mouth feel?" Brooke swirled her own glass and took a sip.

JJ ran her tongue around her mouth. It felt drier, like

cotton wool wicking the moisture away. She nodded at Brooke. "I see what you mean."

"Here." Brooke went over to the bar, dipping the complimentary bread into some olive oil. "Eat this."

She offered it up to JJ, who obliged, the moment weirdly personal as their eyes locked. Was there heat simmering in that look, or was it just her?

Focus on the food. The bread was delicious. Some chunk of artisanal lepinja that matched perfectly with the smooth oil. JJ's eyes fluttered closed. "Delicious."

"Now, take another sip of that wine," instructed Brooke, licking an errant oil drip off her finger. So messy but JJ was transfixed.

The words finally sunk in, and JJ did as she was told. This time as the shiraz swirled around her mouth and coated her tongue, it was smoother, stripped of the astringent notes. Like a completely different wine. "Cool trick."

Brooke shrugged. "It cuts through the tannins, so you get a better flavour profile."

"You've been more educational than the guy behind the bar explaining his own wines," JJ said, hooking a thumb over her shoulder.

Brooke beamed again, and JJ wanted to hold on to the smile. It was the same one she'd given JJ on top of the ridge. She seemed so proud of herself. JJ's chest expanded.

"All right everyone, time to purchase any of those amazing wines you've tried, and then it's back on the bus," Veronica called.

Almost their entire group inundated the poor attendant to order at once. Brooke and JJ opted to walk the grounds instead. Outside, groups of people milled about at tables and under umbrellas, enjoying the mild autumn day: a little sun, a little cloud, and not a breath of wind. As the fresh air hit her face, JJ felt the effects from their first tasting take hold. They must've been strong. She'd only had a mouthful or two of each wine, but still, it added up. The light buzz had her limbs loose and thoughts quiet.

It was nice, slowing down and not having to think about work schedules. It was double nice not thinking about the holiday schedule either. That had, so far, been one of her best decisions. It was a risk, putting her trust in someone else to organise an entire trip, but it had paid off.

"Ooooh, fancy." Brooke pointed at the winery's house up on the hill.

It was more like a homestead. A verandah ran the length of the perimeter, thick grape vines growing along the top.

"I don't know what kind of house I'd buy if I could afford it," Brooke said, taking in the home as they strode past and headed back up the hill.

JJ wasn't sure when they'd looped arms again. But she didn't mind at all.

Brooke turned to her. "You said you own your place, yeah?"

"Yep." And JJ was proud of it. She felt for anyone trying to get into the housing market now.

Oh, that would be Brooke. It was easy to forget how different they were at times.

"Must be nice having a place to call home. What's it like?"

"Hopefully still in one piece when I get back," JJ quipped.

"Huh?"

"My housemate, Jess, is looking after it while I'm gone. You know her—Hayley's friend."

Brooke's eyes widened. "Oh. I didn't know you knew Hayley's friends." She reached an arm out, hand brushing against the vine leaves.

"It's kinda how I got the painting job for your sister. Long story short, Jess just started dating my best mate."

Brooke's eyebrows raised. "Huh. Well, there you go. Such a small world."

"Sure is, Jess is great." JJ caught the stiffness in Brooke's arm. "Anyway, back to my house, it's just a little place—a two-bedder that I've renovated over the years, very mid-century modern. A garden out the front and back. My little slice of heaven."

"Sounds incredible. You'll have to show me some time," Brooke said.

They circled back to the cellar door. JJ tried to picture Brooke hanging with her, along with Jess and Remi. JJ wasn't sure where Brooke stood with Hayley's friends, and Jess didn't seem to know either—more from a place of confusion than any true negativity. Either way, JJ looked forward to finding out. She wanted to stay in touch once all this was over, as more than just travel companions.

JJ took in the carefree blonde, their arms still linked as they strode in perfect sync up to the waiting bus, Brooke's free hand now clasped around JJ's bicep.

Would Brooke want to be friends after the trip too?

SEVENTEEN
Brooke

Brooke felt like she'd blinked and they'd arrived at their second destination. This winery was a little different. The cellar door was attached to a large building that housed a full restaurant and accommodation overlooking the vineyards, but instead of being ushered indoors, Veronica led their group around the side to the rear of the property. There, a single long table stood covered in white tablecloths and swathed in garlands of natives with an array of platters spread between them. Brooke salivated at the amount of food, her stomach grumbling in agreement.

Too busy in their own conversation, Brooke and JJ were seated right on the end. An American couple who appeared to be in their fifties sat opposite them. Their glasses were already poured with their first tasting.

Brooke held her breath as JJ dove into the wine—an extra crisp sauvignon blanc. JJ sipped, her face twitching slightly. Brooke would feel bad, but JJ was the one who'd agreed to a wine tour. She'd wanted the new experience and so Brooke had obliged. It seemed JJ was getting the hang of it now and taking more appropriate-sized sips. She'd even swirled and sniffed the current tasting like a proper connoisseur.

JJ lowered her glass. "What?"

"I feel like you're starting to enjoy that."

"It's fun, and it's either getting easier or I'm getting drunk enough that I don't care."

"Probably the latter, *darling.*" She dragged out the name with sarcasm then popped an olive into her mouth from their platter. They were the stuffed green kind with a satisfying crunch. The tartness melded with the white wine still sitting on her palate.

The outdoor meal was slow and the chatter of their tour group relaxed against the acoustic tunes of a young man strumming his guitar, a mixture of laid-back beats from the last few decades. They'd gone through four more tastings with their latest one of Brooke's favourites so far—a velvety smooth, straight merlot. She'd be buying a bottle of that before they left! Brooke picked a gum leaf off their table's garland. She cracked it in half, the fresh scent wafting into the air, almost like woody menthol.

"So, are you two sisters?" Clive asked across the table as he buttered a piece of bread. They'd been in polite conversation on and off with the older American couple, mostly about the tour and other activities they'd all been up to recently.

Brooke giggled, but JJ frowned, sitting back and crossing her arms. "No," Brooke answered for them. "I'm her tour guide." She wrapped an arm around JJ's shoulders, giving her a quick squeeze, making JJ's arms fall back in her lap.

Clive leaned over to his wife. "Oh really? Hear that, Jen? She's a tour guide." He turned back to Brooke. "Do you have a card?"

"Oh." That was unexpected. Brooke's cheeks warmed. "It's not my job. I'm just helping out my—friend." She stuttered on the last word, unsure of the right way to explain their current relationship. Acquaintance didn't quite fit, neither did client... but she was working for JJ after all. Hmm, friend still seemed to suit best with how Brooke felt around her.

"Well, here." Clive reached into his pocket, pulling out a slim case. He slid a card across the table. "If you ever offer that or trip planning as a service, let me know. Your itinerary so far sounded excellent. We'd have never thought to go helicamping, and it's one of those unique experiences we're always on the lookout for. Appreciate the recommendation."

Brooke tucked the card in her bag. "You're welcome."

It was enough work planning her own travels. Doing this for others? She couldn't imagine that. Though, this trip was more... enjoyable than expected, but maybe that was more to do with the current company rather than the destination.

Lunch drew to a close and they began to make their way over to the cellar door for a few sticky tastings to finish off their meal. Brooke's head spun from the wine as well as the earlier conversation.

She pushed that aside and turned to JJ. "Hey, before, you looked upset about the sister comment. What was that all about?"

JJ pursed her lips before answering, "Because why is it

that middle-aged white dudes always have to ask if you're related to the girl you're with? I don't ask if they're brother and sister when they're clearly together." Her eyes blew wide as she held up her hands, stopping mid-stride. "Not that I'm saying I'm *with* you." She waved it off. "Ugh. It's a lesbian thing."

They continued to stroll along the grass and up to the building.

"Seriously?" Brooke said. "I guess I haven't been in a relationship with a woman before to have had it happen to me. But when you put it like that... that's rough."

"Yeah, it doesn't happen often—clearly, as I'm usually single—but there's a girl at my quarterly work dinners, she has to put up with it on site whenever her girlfriend visits for lunch or whatever."

"Thanks for enlightening me. I'd be happy to correct people in the future, you know, if I had a date that looked like me."

"We don't even look like each other," JJ said. "I mean blonde hair, sure. But other than that, we're chalk and cheese."

"I mean we're basically the same height. But yeah, you're right. I don't see it."

They moved into the cellar door and stood at the back of the line to wait their turn. Where the other winery was rustic, this was all modern whites, straight edges, and oak trims. It didn't really match the vibe of other wineries Brooke had visited. It was like all the personality had been stripped and replaced with a side of pompousness.

"So, speaking of usually being single, what's the dating scene like for a lesbian these days?"

JJ grimaced and pulled her lips in.

"Is this one of those don't ask questions?" Brooke checked in.

"No," JJ replied with a slight groan. "It's just... hard. To be honest, it's been so nice *not* worrying about dating as much as having a break from work on this trip. My parents are—" She ran a hand along the shaved side of her head. "So I told you how my friends recently got together, and it made me realise I hadn't really been putting myself out there in a while—too busy with work, you know? And—never mind."

They moved up a couple of spaces. "I'm listening, not judging."

JJ was quiet for a beat. "Anyway, I went on a bunch of dates over the last month—each one worse than the last, and I'm pretty sure I burned myself out."

"See, this is why dating is overrated. Too much pressure. Just sleep with them and run." Brooke winked, expecting the second horrified look on JJ before she'd even made it.

"I'm kidding," she said. "I get it. Not your style. So, why do you think the dates flopped?" The wine had to be kicking in. Brooke didn't ask these kinds of questions, yet here she was. She twisted her bracelets around her wrist.

"Well, Jess would tell you it's a me problem. I would tell you that once I've chatted with someone for a few minutes, I just know they're not my person."

"So, who is your person?" Brooke bit her lip.

JJ didn't respond right away. Her eyes were focused on Brooke's mouth.

Then she cleared her throat and squinted, as if lost in

thought. "Um. She's... god, it sounds kind of silly to say it now."

"Why?"

"I have a list."

"Of people?"

"No." JJ chuckled. "A list of attributes I'm looking for in the right person. Like to be confident in themselves but not cocky; has their life put together—like maybe they run a business too, manage a company or have a house—you know, stable income, that kind of thing; they're an all-round nice person and a few other points, but that's the gist."

"Wow, I'm like a walking anti-list." Brooke went for the joke, but the list still stung. Did JJ have similar criteria for new friends?

"We're different in some ways, but it's not a bad thing," JJ rushed to say.

Brooke wasn't sure if she was trying to reassure Brooke... or herself.

"I mean—go you for knowing what you want. All I'd say is remember that no matter how much you write a list or plan things, sometimes you can still end up broken down in the outback with goats on your car, you know?"

JJ let out a belly laugh, setting Brooke off at the same time.

"I'll keep that in mind," she said through laughter.

They reached the bar, giggles still dying down. It was nice how much fun she'd been having on the trip. She rubbed at her aching cheeks.

An attendant placed two triple wine flights in front of them then pointed at their first glass. "This is a French style

Botrytis dessert wine. The year of harvest was a wetter season than anticipated, which resulted in the sweeter caramel notes you'll soon taste—all thanks to the fungal rot."

JJ seemed captivated by the story, taking the first sip and nodding along to their pourer. "Mmm." Mouth closed, she made a show of waiting and allowing the wine to sit on her tongue. It was impressive how much JJ was leaning into the fun of tasting.

JJ nodded once more and declared, "I can really taste the wet season."

Both the attendant and Brooke looked at each other, the young woman trying and failing to suppress a grin. Brooke cackled, unable to hold it in.

JJ swung her head between them, brows furrowing. "What?"

"I think, maybe, just stick to the fruit names." Brooke patted her on the shoulder. A gentleman standing next to them also cracked a smile at the show. "You, uh, can't 'taste' the wet season. It's just part of the growing process that shapes the wine and the flavours it presents."

"Oh." JJ already had a wine blush, which deepened as the meaning landed. "That's what I get for trying to be an astute arsehole." She laughed into her glass, taking another sip.

Four wineries down and eight hours later, everyone piled back onto the bus a final time. Brooke's arm hung through JJ's again. Who was holding onto whom couldn't be confirmed as they teetered through the door and toward a pair of empty seats. They collapsed in a heap of messy giggles, somehow managing to clip their seatbelts on. For some reason they were holding hands, and JJ was giving Brooke a glassy-eyed grin, complete with wine-stained lips. Brooke was probably reflecting the same look back, though she couldn't be sure. Her head felt like it was in the clouds. She was so warm and fuzzy.

Her dress had been a good decision at the start of the day, but now the sky had darkened, and a crisp chill was in the air. Heat wafted off JJ, her palm warming Brooke's. JJ's thumb brushed over her knuckles as the bus lurched down the road.

As everyone was dropped off to their accommodations, the boisterous roar dulled to low murmurs, the radio playing gently as they jostled along. JJ's head now rested on Brooke's shoulder, the weight increasing until the faintest of snores began.

Brooke's mind settled. Once again, she found herself with this woman wriggling well into her personal space. But once again, she still allowed it. Her senses were overwhelmed, full of everything JJ: fresh soapy shampoo and an earthy vetiver scent—more warmth seeping in. Her unofficial title of tour guide was becoming blurrier, fading into the background. At some point, this had started to feel like a real holiday, though Brooke couldn't pinpoint when exactly that had happened. As for JJ? Brooke wasn't sure what they were now, but client and acquaintance were definitely off the list.

Brooke had never had a best friend. Plenty of friends, sure. But not best friends. Not those kids she'd see in school making bracelets or having sleepovers, whispering secrets in each other's ears. She'd move from group to group or sit on the log by the school boundary and daydream of adventures. Then once her adventures became real, it was the same thing. New friends almost every week, a growing collection too many to count over the decade. But once again, no one stuck. Just travelling buddies.

JJ felt like more than a travelling buddy.

The realisation was like a gut punch. Brooke wasn't a relationship person—clearly—that shone in lights when it came to someone like JJ, who was looking for Brooke's opposite; someone to settle down with and live their perfect lives together behind their white picket fence. Her thumb rubbed circles on the back of JJ's hand. She visualised yanking her hand free, and nudging JJ awake. Again, her body refused to cooperate.

What was it about JJ that drew her in like a magnet despite their differences? Was it physical touch she was craving? A flash of white teeth and French cologne made her shudder at the memory.

No. Not that then.

The bus pulled up to their accommodation. They were the last ones left. She'd had no idea.

"Hey, wake up. We're back." She squeezed JJ's hand.

JJ stirred. "Sorry, I guess I fell asleep."

"Let's get inside, yeah?"

JJ wrapped an arm around Brooke's waist and kept it there the entire walk up to their door. Brooke soaked in the warmth, not wanting it to end.

EIGHTEEN

JJ

JJ shivered, no longer leaning against Brooke and her warmth.

Stupid door needing to be unlocked.

She craved that heat again.

Her hands came together in a loud clap. "We should get in the hot tub!"

What an awesome idea. Perhaps her best idea ever.

"You sure you're good for a swim?" Brooke checked.

JJ made a *psh* sound, moving past Brooke and into the house. Her shoulder bumped into one of the walls. This place really was small.

"Where are all the ligh—" JJ shielded her eyes as they were dowsed in bright light. "Thanks." Her eyes adjusted, gaze catching Brooke's across the room. "So, swim?"

Brooke pulled in her lips, but her grin still broke free. "All right then, let's go."

"Yes!"

JJ raced off to get changed then headed out onto the deck. The little moonlight they had reflected off the tops of the vines, giving them silver highlights against the dark buildings of the winery beyond. It was Brooke's original idea to turn the hot tub on before they'd left for their tour, and right now JJ could kiss her for that forethought. Pulling back the cover, the tub was steaming. JJ turned on the rainbow light which slowly changed through the colours.

JJ removed her fluffy hotel-style robe and placed it—folded—onto one of the chairs. Her exposed skin prickled from the frigid air. She wobbled as she climbed into the tub, easing in a little slower than usual. It always paid to be careful, especially after all that wine.

Once submerged up to her shoulders, she groaned and relaxed back on the bench seat. Cedar and the faintest hint of chlorine enveloped her senses. Her entire body tingled as the jets drove hot water into her muscles. Yes. This was a good choice. Brooke would be out any minute, and JJ looked forward to her company, even after they'd been in each other's pockets all day.

Behind her, the back door slid open.

"It's freezing!" Brooke exclaimed.

JJ turned. Brooke's purple bikini had an incredible plunge.

Wow.

Eyes up!

She cleared her throat. "Where's your robe?"

"What robe?" Brooke narrowed her eyes as she toed off her thongs.

"Uh, the one on the bed?"

"Oh. I thought they were both towels."

"One's a towel, one's a robe."

Brooke stuck one foot over the edge of the tub. “Well, I’m here now.”

Yes, she was. Very much here.

And looking incredibly attractive.

All feminine curves, tall but not lanky, and those sun-kissed shoulders were absolutely gorgeous on full show.

JJ shuffled over to make room as Brooke collapsed ungainly into the water. Adorable.

“Oops, sorry. It’s deeper than I thought.”

Of all the space in the tub, Brooke settled in right next to JJ, thighs touching.

Now where was JJ meant to put her arm? She shuffled, resting it on her own leg in a way that wasn't resting at all, but rather, awkward and uncomfortable. Why was it so hard to give Brooke some personal space?

JJ inhaled, counting to four. She needed to relax. This was ridiculous. She was in a hot tub for god’s sake! She straightened and dropped her shoulders, her arm moving back until it brushed against Brooke’s.

It was her fault anyway; she chose to sit this close.

“Wanna play truth or dare?” JJ asked in an effort to stop overthinking their proximity.

Could the hot tub just swallow her now? Who suggested that?

She did, apparently. That’s who.

Because JJ wasn’t boring.

She’d had fun today letting loose. Why stop now? Games were fun.

Brooke side-eyed her. “What are we, twelve?” She twisted her lips to the side, then grinned. “Fine. Truth or dare?”

"Truth." How bad could it be?

"What was your worst sexual encounter?"

JJ slid into the tub until she was blowing bubbles.

"You said truth!" Brooke grinned, mischief dancing in her eyes.

"You *had* to ask that question." JJ popped back up, rubbing her hands over her face and hair.

Brooke turned, bringing a knee up on the bench and leaning her arm against the edge of the tub. She was all ears. And her thigh was still touching JJ. Of course.

JJ sighed, tipping her head up to the sky, taking in the stars. They were fascinating, really—

Brooke nudged her.

JJ groaned, kept her gaze on the twinkling lights, and relented.

"I only slept with him one time. His name was Callum, and we were dating at the end of high school when I was still figuring out if 'I just hadn't met the right guy yet'. We'd been to a football game—I know, so romantic, right?—and ended up back at his parent's place. He lived upstairs, and we'd both agreed we'd been dating long enough to take the next step."

Out of the corner of her eye, JJ caught Brooke's wince.

"Ugh. It was so… bad—awkward. Just the most—god. There was the whole—is it in yet?"

"Oh no."

"Then—are we done yet? Umm, lots of silence."

Brooke covered her mouth.

"Then he was, uh, struggling to keep going, as he'd had a few beers. In the end, we just called it, said enough was enough and awkwardly spent the rest of the night facing away from each other with muttered apologies. It was the first and only time I slept with a man. We broke up shortly after, and funnily enough he came out as gay a few years later. Go figure." She chuckled and slid a glance to Brooke.

"Okay, you win with that story. That sounded painful to even recount."

"Oh, trust me when I say that memory is usually blocked. Actually, I don't think I've told anyone that before." She chanced another glance.

Brooke took her hand under the water and squeezed. "Well, thank you for trusting me with it."

JJ relaxed. "That's the game, right? Now—truth or dare?"

Brooke didn't let go of her hand. What was happening between them?

Focus on the game.

"Truth," Brooke said.

Now would be a great time to ask about Hayley, though that would definitely bring down the mood.

"First kiss?" she asked instead.

"Easy. James. It was in kindy. We'd just finished making pizzas as a group and ran out into the sandpit. He declared we were getting married and kissed me on the lips. I screamed 'boy germs!' and ran away."

JJ laughed. "Okay, I revise my question. First real kiss."

"Nope. Ask a better question next time."

JJ shook her head. Absolutely infuriating. Yet she couldn't stop smiling.

Brooke squeezed JJ's hand as she asked, "Your turn again, truth or dare?"

Was she leaning in closer? JJ blinked. The heat of the

tub was making the lingering alcohol go straight to her head.

Brooke's thumb was definitely brushing the back of her hand. JJ swallowed, mouth wicking the moisture away like a strong shiraz. If she picked dare... anything could come out of that woman's mouth.

"Truth."

Did Brooke just deflate a little?

"What's your biggest turn on?" she asked after a brief moment.

JJ's face heated, and it had nothing to do with the water.

She should've picked dare.

"Wait, let me guess," Brooke said, eyes sparkling. "Is it your smutty audiobooks?"

Brooke copped a face full of water. She sputtered and gasped—the resulting shock on her face was everything. JJ was impressed with her own reflexes.

"I deserved that." Brooke chuckled, wiping the water from her eyes. "Okay, I'm listening, because I actually do want to know."

"Do you now?"

"Who wouldn't?" Her eyes flashed.

JJ sighed. "Fine. I... enjoy it when a woman is dominant and knows what she wants in the bedroom. I love seeing them come alive and enjoying themselves."

"Okay, so you *enjoy* that, but is that what *turns you on*?" Brooke stroked JJ's hand in circles.

JJ's stomach swooped low. The circling motion sent an electrical current coursing from her hand to straight between her legs. Her stomach swooped again and she let out a slow breath to steady herself.

That bloody question was turning her on, that's what. Brooke was—*annoyingly*—turning her on. This whole situation was turning her on. Muddling her thoughts.

"Slow physical touch is a turn on," she confessed. *Don't look at our hands.*

"Body confidence is a turn on."

Brooke's shoulders pushed back, just a little.

"And strong eye contact is a turn on. To see that the other person is feeling what I'm feeling reflected back at me."

JJ's heart hammered.

She didn't wait for a response from Brooke. "Truth or dare?"

Brooke bit her lip, looking up through her eyelashes and locking on to JJ.

"Dare." It was basically a whisper.

A half laugh escaped JJ, but it cut off. She couldn't look away.

Brooke's eyes darkened, a mirror of her own.

"Is this the part where I dare you to—"

Head thrown back against the tub, a wave of hot water surged over her shoulders as Brooke lurched forward—and kissed her.

Warm lips on hers, pressing hard.

White noise filled JJ's head. Was this really happening?

Then she was kissing Brooke back, every nerve prickling with energy.

Her free hand dove into Brooke's hair and pulled her in. One of them moaned, or maybe it was both of them.

Somehow they were still holding hands, and Brooke was *crushing* hers.

There wasn't anything soft about this. This was hunger. This was thirst.

This was—over before it had properly started?

Brooke pulled herself away, gasping for breath, hand ripped from JJ's grip as she launched herself to the other side of the tub.

JJ was still in cardio zone four and rising. She licked her lips, breathing hard, trying to come up with what to say, what to do.

Because that was the best damn kiss of her life.

With Brooke. Messy Brooke. Tour guide Brooke. Not-on-her-attributes-list Brooke. Brooke who liked to "have fun with a girl or two". That's who JJ was tonight—fun JJ. Not boring, paint-another-house JJ.

She could be totally chill about this.

Only… that kiss wasn't a dare.

It was a truth.

NINETEEN
Brooke

There was before the kiss and after the kiss.

Before, they were having fun and sharing secrets. Then Brooke saw that look. And yeah, maybe she'd instigated that dare. She'd been brimming with energy, full up on life. She'd anticipated what JJ was about to ask, and she'd be lying if she hadn't already thought about doing it anyway.

Hell, she hadn't been able to keep her hands off her all day. None of it made sense. She'd hoped the kiss would make it make sense. That she just needed to get it out of her system, like she usually did. Bring the energy down to a normal tempo. But her system was broken, because now—in the after—all she wanted was to go back for more. Slide back up and straddle the handsome masc painter, take her head in her hands and lean into the softest of lips.

But she couldn't do that.

Because this was JJ. Sweet JJ. Who specifically wanted and needed an emotional connection with someone to take things further. Not a one-night stand. Not with Brooke. And not now. Not when they were drunk. The last thing she'd ever want to do is hurt JJ or get her into something she'd regret.

And so she'd pushed away. Forced the space.

Now JJ stared at her, lips parted and chest still rising and falling.

Brooke prodded them out of the moment, asking, "Truth or dare?"

She flicked water at JJ, who opened and closed her mouth a few times.

Brooke couldn't blame her.

After the kiss came with more questions than before the kiss.

She'd hooked up with a lot of people over the years. A lot. It was whatever. Part of life, part of her lifestyle. It was fun. And that's exactly what that was meant to be—a passing moment, vibing on the energy, a little teasing. A quick little dare. Harmless.

But right now, there was desperation scraping at the surface. And Brooke wasn't desperate. She didn't *crave* a kiss like she was now. Kisses didn't feel like they plugged you in like a Christmas tree with a train running around the base. Brooke was losing her mind—over a less-than-thirty-second kiss.

"Truth," JJ finally answered.

They stuck to safe zones: most embarrassing moments, weird habits and a dare to sing a favourite song out of key. No more sexual topics, no more touching. The heat of the water had become stifling, and Brooke needed out. Time to collect her thoughts and put a little space between her and JJ.

"Right, I'm calling it a night. We've got an early one

tomorrow and I plan on trying to sleep as much as possible."

JJ agreed, holding out a hand to help Brooke step out safely. How chivalrous. The cold night air had them towelling off quickly, both avoiding each other's gaze. Maybe Brooke wasn't the only one still affected by that dare? Would JJ want to kiss her again?

"Good night," Brooke mumbled as she made her way into their house.

JJ stopped behind her in the tight hallway. "Almost feels weird having our own beds tonight."

"Yeah." Brooke laughed lightly. "Don't worry, there's still time for us to stuff up our future accommodation."

JJ smirked. "I suppose you're right. Good night, Brooke." She turned, heading to the other end of the house.

Brooke moved to her own bed in the loft above the bathroom. It was just as well they were sleeping separately. Brooke didn't trust herself to be anywhere near a bed with JJ tonight.

Brooke's alarm blasted at 4am, the chorus of *Best Day Of My Life* by American Authors serenading the entirety of the tiny home. It was the wake-up song from a Contiki tour she'd ended up on years ago, and she'd stuck with it as her alarm ever since.

A groan sounded from the other end of the house. "Brooke?"

"C'mon, up you get," she yelled over the noise before swiping to shut it off.

Brooke was out of bed in an instant. She switched on all the lights and shot off to the bathroom to get ready. Done in ten minutes, she emerged and—JJ was still in bed. "Oi, up!"

The lump at the other end of the house didn't move, so Brooke stormed down the narrow hallway and jumped on the bed on her hands and knees. She leaned over the form of JJ still hidden under the covers and hopped up and down on the spot, the whole bed bouncing.

"Urgh, no," JJ mumbled. "I'm staying in bed. Wine was a bad choice. You go."

"Wine was an excellent choice, as is today's activity. Now—up!" Brooke ripped back the covers as JJ faced away from the light, pretending to hiss like a vampire. Brooke jumped off the bed and ignored her. "We're leaving in ten minutes."

They left in twelve.

Once they arrived at the meeting site, a local Barossa hotel, it was go, go, go. They were ushered into 4WDs and zoomed through the early morning darkness to their destination. It was a race against the clock to be ready for sunrise.

"Are you sure this is safe?" JJ asked as they climbed out of the car.

Brooke zipped up her jacket and took in the big contraption. "Of course. These are the best of the best in the Barossa. They've been operating for years and it's one of the safest forms of flying. I think you might enjoy it more than the helicopter ride."

JJ stared at the basket. "But there's no glass—we're all out in the open!"

"Wait and see what I mean, the basket feels safer than it looks."

They'd pulled up to a big open grassy field with six other tourists—a young family from Korea, and a couple down from Queensland. Their instructors gave them a quick run down, then it was all hands on deck to help roll out the massive rainbow striped balloon on the ground, ready to fill it with air.

This was only Brooke's third hot air balloon ride, but she'd loved every single one of them. The most unique had been in Cappadocia, when there were over a hundred other balloons in the air beside them. It was such a surreal sight, not to mention the views below. Of course, Adelaide being Adelaide, it would only be the one balloon up in the air. Possibly one other. That wasn't necessarily a bad thing. There had to be more solitude in the sky when it was less cluttered.

The balloon slowly filled with air and began to rise. The nearby trees were still silhouetted against the dark sky, but the birds had started to wake as soft chirps echoed around them. JJ rubbed her hands together and hopped on the spot. The day was meant to warm up, but sunrise was still an hour away.

"Don't you have a warmer jacket?" Brooke asked.

"I'm wearing it."

Brooke rolled her eyes, then grabbed onto JJ's arm and pulled her close.

"Better?"

"Y-yep," JJ stammered, whether from the cold or their current proximity, Brooke couldn't be sure.

After climbing into the basket, JJ's knuckles turned white as she latched onto the edge.

"You good?" Brooke asked.

"I think it's just the whole take-off and landing thing in a new vehicle. Are balloons classed as a vehicle?"

"Sure." Brooke smirked, then caught JJ's look. "You're going to be fine."

The tight-lipped smile Brooke received in return didn't have a shred of confidence in it.

Their pilot, Andrew, pulled down on a handle that caused a burst of flame to shoot up into the balloon. This close, the warmth washed over them from above. Brooke welcomed the heat after standing around on the dewy ground in the dark for so long. As the basket began to lift, JJ's hands gripped harder. Brooke did the only thing she could think of to help further—she placed an arm around JJ and squeezed, hugging her from behind, while still holding onto one of the padded poles herself.

"I've got you."

JJ relaxed back into her.

There were a few gasps from the others as the basket lifted from the earth, making Andrew chuckle as he explained what was happening and increased the heat. A floating feeling took over Brooke, reminding her of dreams she'd had where she could fly.

They ascended into the sky, the first inkling of light rising from behind the hills. She and JJ had picked the right side of the basket to stand for the glowing view unfolding right before them.

The higher they got, the wider JJ grinned each time she turned to say something to Brooke. It was good to see JJ relaxing, just like she had in the helicopter. Was Brooke meant to let go of her now? Because this was kind of comfortable, and maybe… maybe—she didn't want to.

"Look straight ahead," Brooke encouraged JJ.

The sun peeked over the horizon, shooting rays of golden light across all the vineyards. Brooke inched forward, gazing over JJ's shoulder to get a better look as they rose. She had no qualms about peering over the side. The balloon's movement was so slow, calm and soft in comparison to riding in the helicopter.

"This is actually really nice," JJ admitted once they'd gained ample height.

"Told you."

Silence fell between them. Brooke's mind replayed their kiss in the tub last night. Would it happen again? If something did develop between them on this trip, it's not like it could continue when they got back. They'd be living their lives again, separately.

Brooke was an awkward puzzle piece that didn't fit into JJ's life. Or anyone else's it felt like. A little lost puzzle piece, hidden under the couch and forgotten about. Her parents never even bothered to look. They hadn't reached out since Brooke had been back, and surely Hayley had told them by now. Not that Brooke would answer the call if they tried.

She shook her head. *Enough*. It was time to brush off the dust, pull herself out from the shadows, and find where she did fit in the world. The answers had to come soon. Time was running out—she'd be back at Hayley's before she knew it.

Arm still wrapped around JJ and heads close, she glanced at the woman who, a few weeks ago, had been a mere painter in her sister's house. She played with the soft fabric of JJ's jacket. Could there be a future there?

Her fingers froze. *Stop.* What was she thinking? She'd never even dated a girl. Or dated—period. Why was she considering it now?

JJ inhaled and closed her eyes for a moment. "I feel so free up here."

Brooke felt like she couldn't breathe, forcing the air into her lungs as she settled back into the present, back into JJ. Her chest eased.

The balloon sailed over one of the wineries they'd visited yesterday, the same one they'd walked arm-in-arm through the vines. Brooke smiled.

Everyone else had their phones and cameras out, madly clicking and posing against the spectacular backdrop. JJ and Brooke stayed in their own little bubble, tucked away in the corner.

JJ turned to Brooke. "So, about last night..."

Her stomach lurched. Brooke had wondered if JJ would bring up their kiss. It seemed the painter was gaining confidence as fast as their altitude. Brooke had been intent on sweeping it under the rug. She excelled at that.

"Mmm?" Brooke said, schooling her face. She wanted to know what JJ was thinking first. Her chest prickled with heat as she adjusted her grip on the pole, hand slippery with sweat. Was it Brooke or had Andrew just cranked up the burners?

JJ returned her focus to the view ahead, but a blush climbed up her neck. "I—wouldn't be opposed to a repeat." She coughed, sneaking a quick glance at Brooke for a reaction.

Brooke's mouth parted. Was JJ suggesting what she thought she was? But what exactly? To just kiss her again, or more?

And was that... butterflies in her stomach? Pfft. They'd probably just hit a pocket of air. JJ didn't do one-night stands, but... her gaze was definitely on Brooke's mouth.

Loud claps drew their attention. "Right everyone, landing positions!"

TWENTY

JJ

"Coffee?" the waiter asked.

"Yes, please. One latte and a long black," Brooke said.

They were back at the balloon operator's headquarters waiting for their gourmet breakfast as part of the activity's package. JJ picked off more grass from her pants. Even though they'd been warned the basket usually ended up on its side, it was still a terrifying experience to go through it. JJ had clasped at Brooke's hand for dear life and refused to open her eyes the entire bumpy landing. When she did, there was dust, dirt and all sorts covering them.

"And for the Big Breakfast, how would you like your eggs?"

"Runny—for the both of us please," Brooke answered again.

JJ's eyebrows rose. How thoughtful. It wasn't often someone remembered how she liked something. They'd only had eggs once—on the morning of their helicamping adventure.

Even in her drunken state, sleep hadn't come easy for JJ

last night. She'd started a list in her head of all the ways she could go about talking (or not talking) to Brooke about their kiss. Something that mind-blowing wasn't easily forgotten, and while she wasn't looking to date someone like Brooke, she couldn't deny that over the last week Brooke's company had been far better than any date she'd been on recently. It was like trying to bring two opposing magnets together—she liked Brooke, was attracted to Brooke... but Brooke wasn't who she'd pictured herself with. Yet here she was, wanting to kiss her again—and asking to kiss her again.

Explain that to her brain.

The plan she'd come up with was simple. JJ was on holiday, trying new things. Brooke had already opened her eyes to living a little looser, a little more in the moment. So, JJ wanted to do that with Brooke. Without going *all the way*, JJ would lean into whatever was brewing between them and have some fun—Brooke style. More flirting, more touching, and hopefully, more kissing. If they stayed friends, they'd probably laugh about that one time they took this amazing trip together, shared a hook up or two, and that was that. She just had to find out how Brooke felt about everything. JJ had tried to ask, but with their ill-timed balloon landing, she'd been left hanging in the sky.

Her knee bounced. Now to work it back into the conversation... somehow.

"So, would you do another balloon ride?" Brooke asked.

"In a heartbeat." JJ's stomach growled and she laughed. "But I have to say—not a fan of the early morning rise. I'm starving. Though, at least I'm not hungover like I thought I'd be. That could've made for an interesting ride."

"Yeah, same. A good night's sleep can help stave off the worst of it." Brooke leaned back in her chair, crossing her legs. "So, halfway through the trip tomorrow—how are you feeling?"

Wow. Already?

"After that rocky start, I'm glad things have smoothed out a bit."

"Yeah, how's your butt by the way?" Brooke gave her a lopsided smile.

"Fine now, thank you. How's your hate for South Australia going?"

Brooke pursed her lips, a smile tugging at the sides. "Just peachy, thank you. I told you it's not hate; I find it boring—remember?"

JJ cocked her head to the side. "And have you been terribly bored so far?"

"Oh, shut up." Brooke looked away, pink dusting across her face. "It's been... more enjoyable than I thought it'd be. I've even surprised myself with some of the things I planned."

"Maybe—" JJ paused for a moment, not sure how far to push the conversation. "Do you ever think maybe you were basing your dislike—sorry, *boredom*—on your past, like some old negative association, or something? Like you said when you first saw *The Wharf*, things have changed considerably since you were last here, and you're also a different person. Maybe Adelaide deserves another chance?"

Their waiter placed two steaming Big Breakfast plates in front of them. Brooke shifted her plate closer, not replying.

JJ cleared her throat, picking up her cutlery and slicing into her eggs and toast. "I know you get uncomfortable talking about these things, so you don't have to say anything more on the topic. Just think on it and know I'm here if you ever wanna talk."

"Thanks," she finally said, a conservative smile in place.

At least Brooke hadn't bit her head off this time.

Now to spit out what was really on JJ's mind. No more avoiding.

She just had to say it.

Right now.

Her heart picked up speed.

"Okay, new subject. What do you think we're doing?" There. Conversation initiated. JJ had her plan, but first, did Brooke even want a repeat?

Brooke covered her mouth with a hand as she finished chewing, then spoke, "As in tomorrow? We're heading to Deep Creek."

How was Brooke making this even harder? "I mean *us*." JJ waved a hand between the two of them. "Was the hot tub just a one-time thing for you? Or..."

"I don't know yet. As of half an hour ago, I only just learned you wanted a repeat."

God, Brooke kept her cards close to her chest.

"But do *you* want to?"

She still hadn't answered the bloody question. JJ's knee continued to bounce.

Brooke sipped her coffee, eyes flicking to JJ. "I... wouldn't be opposed to that." A twitch of a smile as she set down her mug.

JJ's stomach swooped, heart now thumping. "Well,

would you, uh, be open to multiple repeats, but maybe establishing some rules?"

"Rules?" Brooke said, eyebrow arching.

"Yeah, like this." JJ brushed her leg against Brooke. "Don't think I haven't noticed your arm and hand holding lately. Do you want more touching?"

Brooke scoffed and looked away, cheeks reddening. "I don't hold your hand." She frowned.

JJ leaned forward. "Uh, yeah you have. Multiple times. During that hailstorm—"

Brooke folded her arms, eyes flicking back to JJ. "We were running for our life down a mountain."

"Still counts. Then again—on the bus."

Brooke shifted in her seat and shook her hair over her shoulder. "I thought you were asleep. We were drunk." Her neck was flushed now.

"Okay, fine. I'll take touching as a no then." JJ pretended to strike it off her imaginary list.

"Hey, I didn't say I didn't want more touching!" Brooke unfolded her arms, face scrunched.

It was like arguing with a toddler. JJ couldn't help but smile, a light huff coming out with it.

"Why are you laughing?"

"Do you ever hear yourself and think: hmm, maybe I'm just arguing for the sake of arguing?"

"No," the stubborn woman argued back.

"Right. Think I'm just going to drop this topic."

Heat rolled through JJ as she ran a hand through her hair, dropping Brooke's gaze and going back to her breakfast. What was the point? At least she'd asked.

Maybe Brooke wasn't interested after all?

Everyone else sat around laughing and swapping stories of their balloon ride experiences. JJ cut into her bacon, intense focus on her next mouthful.

After finishing her bite, Brooke piped up, “I do.”

JJ set her fork down, heartbeat ramping back up. Did Brooke just say what she thought she said?

“Do what?” JJ wanted to make her say it.

“Want to hold your hand... more.”

JJ’s grin bloomed.

This time Brooke moved her leg under the table, brushing against JJ’s. Back and forth. Brooke looked up through her eyelashes, but instead of the usual playfulness JJ had come to expect, a vulnerability shone through. Uncertainty? Nervousness? *I don’t date* echoed in JJ’s mind, a reminder that while Brooke happily slept around, maybe she hadn’t explored the softer sides of a relationship. And though this wasn’t technically a relationship, it was more than a one-off fling. An extended fling of sorts.

“Well, I do want to kiss you more,” JJ said. “Preferably, beyond just hooking up in the hot tub. But just kissing might be as far as—um—what I’m comfortable with.” Her face heated again, burning all the way to the tips of her ears.

Brooke nodded. “I can do that.”

“What if—”

Just say it. It's time for fun JJ.

“What if we made this a holiday fling for the rest of the trip. Nothing serious. No dates. We enjoy the week for what it is.”

Brooke stared, as though checking if JJ was serious.

A smile slid into place, another brush against JJ’s leg. “You're on.”

The rules were set.

Brooke in bathers had JJ wanting to break all her rules.

JJ tried not to spill the wine she was pouring while Brooke climbed into the hot tub.

The rest of the day had been relaxed. A walk around the grounds of their accommodation's vineyard, a chat with the owners and a late afternoon nap. Afterwards, they'd enjoyed a lazy dinner beneath the stars before changing into their swimwear and heading back for the tub.

JJ handed Brooke a glass and stepped into the hot water. "Cheers—to one more week of bliss."

"Cheers to that." Brooke clinked her glass to JJ's.

JJ's whole body buzzed with the high of the moment.

She took a leaf out of Brooke's book and wedged herself right next to her on the bench seat. Skin slid against skin. JJ sipped her wine. Anything to keep her hands busy. Her fingers twitched on the stem. JJ's mind was fixed on the tanned shoulders pressing against hers.

She'd been thinking about this moment all day, playing out all the possible scenarios.

How she'd go about it. Would she be the one to initiate the kiss this time?

The courage she'd found this morning sunk to the bottom of the hot tub, drowning in thoughts, decisions and what-ifs.

She took a steadying breath, eyes catching Brooke's. They held, neither saying a word. JJ's heartbeat spiked as she found herself drawn toward the blonde with the sparkling smile.

She could do this.

Her eyes fluttered closed. She leaned forward—

A phone rang out on the outdoor table. *Her* phone.

JJ blinked several times, head whipping toward the noise. She huffed out a breath.

"Sorry, I better get that." JJ launched out of the water and ran to the table, wine still in hand and not a single drop spilled over the edge.

Brooke sat with a greedy grin. "Make it quick!"

JJ answered the video call. "Hey!" Jess was reclined against Remi, and they appeared to be at JJ's house on her leather couch. "How are we this evening, ladies?"

"We were wondering the same about you," Remi said, leaning forward to rest her head on Jess's shoulder, arms wrapping around her.

"Yeah, how's our favourite tradie lady?" Jess asked. "We didn't want to bother you on your trip, but we haven't heard anything from you, so we wanted to check in."

"Well—" JJ spun around on the spot with the phone. "You can see the magical view of the vineyards behind me. I've just poured us a wine"—she held up her glass—"and Brooke and I are in the hot tub at a tiny house. Say hi, Brooke!"

Brooke gave a polite wave, one side of her mouth barely flicking up. JJ focused the camera back on herself.

"You girls look like you're enjoying yourselves," Jess said.

JJ's smile faltered. Could Jess sense her attraction to Brooke through the phone?

No, she was over thinking it.

"It's nice to see you actually relaxing," Jess continued.

"And I can't believe you're drinking wine," Remi added.

"Go to enough wineries and apparently it starts to taste good. Who knew? How's work, Rem?" JJ took a sip of said wine.

"The new girls are keeping me on my toes, but I'm loving it."

"I still can't believe you have an entire team now," JJ replied. "And Jess, house all good?"

"Great." Her face blushed pink as Remi coughed and looked away.

Bloody rabbits.

She gave the girls a quick rundown of the last couple of days then wrapped up the call, not wanting to leave Brooke waiting too long.

"Sorry about that," she said, slipping back beside Brooke. "Were you friends with Jess back in the day?"

Brooke's glass halted midway to her lips.

"I hung around her occasionally." She shrugged and took a drink. "Mainly at game nights. I was surprised when I got back to see their little tradition still going."

"You didn't join in again like old times?"

"Nah, I'd just be in the way." Brooke tried to pass it off like she didn't care, but the furrow in her brow told JJ otherwise.

"Pretty sure Hayley would be the last person to think that. She's one of the most hospitable people I've met—as you'd know."

"Mmm," Brooke replied, frown deepening.

"You don't agree?" Sirens blared that JJ was pushing too hard, but she couldn't stop. Surely Brooke didn't truly believe Hayley wouldn't want her around?

Brooke looked at her then, emotions swirling and eyes shining. There was a question there, asking JJ to—to what? A plea to stop or a push to open this conversation further, JJ couldn't tell.

"Did..." JJ took a breath. "Did Hayley do something to you?"

Brooke's eyes blew wide. "No!" She placed her wine glass on the decking and faced JJ. "No, of course not." She shook her head. "No."

JJ put her glass beside Brooke's, then she waited.

Brooke's eyes were moving but staring past JJ to the vineyards beyond.

JJ was about to suggest they drop it and give Brooke an out, when Brooke spoke up.

"Hayley reminds me of Mum. Of my past. Our childhood. Of certain things that were the reason I left. Coming back has been... not what I expected, and—and I don't like who I am here."

Brooke whispered the last sentence so low, JJ had to lean forward, breath held.

"Not here with you, but back home. The me when I'm not travelling." Brooke met JJ's eyes again, the raw truth of the words sitting between them.

"Is that why you wanted to come on this trip?"

A pause. A slow nod. Brooke licked her lips, eyes cutting away then returning.

JJ reached for Brooke's hand and started to trace the circles this time on her palm.

"I haven't been the best sister. When I left, I never looked back. I kept in touch with Hayley and our brother, Steven, but barely. I never spoke to my parents again."

The edge of Brooke's mouth crooked up. Tight. A front. How did Brooke keep these emotions buried so deep? JJ couldn't imagine. It was hard enough watching her hurt like this. JJ's fingers stilled on Brooke's palm. She'd almost started to quiver, hanging onto every word.

"I *want* to like Hayley, but it's like whenever I'm around her, all our past is dredged up, and my emotions boil over. All I feel is anger and shame. And you know what the funny thing is? It's not even *at* her. She's just the scape-goat, the constant reminder of everything I wanted to forget."

"Have you ever spoken to her about this?" JJ asked.

Brooke scoffed. "Yeah, right. No one fixes problems in my family. We ignore them. Or, if you're like me—you just run away. Get on a plane and go."

"And how's that working out for you?"

"Well, it seems they don't just disappear like I first thought."

JJ squeezed Brooke's hand.

If there was a way JJ could help erase Brooke's prob-lems, her pain... she would.

While this night hadn't gone as planned, Brooke opening up like this had JJ leaning in even more. Each little truth, a peek into who Brooke was behind the curtain.

JJ's gaze held firm.

TWENTY-ONE

Brooke

A wave of nausea rolled through Brooke as the word vomit kept spilling from her lips. Now she'd started, she couldn't stop. She couldn't even blame the wine—she'd only had a sip before casting it aside. Brooke's heart hammered, but JJ's solid brown eyes were warmth, comfort and caring all rolled into one. They pulled the words from her. Words she'd tamped down, the ones she didn't want to hear.

Brooke's free hand traced the edge of the hot tub seat. "Some part of me thought coming back home would be different. I thought enough time had passed that everything would be magically fixed. I thought *I* was fixed. I rocked up on Hayley's doorstep—because that's the kind of person I am now: the Queen of Spontaneity and Adventure—thinking I'd crash with her for a bit, give myself some time, then decide what my next steps would be. Instead, my confidence dissolved into nightmares, flashbacks and this sense of hopelessness. I hadn't felt anything like it in a long time."

Heat filled Brooke's body. She dropped her chin,

staring at their joined hands underwater as they shimmered with the water's movement. The hands blurred.

"After everything I'd done, everything I'd achieved while travelling full time—all I had to my name was myself and my backpack. I saw Hayley's house, her wife and her life, and suddenly I was the little sister again. The one who wasn't enough, who didn't fit the mould, who was a bit out there. It made me realise how little I'd made of myself and how much I still don't fit in with the Mayfields. I don't have the accolades, the house or the partner, I just have... me. That's all I've ever had."

Brooke took a shaky breath then clamped her mouth shut. Her chin needed to stop quivering. The flush of heat intensified, rippling in waves down her arms and up her neck.

Brooke's eyes lifted back to JJ, then past her, to the blurry, blurry stars.

Fuck. I'm a mess.

"So, yeah, it's not Hayley. She's never done anything but be her perfect self."

JJ reached forward and wiped at her cheek. "Brooke, I don't think there's anything about you that needs to be fixed or made differently to fit some mould. There's nothing wrong with just being you; that's more than enough. It's admirable."

"I don't think so," Brooke said through a watery laugh, swiping at her own eyes.

"I'm serious. I don't think Hayley expects you to be anything else either. I'm sure if you did talk, you'd find—"

"I can't." Brooke stiffened, a pain pulsing between her shoulder blades.

"Okay." JJ twisted her lips to the side. "So, it's not that you don't want to. Why do you think you can't?"

"I freeze up. It's all in my head and nothing comes out. Or I'm an absolute bitch. I'm not delusional, I know I'm doing it, but I can't stop it. It's like a bad reflex."

Her stomach churned, wringing itself tight. Just the thought of...

JJ shifted closer, facing Brooke, her leg now pressed against Brooke's thigh, their hands still clasped. "Okay, well you're talking to me now. If I was Hayley, what would you want to say to her?"

Brooke watched the bubbles in the water in a slow trance. What would she say? She closed her eyes. JJ interlocked their fingers, thumb stroking the skin. Brooke's heart slowed.

She steadied her breath then straightened and focused on JJ. On those warm brown eyes.

"I'd say..." Brooke let out a slow, wavering breath. "I'm sorry I left and never properly kept in touch. I wanted to, but I never knew how. We never properly talked, even when I was home. I never thanked you for all the things you did for me, because I could never get past the fact Mum and Dad liked you and Steven more than me. I know that's not your fault, but my brain doesn't let me see it that way, no matter how many times I remind myself. You were always there for me, even now, when I know I have been absolutely horrible to you. If you want to start over, I'd really like a chance to be a proper sister."

JJ's eyes shined. "Wow. I think—uh—man. She'd really appreciate those words, Brooke."

"But it's you, so it's different. It's weird, but you make it easy. I wouldn't be able to say any of that to her."

JJ squeezed her hand. "What if you wrote it down instead? Say what you just told me but put it in a letter. Sometimes when I'm emotionally vulnerable—like if I've got a really horrible client or had a bad work mishap and I know I'm angry or frustrated, I'll always make sure I write my response out rather than calling or doing a face-to-face meeting. Say if it's an email, I'll write it out, sleep on it, then edit it the next day when I've calmed down—take out that layer of emotion, and say what truly needs to be said."

That almost sounded easy. Doable.

"I guess I could try. I've never thought of that. Thank you." Brooke inched forwards, lips pressing to JJ's. *So soft.* They held a moment and Brooke melted into the touch. Warmth. Comfort. She almost sighed before pulling away. JJ's eyes fluttered open, face slack.

"I appreciate the advice." Her head dropped, a smile flickering.

"Anytime," JJ said, releasing Brooke's hand and picking up her wine. "So, crappy parents huh?"

Brooke's insides twisted. So much for that being the end of the conversation.

"You don't know the half of it." She kept it light. Tree tops. "They're academics, involved in everything under the sun that can take time away from family. If you were getting straight A's and talking about university, they were all ears; otherwise, have fun trying to get their attention."

"Ah. Those types. Couldn't imagine why you'd want to just pack your bags and leave that behind." JJ smirked.

She wasn't wrong.

Brooke leaned on the edge of the tub, goosebumps prickling her arm as a crisp breeze blew past. "What's your family like?"

JJ swirled the wine in her glass, lips ticking up. "We're super close. My gran lives out the back in a granny flat and loves driving my parents mental. I try to visit a few times a week."

"A week! Whoa. Sounds like my idea of hell." Brooke laughed, then added, "Though, it sounds nice to have a close family like that."

"Maybe I'll drag you around some time. Change your mind. Dare I say, you might even enjoy it." JJ quirked an eyebrow and took a sip of her wine, only half-wincing. "They don't bite, promise. Gran would love to show off her garden to someone new."

"I'll think about it." She was flattered JJ thought she was good enough to bring over to meet her family. "Do you usually take your dates to see your gran's garden?"

JJ looked away. "Dates—no. Friends—yes."

Brooke sat back. Right, she was a friend to JJ, and this was a holiday fling. Why did she feel almost... disappointed? She wasn't looking for a relationship either, so why would it matter that JJ didn't see her as dating quality?

Brooke's lips pulled tight. That was fine, because she didn't date, so it didn't matter. This is what she wanted, who she was.

"Is there a reason you don't bring dates over to meet your family?" Brooke asked.

JJ scratched at the back of her neck. "Over the last couple of years they've been a bit more vocal about me settling down with someone. It's like they saw the ticking clock as I reached my mid-thirties. I used to brush it off, but it started to get to me after a while. Started playing on my mind. When I began to date properly, I thought it'd get them off my back, but it only made it worse. Now they ask even more questions."

"Tell them to back off," Brooke said simply.

"I can't do that."

"Sure you can. It's your life, do whatever the hell you want. Not what someone else says is best for you."

"They mean well." JJ shrugged.

"If they love you as much as you say they do, they should also respect your boundaries. If you don't want to talk dating with them, just say that's private or you want to keep that to yourself."

"I just don't want to upset them." JJ fidgeted with the stem of her wine glass.

"JJ—while these people are your family, they don't get to dictate how you live your life based on how they feel. They don't get to control when and how you date. They don't get to make you feel less than if you tell them the truth or put a rule in place. You are your own person."

JJ stared into her wine, swishing it around. Her eyebrows knitted together. "I do want to date, but it's been nice to be away from that pressure. Both from my family and with dating as fast as I was before we left. Even though we've been doing so much on this trip, it's weirdly felt like I've been slowing down."

"Do you know why that is?"

JJ shook her head lightly, frown still in place.

Brooke's hands danced on top of the water's surface. "When we get stuck into habits, or everyday life, it can seem like life speeds up. Every day is frantic. Every day becomes monotonous. Forgettable. Your head hits the pillow. Alarm goes off. Repeat."

"Why do I feel like you're recapping my life at home?" JJ chuckled and raked her hand across her shaved hair.

"Because I probably am. But going away on holiday and having new experiences literally slows down time. It's called the Novelty Effect. It's one reason I think I'm so addicted to travel. Chasing those dopamine hits of a new place has to be healthier than scrolling on our phones or working the same job—day in, day out. No offence." Brooke winced.

"None taken. You're right. I can whole-heartedly say I've felt nothing but the Novelty Effect since we left. It's like magic."

"It is. You should look up ways you can squeeze some novelty into your life when you're back."

"Maybe I need to keep you around to plan that for me." JJ winked.

Brooke's stomach fluttered. Did JJ really mean that?

She dropped her gaze to her hands, then her eyes widened. She waved her hands at JJ. "I think it's time we got out." Any longer in the water and they'd be shrivelled enough to pass for old grapes in the vineyard.

JJ chuckled as she inspected her own hands. "You're not wrong." She climbed out of the tub and turned, holding out a hand for Brooke.

So thoughtful.

JJ's teeth chattered, hairs standing on end as her outreached hand shook. "Bloody hell it's cold," she said as Brooke took her hand and stepped out.

Brooke padded quickly over to the deck chairs, picking

up their towels and throwing one at JJ, who wrapped herself in it within seconds.

The night hadn't gone as anticipated. Ever since their talk that morning, Brooke had been picturing her straddling JJ in the hot tub, hands running through JJ's wet hair and losing herself in JJ's touch. Her usual. That's how things went. Her body knew what it wanted, and she went after it. Especially after the rules they'd established, that's what she'd expected to happen. Not an hour session talking about feelings and childhood trauma. Not Brooke giving JJ a single, soft kiss in gratitude for said conversation. Would she get another tonight? Her eyes slid to JJ towelling herself off.

Slow wasn't Brooke's forte, and with the boundaries JJ had set, she wanted to leave the progression in JJ's court. Even if it felt like her hands were tied behind her back.

Fifteen minutes later, Brooke came out of the bathroom, ready to say good night. JJ stood checking her phone. Her PJs were a cute mismatched set of striped shorts and an oversized T-shirt with *Punky Brewster* written on the front.

Brooke leaned on the wall. "Okay, I have to ask—what's a *Punky Brewster*?"

JJ's eyes widened. "Um, only one of my favourite shows from the eighties. Don't tell me you've never seen it?"

And that's how Brooke ended up shoulder-to-shoulder in JJ's bed, a phone between them, watching the retro show for three hours straight.

"Okay, I'll admit, that was great. Brandon is so *cute*," Brooke said through a yawn, arms stretching above her head. "Now, we better get to bed. Time to hit the road in the morning!"

"More novelty time!" JJ replied, placing her phone on the bedside table. "You're welcome to crash here, if you want."

Brooke bit her lip. She should really stay in her own bed tonight...

Yet, her body betrayed her, legs slipping under the covers.

"Sure."

JJ switched off the light, bathing the room in darkness. A faint glow emanated from the microwave in their kitchenette. Though they'd spent numerous nights sleeping next to each other on this trip, this was the first time since they'd kissed. Twice. While the second kiss was quite chaste, lying here thinking about said kisses had everything *but* chaste thoughts running through her mind. Brooke lay on her back overthinking every movement, every rustle of the quilt.

They'd agreed on more touching and more kissing, but there'd been basically nothing. The deep conversation in the hot tub had put a pause on that, but they'd just spent three hours on the bed together and JJ hadn't made a move.

Should Brooke just instigate it? Was that too forward for JJ? Brooke *had* been the one to kiss her in the hot tub, and JJ hadn't seemed to mind then. Her fingers twitched, confused about which orders to take. Her breaths seemed too loud to her ears—even her blinking was at an audible level. The fridge clicked over, humming away. JJ swallowed next to her.

Oh, fuck it.

She rolled over and—*ow*!

JJ had rolled over at the same time and headbutted her chin.

"Shit, sorry!" JJ placed a hand on Brooke's shoulder. "You all right?"

"Fine, you?" Brooke whispered, the heat of JJ's hand spreading through her.

"Yeah," JJ whispered back.

Why were they whispering?

Now propped up on their elbows, they faced each other in the dark.

Slow breath in. Slow breath out.

Oof.

Brooke's back hit the mattress. JJ leaned over, pressing their lips together, her hand squeezing Brooke's shoulder as she deepened the kiss. Oh. Oh wow.

JJ had it in her after all.

Brooke's hands played catch up. Reaching around, her nails scraped at the nape of JJ's neck—making her groan into Brooke's mouth. Need centred low in her gut, chest flushing at the sound. JJ licked Brooke's lip, sucking it in with a gentle bite, causing heat to ripple through her entire body. Her hips lifted instinctually.

Get a grip!

She needed to slow this down before she lost control. It was too good, too quick. She allowed the kiss to continue a few more moments, a slave to JJ's mouth, then she broke away, sliding to the far edge of the bed.

"Sorry, that was—great." She tried to get a breath in. "But I need to—I think I should stay in my own bed."

"Hey, wait." JJ sat up, eyes wide and arms dangling limp at her sides.

"Sorry," Brooke mumbled again, climbing out of the bed.

Brooke didn't want to be the reason why JJ broke her boundaries, then later regretted it. No, sharing a bed was a bad idea.

She scrambled down the hall and up to her own loft bed, crawling under the covers only to sit straight back up.

Tomorrow they'd be sharing a tent again.

Juuust great.

TWENTY-TWO

JJ

It was like someone else had overtaken JJ's body. She didn't maul people like a lion being fed at the zoo.

JJ threw her suitcase in the roof cargo and climbed in the passenger seat, waiting for Brooke.

Previous partners were usually the ones to start anything physical; initiation was an area she struggled in, needing that deeper connection to help quiet her brain, keep her present and awaken that assertiveness inside. To find that trust in the other person.

She had no idea what she was doing with Brooke, this playing around—though clearly Brooke had been enjoying herself. Feeling her arch off the bed had set JJ into overdrive. She was thankful Brooke had cut things off in the end, or she wasn't sure she could've. But she wasn't ready for more—not yet anyway. The fact she'd started contemplating the possibility of more with Brooke was... confusing.

Brooke hopped in the car and they set off. It was weird not to be driving, making JJ feel a little out of sorts.

"Sure you don't want me to drive?" JJ asked, knee bouncing.

Brooke flicked the indicator on to change lanes. "It's fine, I got this. You relax."

JJ couldn't relax. Everything itched around Brooke this morning. This holiday fling had her both antsy for more and a little uncertain. Yeah, she'd asked for all this, but now JJ had time on her hands—*thanks, Novelty effect*—her mind raced, and her knee bounced: At the possibilities of touching her again, the fact they only had less than a week left of their fling and... what that meant for them once it ended. So many thoughts she had no concrete answers to.

Maybe she could organise her emails? No, she was on bloody holiday. That'd only open up a can of worms. She bit her lip and looked out the window.

A hand landed on her bouncing knee and squeezed.

Her knee stilled. JJ stared at Brooke's hand.

"You good?" Brooke asked.

"Huh? Yeah."

Her leg tingled under Brooke's touch.

"Why don't you put some music on?" Brooke started pressing buttons on the car's head unit.

"*Paired*—rolled the nipple between her thumb and—"

JJ shut off the audio, eyes wide. *Not again!* Where was the eject seat button in this car? JJ's face heated. No words.

"You don't have to turn off your naughty lady books on account of me being here." Brooke's grin widened, her hand returning to JJ's leg.

JJ gave her a look.

"I'm serious," Brooke continued. "We've got a long drive ahead of us, might as well put something on. I usually listen to podcasts and stuff while travelling, so I'm happy to see what these books are actually like. You're always trying to make me listen anyway." Brooke winked and chuckled.

JJ gave it another moment, but Brooke waited.

"Okay," JJ said. "But let me pick something from the start—one of my good ones."

Once the soothing tones of her favourite narrator came through, JJ relaxed. Apparently, it was exactly what she needed.

Brooke's hand didn't leave her leg the entire ride.

And neither did the tingles.

Deep Creek was a windy location, atop cliffs that sunk into the dark ocean below. Rolling green hills stood proud the entire length of the coastline. South of Adelaide, this area was known for its harsh winds, heavy rains and lush but rugged environment. Their camping spot was nestled in a small clearing, enough to fit the tent and car with a little privacy from other campers. Brooke knew how to balance the accommodation well with a mix of comfortable sleeping arrangements, then nights like tonight, roughing it a little.

They'd set up their tent, a simple four-person dome, so they had enough room to stand inside with ample storage space left over. Thankfully, there were also flushing toilets and hot showers nearby—no long drops in sight!

Brooke had planned another day hike, and this time she'd triple checked the weather before leaving to make sure there were no storms on the horizon. JJ was thankful for the attention she put into the trip. She was constantly checking, updating and tweaking as they went. It made JJ realise how much time and effort truly went into organising travel, and it reiterated how good her choice had been to bring Brooke along, leaving *all* those decisions to her. Thank god. If she'd cancelled way back at the start and had that home holiday, she'd never have gotten to know Brooke. Her gut twinged at the thought.

JJ led the trail today, and it felt good to be in control of something again—even something as simple as a circuit hike to try and get that head of hers cleared.

"There's a waterfall just up ahead," JJ said, a third of the way into the walk. It had rained the day before, and fresh petrichor still clung to the air. They rounded a corner, heading up a steady incline to a spot overlooking the falls. The roar wasn't too loud, and the soft spray that reached them was refreshing after the long walk. They sat on an overhanging rock, legs dangling and thighs touching. Snack time!

"JJ, how many boxes of BBQ Shapes did you pack?" Brooke asked, incredulous as JJ opened the packet between them.

"I didn't hear you complaining every time I saw you shoving a handful in your face."

Brooke poked out her tongue. "That's not an answer."

"Well, it's personal and I don't want to tell you."

Brooke chuckled, digging her hand into the box. "Good practising."

JJ didn't think any amount of practice would really help her when it came time to try standing up for herself. Her family meant everything to her, so offending them was the last thing she wanted.

JJ stole a biscuit out of Brooke's hand and winked. "So, have you thought any more about Hayley?"

Instead of shutting down, Brooke considered the question. "It's been gnawing at me since we spoke. I finally feel like I have a way of communicating that might lead to some sort of resolution. That feeling is... liberating. Or at least, writing out what I want to say feels somewhat achievable. I've been trying to come up with things in my head on our walk. It's dredged up more memories, but I've started to see them differently."

"Oh?" JJ leaned back on her hands, the warm, rough rock prickling into her palms.

"I think I'd been ignoring how much Hayley used to do. Not just for me, but for herself and Steven too. Well, maybe not ignoring... I didn't see it."

It was refreshing to hear Brooke revisit her past without the emotional burden overtaking her.

"Really? Like how?" JJ asked.

"There was this one time I remember sitting down for dinner and Hayley looked exhausted. Mum and Dad were out at a gala for the night, and Hayley was meant to be finishing up a uni assignment. I'm not sure how much study she did between washing our clothes, shopping for food, and cooking us dinner—because Steven wasn't about to get off his arse and cook." Brooke rolled her eyes and munched on another biscuit.

"At the time I'd been thinking—of course Hayley can do it all. Even when our parents are away, she's *still* got it all together. But... I never stopped to consider if she wanted to take on that work, to make sure the house ran smoothly when our parents were out or interstate. How did that make her feel?"

JJ folded in her lips and shook her head. She couldn't

imagine being in that position with that kind of pressure. Her family and upbringing were so different.

Brooke brushed a few stray crumbs off her lap and continued, "I'm honestly not sure I could've seen her side at the time, I was too in my own feels. Now, coming back home and heading away again so soon has me questioning everything. There's a lot to unpack. I just hope Hayley is open to talking about it."

"Well, time will tell. All you can do is ask." JJ wished she could give Brooke the answers she sought, but this was her journey. Who knew what the future held?

The trail from the waterfall to the coastal cliffs was quiet and contemplative. That was the beauty of hiking, the brain had time to process. Instead of a million to-dos or distractions, each simple step in front of the other allowed for past memories and thoughts to collide with what-ifs and maybes of the future. And after their recent conversations, they both had *a lot* to work through. JJ's ability to think abruptly halted as the path led them to a particularly steep climb.

Brooke took the lead on this section, her manoeuvrability and skill a notch above JJ when it came to finding the right hand and foot holds to use. She constantly checked back to see if JJ was okay, offering her hand a few times to help climb up some particularly precarious spots. By the time they reached the top, JJ's back was drenched and her chest burned, but they'd made it.

Brooke gave her a lazy smile.

"What?" JJ asked.

Brooke took a step closer. "Nothing. You look cute, is all."

JJ poked a tongue into her cheek. "I doubt that. A drenched, sun-baked rat is probably more accurate."

Brooke closed the gap, and JJ sucked in a breath as Brooke planted a kiss straight on her lips. Sunblock and sweat filled her senses.

"Disagree." Brooke turned on her heel and continued down the now very, very steep slope on the other side.

JJ couldn't stop the smile that followed. She touched her lip where it still tingled.

Moving to follow Brooke, she caught a glimpse of the path down below. Well... the not-path. The trail disappeared straight into a large body of water.

"Uh, Brooke. We have a problem."

Brooke swivelled on a rocky outcropping, one foot still in the air as she searched for what JJ was pointing at.

"Do we need to turn around?" JJ asked. It was going to be more difficult to backtrack, and she was so exhausted. They'd even run down one of the previous declines; it was so steep.

"Why?" Brooke asked.

JJ gestured wildly in front of them. "Oh, you know, just the entire ocean coming in through the mouth of the cliffs and covering our path."

"Easy," Brooke replied, continuing her descent. "We just wade through it."

"What!" JJ squeaked.

"It's not that deep. A little water never hurt anyone. It's gotta be better than getting hailed on." Brooke lifted an eyebrow.

"But I didn't bring a towel. I'll get sand everywhere." Despite her argument, JJ started the climb down.

Once they reached the edge of the water, it stretched further than she expected. "We can honestly just turn back—"

"JJ. Just take off your damn shoes," Brooke said, stuffing a sock in her already-removed boot.

JJ made a face but obliged. Her toes sunk into the warm sand. Brooke stepped into the water, having rolled up her pants over her knees.

JJ took a deep breath. *Here goes nothing.*

"Fuck, that's freezing!" She froze in the ankle-deep water.

"The faster you walk, the faster you'll be across," Brooke said. She waded back and grabbed JJ's hand. It was slightly sandy, giving JJ the urge to wipe her hands. *Let it go.* She blew out a breath, following Brooke and hissing with each step as it deepened. The water was a muddy brown from the waves pushing into the mouth of the outlet and flowing back out to the ocean. With her free hand, she held her shoes above the water as it hit their knees. They paused, finagling their pants as high as they could go.

"Okay, so it's a little deeper than I thought," Brooke confessed, grabbing JJ's hand back to continue on.

"Well, it's a little late now!"

JJ shrieked as a small, cold wave hit the back of her knee.

"Well, when life gives you lemons..."

"You turn into a lesbian?" JJ quipped.

"No, JJ, you keep going!"

"That doesn't even make sense."

"You don't make sense."

"I make perfect sense. I'm a lesbian aka—a lemon." JJ grinned proudly.

Brooke sputtered out a laugh and pulled her along. "I think we have heat stroke; we're losing our minds."

"You can't have heat stroke if you're knee deep in freezing-arse water. You just need better sayings that make sense."

"I'm not justifying that with a response. And I've never heard of a lesbian being called a lemon."

"That's because you haven't spent enough time back in Straya. You're losing touch with the slang, mate. Gonna have to take your Aussie card off ya." She went to laugh but yelped instead. Her toes sunk into a particularly deep patch of mud-like sand, the cold water hitting her bare thighs and licking at her pants.

"Jesus!" JJ cried.

"I've got you." Brooke gripped her hand tight, pulling her up and preventing her from getting drenched.

"That was close, thanks."

Turns out they'd crossed the halfway mark, their wading steps getting surer and steadier as the water line dropped. Any deeper and JJ would've turned back.

"C'mon, you lemon. Let's get you on dry land." Brooke said, pulling JJ along by their still joined hands.

"What—you don't like a wet lemon?" JJ cocked her head.

"Oh my god, stop." Brooke laughed.

JJ tugged her in close and kissed her instead.

Brooke's unbreakable smile against her lips was everything.

JJ still had a lot of unanswered questions about their relationship, but one thing she knew for sure: not only could she and Brooke have the heavier talks, they could also have a hell of a good time together.

TWENTY-THREE

Brooke

Brooke had a problem. The further they got into their holiday, the more each day felt like a date. Their whole trip was starting to feel like one big, mega date. And Brooke didn't date. She didn't tie herself to people. She didn't *want* to rely on anyone else. That was just a recipe for getting hurt. But here she was, constantly touching JJ or watching her, taking notes of the way she'd fold up her clothes perfectly every night before bed—even her dirty laundry, or when she'd lock her car twice, every single time, just in case. Then there was her absurd obsession with BBQ Shapes.

Brooke didn't notice this kind of shit about people. Small things. Everyday things. Boring things.

But god—they weren't boring to her.

And Brooke didn't know what to do with that information. Not one little bit.

Everything had become a tease. This game they were playing. Their stupid rules.

Now even her thoughts were turning her on.

Brooke squirmed and readjusted her legs. She sat in a fold-out chair at their campsite. They'd finished their hike and had a luxurious—and necessary—hot shower at the nearby amenities block. Dinner had been a quick affair of baked beans and toast cooked over the fire, giving the simple dish that little extra something after being infused with the smoke.

Now, in the distance, laughter could be heard on and off from another group of campers. Brooke pulled her hands into her sleeves and tucked them into her armpits as she stared at the embers slowly turning to coals. Crickets chirped all around them.

The sun had set a while ago, and JJ was currently sweeping sand out of their tent by lamp light. According to JJ, Brooke had apparently trudged it in after their hike, but she'd sworn she'd stamped her feet before entering.

Oh—but she had walked back in to grab her hoodie... and back once more for her beanie. Oops.

Well, still. She'd *tried* to be careful.

"Much better." JJ placed the banister broom back in her car and locked it—twice. "No more shoes in the tent!" She pointed at Brooke and dropped into the seat next to her.

Brooke stood and moved in front of JJ with her eyebrow raised. "Sorry, I... really should apologise."

JJ frowned for a second, her eyebrows shooting up the next as Brooke stepped toward her.

Brooke needed to touch her, just a little—a quick taste. The restlessness had been growing all afternoon. And then JJ had come back from her shower with wet hair again, and god damn if that didn't do it for her. But the last straw?

Seeing JJ all haughty over Brooke's sandy mess, her wrinkled nose only adding fuel to Brooke's fire.

She stepped either side of JJ's legs and lowered herself—inch by slow, torturous inch—onto JJ's lap, the camp chair groaning with the added weight until they were face to face. JJ's gaze raked over her face, her chest... drinking her in, and Brooke revelled in it.

Apparently even in crappy worn PJs and a hoodie, she could still turn it!

Brooke leaned in and captured JJ's lips. *Yes, finally.*

"I promise I won't let it happen again," she whispered against JJ's mouth.

"Wh—oh. Apology accepted." JJ squeezed Brooke's hips and kissed her again.

Brooke hummed. Lips that soft should be illegal and her minty fresh taste was an absolute delight.

Brooke wrapped her arms around JJ's neck, sinking onto her further and pushing out her chest. It brushed against JJ's.

Was this flirting with the rules?

Tongues lashed and swirled as JJ deepened the kiss, each stroke sending electricity straight down Brooke's body, like a physical pulsating current. She moaned at the sensation, her hips beginning to move of their own accord. The chair squeaked as they ramped up.

"Maybe we should—"

"I know," Brooke replied, not wanting the moment to end. It always needed to stop. Just give her this. A little longer. She made a pitiful sound, disbelieving it had come from herself. JJ's arms pulled her in closer, tighter. Exactly what she needed.

She felt like she was floating.

No, they were definitely moving.

A loud snap ricocheted into the night, scaring a flock of cockatoos from the trees nearby, their raucous screeches echoing as they flew off.

"Oof!" Brooke landed on JJ in one unholy heap, the grass cushioning their fall with a dull thud.

They stared, stunned for a moment. Even the crickets fell silent.

Giggles erupted, increasing in volume until Brooke's ribs hurt, and JJ's stomach felt as if it was punching her.

"I guess we should take this to the tent?" JJ asked once their chuckles had subsided.

Brooke couldn't scoot up fast enough, their broken chair left on the ground. This time, she made sure to take her shoes off at the entrance.

Inside the tent, there was nowhere for Brooke to run tonight. She needed to be careful, keep herself in check. It was so easy to lose herself in JJ's touch, but she couldn't forget JJ's boundaries.

JJ zipped the flap behind them and came to Brooke, a hand cupping her cheek for a soft kiss. The hand slipped into her still damp hair, gripping and pulling, lighting up all her nerve endings. Every move from JJ was a calculated dance, the touches and kisses combining into a rhythm that played Brooke like a perfectly executed song. Everything in tune, every note striking at just the right time.

And this was just a kiss.

But Brooke felt it everywhere: fire dancing through her veins, hairs tingling on the top of her head, heart drumming to the beat of JJ's movements. Brooke was lost in it.

How long they were standing there, sock-footed and lips-locked in their little tent, she couldn't say. The outside world no longer existed.

At some point, JJ pulled her down to the floor. They'd pushed two camp mattresses together and unzipped their sleeping bags to create one big bed. Well, big was pushing it. Their one barely-larger-than-a-twin bed.

JJ switched off their lamp and moved on top of Brooke, half off to the side, propped up on an elbow but still pinning her down. Her leg draped over Brooke's and the feel of their cosy pyjamas mixed with soft skin had Brooke's hands exploring, skimming past any red zones—though surely a little butt squeeze was okay?

There was something different about tonight; their pace remained slow and unhurried. Brooke stopped worrying about needing to be careful. With boundaries firmly established, she was content kissing JJ for hours.

And so she did.

Her body vibrated at a low hum instead of the increasing ache for a climax. But she found with JJ, she really didn't mind at all.

Somewhere in the middle of the night, their movements slowed. Brooke placed one last kiss on JJ's forehead, a hand resting on her chest. A sign to say good night, not a suggestion for anything more.

With that, they rolled over, and JJ tucked herself in behind Brooke, a hand sliding onto her stomach as though they did this every night. How did they fit together so perfectly?

"Okay?" JJ asked, a soft mumble into her hair.

Brooke thought of cutlery again, imagining her fork's

tines curling, fusing together into a smooth, curved utensil. Maybe she wanted to be a spoon after all. At least, for tonight. She shuffled back into JJ, body easing into JJ's warmth... until it began to feel like torture. Brooke shut her eyes but her mind was anything but ready to settle down.

What grew between them tonight felt heavier than just touches and kisses. At least for Brooke. Intimacy for her had always been fast, frivolous and... in a sense, selfish. A means to a *hopefully* climactic end. But tonight? This was deeper, shared. Brooke's thoughts focused on how she hoped her touch and her actions made JJ feel as good as she did.

JJ moved, pulling Brooke closer.

In less than a week they'd be saying goodbye.

But what if they didn't?

Behind her, JJ's breathing evened out. Brooke wanted to roll over and look at her.

Was she seriously wondering what it would be like to date JJ?

TWENTY-FOUR

Brooke

The next morning, the ferry over to Kangaroo Island was anything but smooth. The bumpy forty-five-minute trip had them both on the top deck sucking in fresh air. It was Brooke's least favourite mode of transport thanks to the guaranteed nausea it brought her.

Kangaroo Island itself was the only place JJ had requested be part of the itinerary, so Brooke thought it fitting to end the trip there. They had a handful of nights left and she wanted to make the most of it.

Brooke was four on her last visit to KI. It had been one of the rare family holidays the Mayfields had gone on together. She didn't remember much. Only the large amount of roadkill and her dad pressing his finger to the windscreen whenever they passed another car on the dirt roads.

Time to upgrade those memories!

It was a short drive off the ferry to their accommodation.

"Aren't we too old to be staying at a backpackers?" JJ asked, eyes narrowed.

Nondescript from the front, the place appeared to be a regular single-storey home. A simple swinging sign out the front was the only indication they were at the right place.

"It's part of the experience," Brooke replied. Hostels and backpackers weren't her favourite sleeping arrangement, but they sure were entertaining. "Come on."

The door creaked as they entered the old cottage, the ceilings low and walls thick with history.

Mary, the hostel's owner, greeted them on arrival, ushering them through the communal lounge and dining, down a long hallway and into their room. While they were lucky enough not to be sharing with others, they were unfortunately—

"Bunk beds?!" JJ rounded on Brooke, eyes wide. "This is so exciting. I've got the top." After Mary left, chuckling, JJ pushed past Brooke into the room.

Brooke blinked. This was not the reaction she was expecting.

JJ pushed her suitcase into the corner, scurried up the bunk's ladder, and jumped onto the mattress on her hands and knees. The whole thing squeaked and groaned with every move.

JJ's head popped over the edge. "How cool is this?" She beamed, cheeks ballooning. "It feels like we're having a sleepover." She bounced on the bed to make her point.

Brooke sighed. She wasn't going to get an ounce of sleep tonight with that squeaking.

"You really haven't stayed in enough hostels." Brooke pushed off the doorway and moved to the bottom bed. "I don't mind sharing with you though, just make sure you sleep really still."

JJ bounced again with a mischievous grin.

Back out in the lounge, they met a small group of travellers and introduced themselves.

"I'm Zed, they/them," said a short person on the couch with spiky green hair and the coolest pair of metallic rainbow Doc Marten's Brooke had ever seen.

"Ameera," a petite Indian woman waved, then gestured next to her. "And this is Dan."

"Sup." The tall guy gave a quick head nod, moving dreads out of this face. "Wanna join us?" He held up a deck of cards.

JJ looked at Brooke.

"We've got a bit of time before we need to leave, so sure —why not?" Brooke shrugged and sat on the empty couch across from him. JJ scooched in next to her.

They played a few rounds of *Bullshit*, chatting easily with the group about their adventures so far. After an hour, JJ nudged Brooke to leave.

"Where are you off to?" Ameera asked.

"The lavender farm."

She bobbed her head as if weighing up the answer. "Sounds all right. Or—you could come jet skiing with us?"

"Oh no, we've already—" JJ started.

"I'm listening." Brooke pretended to tuck a lock of hair behind her ear and grinned.

"Dan's mate runs the place," Zed said. "You can just hop on and go."

"The recommended sights usually take a couple of

hours to see everything. You got a boat licence?" Dan added.

"Sure do," Brooke said, eyes bright.

JJ cleared her throat. "Thanks for thinking of us, but we have plans."

Brooke turned to her. "You sure you'd rather go to a farm rather than on a jet ski adventure with me?" Brooke batted her eyelashes, making Ameera chuckle. "Promise I'm a good driver."

JJ's eyes slid to her hands twisting in her lap. "Can we think about it?"

"Of course," Brooke replied. "Give us five minutes?" she said to the group, standing and pulling JJ up with her into the hallway.

"Okay, talk to me."

"Our plan was to see the lavender farm."

"It was," Brooke said. "And this is your holiday, so what would you like to do?"

JJ's eyes darted around as she let out a sigh. "I don't know. I feel like we should stick to the plan."

"Not what we *should* do. What do you *want* to do?"

"But they were expecting us."

JJ was slipping back into old habits, so it was time for a rephrase and a little extra push. Try to get her to shake things up a little. Plus, Brooke really wanted to get on that jet ski... and unlike queasy-inducing ferries on rough seas, jet skis were *so* much fun.

"It's only a cafe and not like the farm is in bloom this time of year anyway. Just something different to see. I can easily cancel the booking." Brooke pulled out her phone and waved it around. "It's okay if we change our mind and try something new. You're allowed to pivot."

A small smile curved at the edge of JJ's mouth. Brooke wanted to kiss it.

Her smile widened. "Stuff it. Let's do it."

Brooke did kiss her this time.

What a day to head out on the water. There wasn't a cloud in the sky and the sand felt so good between her toes. The fresh ocean breeze played with Brooke's hair as she clipped her lifejacket together and tightened the straps. JJ stood next to her, face down as she tried to wrangle her own jacket on.

"Here, you've got it all twisted." Any excuse to step into JJ's space.

JJ's arms dropped and she let out a growl. "Argh. It should not be that difficult."

"It's because you've got something here." Brooke pointed at JJ's chest, making her look down. Brooke flicked her on the nose, JJ's eyes going comically wide before narrowing.

"Hey!"

Brooke laughed. "Can't believe you fell for that."

"You're such a shit sometimes." JJ was smiling at least.

Brooke went to fix her life jacket for real this time, but JJ grabbed onto her wrist.

"Oi! I'm trying to help!" she whined through more laughter.

Brooke tried to wrangle free, but JJ's grip tightened,

eyes locked on Brooke's. Heat flashed and Brooke's stomach flipped, their hands frozen in place. JJ's tongue darted out to wet her lips.

"Can you two hurry up already and stop making googly eyes at each other?" Zed yelled from their jet ski, driving in slow circles, while Ameera and Dan pushed theirs into waist-deep water.

Brooke yanked her hand free and finished buckling up JJ's jacket. "There." She pulled extra tight on the last strap, making JJ suck in a breath.

"Race you to the water!" Brooke yelled, turning and sprinting down to the shoreline. Legs pumping like a machine, Brooke cut through the sand; the heavy foot falls of JJ right on her tail. She squealed, crashing into the cold water. She made it knee-deep when hands wrapped around her middle and launched her into the water. The last thing Brooke heard was her own screeching cackle before she plunged underwater head first.

Heart thrashing, she pulled herself up, still laughing, and flipped her now-wet hair up and out of her eyes.

"Hot," JJ mouthed, and Brooke shoved her playfully in the arm.

"C'mon, these guys are probably regretting asking us along," Brooke said, grabbing their jet ski and pushing it into deeper water. She hopped on, then helped JJ get on behind her. They'd already been through the safety training and while Brooke knew what she was doing, this was JJ's first time. She sat with way too much space between them.

"Squish up. You want to be as close as you can get. There's a handle there, but honestly, you're better off holding onto me for the best balance. Then like the operator said, make sure you're leaning with me on the turns, yeah?"

"Got it." JJ scooched up, the warmth hitting Brooke. She paused, momentarily forgetting what was next. Right, the kill switch! She strapped the lanyard on her wrist and clicked it in.

"You both good?" Dan checked in. Ameera had already taken off to join Zed.

"Ready." Brooke gave him a thumbs up, then called over her shoulder, "Hold on!"

JJ's arms tightened around her as she started the motor and fluttered the throttle, testing the power. Not bad, very responsive. She tried turning to check on JJ, but her vision was blocked by a giant row of white teeth. JJ's grin could blind.

Yeah, this was better than taking her to a flower cafe.

Brooke squeezed the throttle, propelling them forward to catch up with the group. The faster she went, the harder JJ's thighs pressed against hers. She'd never been so thankful for the roar of the engine to drown out her inadvertent groan. The spray blasted them as they sped through the slightly choppy waters, even with Brooke trying her best to keep the ride as smooth as possible for JJ.

They hit full throttle, the wind whipping at her face and a smile that couldn't be wiped off. Adrenaline rushed through her as Brooke leaned forward, thighs burning, JJ clinging to her, and the jet ski smacking against the water. They were going to be sore tomorrow.

"Woohoo!" JJ cried out behind her, squeezing Brooke around the waist. "I can't see anything!" She laughed.

The group rode in a line with Dan in front for them to

follow. He'd done the course numerous times and was their unofficial guide. After ten minutes of speed mania, Dan held up a hand and everyone slowed, pulling up together.

"Look over there," he said, pointing.

To their right, seals played in the water and lazed on the beach. They kept their distance and watched from afar.

"Amazing," JJ commented. "Now we're going to have to cancel the seal tour after seeing them like this!"

Coming off the high of the ride, Brooke was still trying to calm her breath so she could zone in on the simple moment of watching the seals play and feed.

JJ gripped her suddenly. "Uhh, if there are seals, does that mean there are sharks around?"

"Listen. There's a chance. But the good thing is, we're on these bad boys and not in the water." Brooke patted the handlebar of the jet ski.

"There're sharks around all the time," Dan said with a massive grin.

"That's not comforting in the slightest." JJ turned to Brooke. "You better drive *real* careful on the way home."

"Yes, ma'am."

After chilling in the calmer waters watching the seals, spotting a pod of dolphins that were *thankfully* not sharks (like JJ first thought), and chatting with their new-found friends, it was time to head back. They made the most of the last stretch with a few doughies, getting air off each other's wakes, all while JJ screamed several times about not getting her thrown off to the sharks.

They arrived back in one piece, as promised. Once they cut the motor, JJ collapsed into Brooke.

"Thank god we're back. Jesus, Brooke. You're a maniac

on that thing. It felt like I was gonna go flying! More than once."

"But we didn't, did we?" Brooke said sweetly, leaning back into her.

"No, we didn't. Thanks for today. That's not something I'll be forgetting anytime soon." Brooke felt lips press to her neck, and she resisted the urge to push back into JJ, reminding herself there were people around.

Instead, she cleared her throat. "You're welcome."

Though Brooke had every intention of making it up to JJ tonight.

TWENTY-FIVE

JJ

Day two and three on KI had been a whirlwind. Brooke had shown her wildlife sanctuaries, lighthouses, and so many lookouts, JJ was blissed out on nature, and well... Brooke. The perfect balance of sightseeing and kissing in JJ's opinion. It was now just after lunch on day four, and with so much crossed off their itinerary, they'd just pulled in for a quick stop at the lavender farm. JJ nabbed a jar of their signature Ligurian lavender honey from the gift shop, then they headed outside to the cafe.

After ordering, JJ led the way to some chairs under an umbrella and table combo overlooking the rows of fragrant green-grey shrubs, albeit without any flowers. Their arrival had been perfectly timed as a swarm of tourists left the farm, allowing them to soak up the scenery without the bustle and chatter coming from the busload of grey nomads.

JJ bit into the warm lavender scone with fresh cream and apricot jam. She closed her eyes and chewed, an obscene hum escaping her throat. The scone was so light and fluffy, crumbling into her mouth. The sweet jam and cream combo paired perfectly with the light floral notes.

"That good, huh?" Brooke sat across from her with a smirk, spreading cream onto her own piece. "You're making me kinda jealous I'm all the way over here." She rubbed her foot against JJ's.

JJ tried her best to give Brooke a sexy smile back, but her face was too full of food. Brooke laughed, the sound so carefree. Her eyes crinkled and shoulders shook.

It made it hard for JJ to keep chewing, JJ's lips tugging at the edges and wanting to join in on the fun. She covered her mouth, trying to preserve a last semblance of decorum as she forced down her bite, then let her smile run free.

This is what she wanted her dates to be like.

Not checking the clock every minute or working out ways to bail. Not sitting there spending the entire time judging the person across from her.

She wanted this.

Quiet moments. Enjoying each other's company and sharing laughs that warmed her from the inside out, the kind where each note sent off another kaleidoscope of butterflies in her stomach. Even though this wasn't a date, this shared time with Brooke was exactly what she needed—to see that it was possible to find this with someone. It could exist in her future... somehow.

And when she did find it, she'd bloody hold on for dear life.

As her blue eyes continued to sparkle, Brooke reached across the table, fingers stroking JJ's arm, then her hand. Brooke intertwined their fingers and JJ forgot to breathe.

The touch was soft and lazy with a gentle squeeze as

Brooke took a bite of her scone, errant crumbs catching in the corners of her mouth. JJ leaned over to brush them away, the pad of her thumb then swiping along Brooke's jaw. Brooke paused mid-bite, watching the motion with the lightest pink blush dusting her cheeks.

"What do you think?" JJ asked.

"Hmm?" Brooke seemed lost in thought. "Oh, yeah, g-good. Great. Delicious." She shook her head, her features settling back into smiling and carefree Brooke.

JJ wished she could kiss her then and there, to make the most of the time they had left. But they had food to eat. There'd be no finishing if JJ leaned over now. Instead, she tried to sit still as they ate their scones and sipped their tea —lavender of course. As soon as they were done, JJ was out of her chair and pulling Brooke down the rows of lavender. The sun warmed her skin, hairs standing on end as they celebrated being out from under the shade of the umbrella.

"Where are we going?" Brooke laughed, clomping along behind JJ to keep up with her long strides.

"You'll see." JJ guided Brooke through the fragrant gardens, the bees still buzzing around in hopes of finding a stray flower or two. Brooke had taken the lead on so much of this holiday, it was JJ's turn to take *her* on a little detour. Something just for fun.

They came to a large gum tree, tall and old with a trunk so wide it would take four people to reach around it. JJ slowed, taking Brooke's other hand in hers and walking her backwards, each step crunching and crackling on the dense littering of twigs and leaves. Brooke held her gaze with a single arched brow.

"What are you—"

Brooke's back hit the tree, eyes darting from eyes to lips to—

"This." JJ raised both hands over Brooke's head, gripping them tight against the rough bark.

And she kissed her.

Stupid cute crumbs.

JJ kissed her harder.

Stupid not-date dates.

She stepped closer, pressing up against Brooke, a thigh sliding between her legs. Just a little closer. A little more friction.

Stupid bloody rules.

Her hands itched, wanting to roam further, under... lower. To more than *just kiss*.

Brooke squeezed JJ's hands overhead and opened their kiss, her tongue slipping into JJ's mouth. Lavender and apricot.

God, she'd needed this.

The more she kissed Brooke, the more she craved. It only grew worse the closer they got to the end of the trip. To wring as much out of this as possible before JJ was back to square one.

No Brooke. No partner. Just dating apps.

The inner swell inside her grew, the familiar heat building, wanting to be flamed.

JJ broke off the kiss, forehead leaning on Brooke's, their chests pressing into one another with each breath.

"Fuck, that was hot," Brooke said, gaze on JJ's mouth.

JJ closed her eyes, remembering where they were—in the middle of a lavender farm—and only slightly hidden from view. She exhaled slowly and placed one more kiss on Brooke's lips.

"We better get back."

The hostel was abuzz with new people when they returned. Two girls stood talking to Mary, their backpacks at their feet, ready to be shown their room. A father and son sat at the dining table playing an intense looking board game, both animatedly waving their arms with each turn. Zed sat on their phone on a corner couch and looked up as they entered. JJ gave them a wave.

"Ey—JJ, Brooke—timing!" Zed said.

"For what?" JJ asked.

"Sandboarding!"

And that's how JJ's quiet afternoon turned into bumping along on a tour bus out to the famous sand dunes of Kangaroo Island. Though she wasn't complaining about the woman sitting next to her. Brooke stared out the window, JJ's arm in her lap, drawing endless shapes on her open hand. Ameera and Dan had joined them, and the five now affectionately coined themselves *The Hostel Crew*.

JJ gulped on arrival.

Standing at the base, the dunes were much, much higher than she'd anticipated. Like a tidal wave made of sand. Back home, she'd head down to Karkalla Beach, where the dunes were something you could run up and down as a kid. Usually a metre or two high, tops.

This... was not.

It was as though JJ had been shrunk, standing at the bottom of a large ant hill. The ants at the top of the hill now waved and screeched before barrelling over the side and riding down the sand.

Dan and Zed pushed past JJ, sandboards in hand, and raced to the top, kicking up sand with every step.

JJ swallowed again. There was so much sand. And it was so tall.

She turned to Brooke, who burst out laughing.

"Oh my god, JJ, you look like you're about to pee your pants. Relax those eyebrows of yours before they turn into a monobrow." Brooke cupped either side of JJ's head, smoothing out JJ's eyebrows with her thumbs and planting a kiss on her lips. "There. Much better." She smooshed JJ's cheeks with her hands, then dropped her arms. "And don't worry, you and I are tobogganing. Unless... you want to try the boards?"

"The toboggans are better, way more stable," Ameera said, pulling one past them.

JJ took another glance at the gleaming white slope.

The trip was coming to an end, and though she'd already stretched her comfort zone, this was a whole new level.

"I want to try the boards."

Because when on KI...

Brooke squealed and did a little dance on the spot. "Yes! Let's do it!"

Shoes off and freshly waxed sandboards obtained, they made their first trek up the giant dune.

Halfway up, Dan and Zed careened past them on their boards, hooting and hollering at each other until Zed crashed out near the bottom, and Dan ended up on his back in a bush.

JJ licked her lips and shoved the board into the sand like a walking stick to leverage herself up. What was she getting herself into?

The climb was rough. The sun belted down, reflecting off the sand and making it feel twice as warm. The air was as hot as a sauna, read: stifling. JJ's heart pounded harder than when they hiked in the Flinders Ranges. She wiped her forehead and started daydreaming about her water bottle stuck in her bag all the way back down at the base. She hadn't even got on the board yet and she was stuffed! The afternoon nap she had planned was looking mighty good right now. Brooke huffed and puffed next to her, their footsteps pummelling the sand as they reached the crest.

JJ turned to see how far they'd come. Mistake. "Holy shit." She wobbled on the spot, vertigo taking over with how high up they'd clambered. She stuck the board in deeper and stabilised herself.

"It's steep, but we'll hit the bottom before we know it," Brooke said.

"It's *how* I hit the bottom that I'm afraid of." JJ chewed at the inside of her lip.

It was weird to be on an inland dune. The coast and ocean were still visible from the top, but a few kilometres out. Instead of water, the dunes were surrounded by thick, dark green shrubland from all directions. Now at the top and unblocked by the dune itself, the salty beach air was strong, and the breeze blowing was enough to cool JJ off after their arduous climb. She'd expected it to be flat at the top, but instead it was more like a ridgeline where it dropped off on the other side, albeit at a shallower decline.

JJ turned to face the other direction. "Maybe we should test going down this side first."

"Nope." Brooke swung her back around. "Come on. You chose the board. Let's do this."

JJ stared at the drop, heart thrashing. Her hands were clammy, sand already sticking to them. She tried brushing it off on her shirt.

"We can go together." Brooke placed her board on the ground and slipped her feet in. "Just remember: knees bent, back straight and arms out for balance."

JJ blew out a rough breath and copied Brooke's movements.

Don't overthink it. This is fun. You'll be fine.

"Okay, I'm ready." She nodded to Brooke and shook her arms to clear her nerves, only it made the board see-saw and tipped her over the edge.

Warm air whipped past her face as she wobbled, her arms making frantic windmills as she attempted to catch any last semblance of stability.

"Ahhhhh."

JJ's scream lasted the entire five second slide until she flipped, her entire body cartwheeling in the air with fountains of sand blooming around her.

She landed with a hard thump, sliding a short distance until she came to stop.

She blinked.

Sand was everywhere. Her mouth. Her hair. Between her fingers, her toes. Her—god, don't even think about it.

JJ laughed, lying in the sand flat on her back.

And she'd thought the jet skis were crazy! This was the wildest ride she'd ever taken. But she'd done it.

"That was sick!" Dan called out from somewhere behind her.

"Is she okay?" Ameera's soft voice asked from somewhere.

Brooke's face entered JJ's vision upside down, blocking out the sun. "You right?" Her forehead was wrinkled, brows knitted together as she studied JJ's face. "That looked insane—you went flying."

"I'm good," JJ said, her laughter dying down. "But I think maybe I'll stick to the toboggan from now on."

She stuck an arm in the air, and Brooke pulled her upright. JJ shook out her hair and patted herself down until she was relatively certain most of the sand was taken care of. She really hadn't thought that gritty part through... too late now.

Brooke stepped into JJ's space and planted a kiss on her lips as she took JJ's hand and threaded their fingers together. "Proud of you."

JJ stood straighter, chest puffed and a grin that couldn't be wiped off. "Let's grab those toboggans."

Sand be damned.

JJ finished the afternoon on a literal high: climbing again and again to the top of a deceptively steep sand dune, strapping herself to the toboggan, and flying down sand hills so fast she expected to take off into the sky. She still crashed out more times than she'd like to admit, adding more sand to places she never thought possible.

That night, JJ lay in her squeaky bunk bed, staring at the too-close ceiling. Her body ached everywhere, worse than if she'd been home painting houses. She shuffled her feet, stray grains of sand scratching under her heel. JJ suppressed a shudder. Even with the shower and scrubbing, those tiny grains were insidious. She found herself smiling though, at the friends she'd found, the memories she'd made and her own boundaries she'd pushed: to try new things, fun things and scary things.

Flashes of Brooke floated through her mind. The catalyst for it all.

And it was almost time to say goodbye.

JJ's stomach sank.

It's a good thing.

She didn't want to end up getting hurt or real feelings to develop. It was all just for fun, but currently her body didn't give a crap about her list, her ideals.

It didn't help that the hour spent rolling around in Brooke's bed earlier had ended when the intensity rose and Brooke had called it off once again. JJ had slunk to her top bunk, heart racing and heat simmering.

It's a good thing. It had to be.

TWENTY-SIX

JJ

While JJ was still riding the high, refusing to believe this was truly their final day, Brooke had grown cagey, eating away at JJ's euphoria until it had been completely eroded. Every question was met with another question or a diversion away from their evening. Now they were in the car and Brooke was driving. JJ still wasn't allowed to know where and sat pretend-sulking in the passenger seat. She trusted Brooke, so whatever she had planned had to be good. The only clue Brooke had given her: *Look nice. And throw on some perfume, if you like.*

So she had.

"Put this on," Brooke said after she'd pulled over to the side of the road.

"Is that a blindfold?"

"Uh-huh." Brooke passed over her earthy-coloured bandana. Her face remained passive. God, she had such a good poker face.

"Fine." JJ tied the cloth around her head. Not a sliver of

light poked through. "Is this the part where you tell me you were a serial killer all along?"

"Totally," Brooke deadpanned. "I'll get you to hop in your boot in a minute."

JJ laughed. "Sure, that totally works in the SUV. I'll just climb over the back seat."

"Maybe I want you in the back seat."

JJ's response died on her lips. She tried to laugh, but it almost came out as a whine, so she coughed. "You'd make a terrible serial killer," she finally said.

Thinking back to the bumpy start of their trip, she didn't expect to end up here, feeling like *this*. A holiday that had exceeded all expectations.

And it wasn't over yet.

The car turned off the main road at some point, bumping along a dirt driveway. JJ had lost all orientation. The car slowed, swivelling into—presumably—some sort of park, then stopped.

"Wait there," Brooke said.

JJ's door opened and Brooke took JJ's hand to help her out of the car. Brooke then looped her arm through JJ's, her spiced vanilla perfume invading JJ's senses as she guided her along. A breeze blew past them, and JJ shivered. She'd worn her nice shirt, and now she wished she'd brought a jacket.

"Can I take this off now?" JJ reached up and her hand was swatted away.

"Nope."

JJ pictured the blonde's grin, enjoying every part of being in charge this evening.

With careful steps, JJ's feet shuffled from dirt path to soft grass. Faint music played from somewhere in front of them. Was that voices? Brooke stopped walking and JJ stumbled on the spot.

"Okay." Brooke stepped behind her, a gentle caress on JJ's arm as she moved.

Steady hands untied the blindfold. It slipped from JJ's face, and she blinked, adjusting to the light.

"Surprise," Brooke whispered in her ear.

Goosebumps pricked up on the back of JJ's neck. She blinked several more times, frowning at the scene in front of her.

"We're at a big... tree?"

"Yep." Warmth radiated from Brooke's blue eyes as they darted across JJ's face, waiting.

JJ gave her a blank stare.

Brooke leaned in conspiratorially. "It's a restaurant."

"Oh!" JJ's brows hit her hairline. Now she noticed the well-trodden trail disappearing between branches laden with big yellow and green leaves. A glow of light could be seen as they stepped closer. JJ realised it was also the source of the music.

A waiter stepped out as they made it to the tree line, leading them inside.

"Wow." JJ had never seen anything like it. They entered the thick canopy of a fig tree, rows and rows of soft fairy lights strung about from above and small walkways branched off to what looked like separate rooms, each with a single table. JJ felt like she'd just stepped into a fantasy land, like *The Magic Faraway Tree* of her childhood.

Ushered to their table, the waiter pulled out a chair and JJ sat, speechless. Brooke took a seat across from her, thanking the waiter as he brought over fluffy cream blankets for each of them. JJ was grateful for the extra layer of warmth and draped it over her legs. Brooke beamed at JJ. A single candle flickered between them, the golden light dancing in Brooke's eyes.

"So, what do you think?"

"Brooke, what is this place?" JJ took it all in, shaking her head slightly. How was this a real restaurant?

"So, I know this wasn't on the itinerary and that's because this was a little something from me. A thank you for trusting me with your holiday, for letting an almost-complete stranger tag along, and for making this trip something I won't forget anytime soon." She adjusted the blanket on her lap. "I thought it fitting that this was the last night the restaurant was open for the season, but like our holiday, all good things must come to an end."

A single yellow leaf dropped from the canopy above and floated to the floor.

"You really didn't have to—" JJ started, touched at the thoughtfulness.

"I did though. You said you enjoy nature the most, and I thought this could be special." Brooke knocked their legs together under the table. A breeze fluttered through the leaves, playing with Brooke's hair.

JJ went to reach out and tuck a loose strand behind Brooke's ear. She paused.

A pang hit her chest knowing this was it for their fling after tonight. The rules *she'd* put in place—and for good reason. For several *many* ideal reasons. This was all just *a little fun* for the world traveller before she probably took off again anyway.

JJ dropped her hand and attempted a smile. "Is this the

part where you admit that South Australia isn't that bad after all?"

Brooke blew out a breath, a small smirk in place. "I've been thinking on that, you know?" She tucked her own hair behind her ear. "I don't think any place is inherently bad, but sometimes it's our memories or experiences that can make it seem so. These new memories definitely top my past and are a good reminder you can enjoy a place, no matter where you are, with the right mindset. So maybe it's time for me to confess that South Australia isn't so bad after all."

She cleared her throat. "I didn't expect to fall in love with it as much as I have."

Why was it when Brooke spoke those words, JJ's heart wished they were for her instead of this place? Brooke wasn't right for her; they were too different. Besides, Brooke didn't date. So even if JJ was starting to think maybe she could go out with someone so opposite, it wouldn't matter. Tomorrow, she'd be back to real life—to dating apps and finding a person who could choose her back. The perfect person.

Even those thoughts felt like a lie, bitter and wrong. But it was part of her plan. And she was determined to stick to it. She had to. Didn't she?

JJ pushed the thoughts aside, focusing on her meal. It was as beautiful as the woman sitting across from her. Everything was locally sourced, from the vegetables to the freshly caught seafood—even the wine. Well, Brooke was enjoying the wine, her arm casually slung over the chair as she sipped. JJ had caved and ordered a beer instead. The icy bubbles were welcome on her tongue. Biting.

"Last night in the bunk beds," JJ said.

"What a shame," Brooke replied dryly. "I'll miss the *Hostel Crew* though, they've been fun."

"Not as much fun as me, I hope," JJ said.

"No." A small smile pulled at Brooke's lips. "You've been quite the surprise."

"A good surprise?"

"Debatable." Her eyes sparkled. "When I'm not trying to—literally—save your butt from prickle bushes."

"Urgh, don't remind me. So embarrassing."

"I wonder how Nancy's doing?"

"Probably raising hell on another poor soul's car."

"Stealin' BBQ Shapes," Brooke added.

"Exactly! Can't have them wrangling my stash. Speaking of—my current box looked emptier than usual—you wouldn't have anything to do with that, would you?"

Brooke slurped her wine. "Not me."

"Uh-huh." JJ narrowed her eyes before breaking into a grin. "So ready to go back tomorrow?"

"No. We can just stay here forever. Move into this tree. No need to go back home."

It was the first time Brooke had called Adelaide home. Things really were changing for her.

JJ tilted her head. "We can just pretend for tonight."

"I'd like that." Brooke reached across the wooden table and took JJ's hand.

It was a long drive back to the hostel, and JJ was thankful to be climbing into her bunk bed one last time. The novelty was wearing off, as she pictured her very comfortable, very large queen bed at home—aka her sleeping kingdom.

They'd shared a few kisses before bed, but they'd been brief, like they were both pulling away already. What was going through Brooke's head? JJ could barely make sense of her own thoughts, let alone truly consider asking about Brooke's. So she'd said good night, not wanting to dampen the memories of everything else they'd shared.

After an hour lying awake staring at the ceiling, the bottom bunk squeaked for what felt like the twentieth time.

"You awake?" JJ asked.

"No."

JJ smiled. "Can't sleep?"

"No."

JJ leaned over the edge. "Want company?"

"N—maybe?"

The bed groaned and wobbled as JJ shuffled to the ladder. Her feet hit the carpeted floor with a dull thud. It felt so much like being a kid up in the top bunk that she half expected to land on a bunch of toys.

Brooke moved back against the wall, allowing JJ to slip in next to her. JJ lay on her side, propped up on her elbow. "What's going on in that pretty head of yours?"

The quilt rustled between them as Brooke changed positions.

"I don't want to go back. I still have no idea what I'm doing with my life, JJ."

"You don't have to have it all figured out. You've already started applying for jobs, and you should hopefully be able to connect with Hayley again in some way, just like we talked about."

"But then what? I don't have a solid income or my own house like you, and—"

"Well, comparing your life to mine isn't going to help. We're two very different people."

Brooke scoffed, "Don't remind me."

"Hey." JJ found her hand. "I didn't mean in a negative way. Just that we're two completely unique humans. Like every other person on this earth. Comparisons like that are only going to make you feel like shit. And you know why?"

"Why?"

"Because sometimes the questions we ask ourselves aren't the right ones." JJ sat up, crossing her legs, careful not to hit her head on the bunk above. "Okay, so you've said a couple of times you don't have the stable income or a house. But do you even want those things? Are they goals you want to pursue? Because when I started my business, there was nothing stable about my income. It was terrifying, but—my goal wasn't a stable income. It was to work for myself, and so I made it happen, even if some months I made almost nothing."

She was on a roll now, gesticulating into the darkness.

"When you were travelling, was your goal to have a stable income? Or just to make enough to get by in whatever country you were in? And I assume you wouldn't have wanted to save for a house either if you weren't staying in the one place. So that's what I mean by two different people, two very different goals. One is not better than the other."

"I guess I hadn't looked at it that way," Brooke said.

JJ squeezed Brooke's hand. "If I was to turn the tables, I'll admit I'm jealous of your constant stories of experiencing *life*. You've seen so much, done so much and met so many people. You're skilled in so many areas and so effortlessly cool being able to just hop on a jet ski and say, "jump on!"—like, who does that? I couldn't travel full time for so many reasons, but mainly, I couldn't cope without my job—and that income. Sure, I could leave my house and rent it out, but that's still not without its issues. I'm tethered to where I am. You have freedom, choice and a fresh start to do whatever the hell you want with your life.

So, the question is Brooke: what do you want?"

TWENTY-SEVEN

Brooke

There was a lump in Brooke's throat.

JJ kept saying words and the lump got bigger.

She swallowed, mouth dry.

Brooke ran her hand over the quilt, the other one still in JJ's hand, the warm tether quietening her usual overwhelming thoughts to be something more. Like a rushing tap had been turned off.

She sat up on the bunk, mirroring JJ.

What do I want?

The question bounced from side to side in her brain. The same one JJ had asked her on top of the ridge.

She'd been mulling it over ever since.

"As much as I enjoy this—being away, on the road, I'm not sure I want to keep travelling like I used to. At least not full time. And I want to stop long enough in one place to allow myself the time to come up with an answer to what I want. If I'm able to fix things with Hayley, maybe staying around here wouldn't be so bad."

Her hands were sweaty and clammy. She hoped JJ didn't notice.

It was the first time she'd admitted it out loud: that maybe home could be a place to stay, to put down a root or two.

To stop running.

Talking to JJ made it seem like it could be possible, and that being *just Brooke* in the meantime was okay. Not a failure. Brooke's shoulders shifted back as their conversation tamped down her negative thoughts. Maybe she could take control of her life and leave her past in the past?

"Well," JJ said, "sounds like that path is starting to show itself to you. Just take it one step at a time."

"That's only as far as I can see at the moment anyway." Brooke laughed, now fiddling with her bracelets.

"Well, sometimes all you need is that next step and just make the rest up along the way. Feel better?"

"Actually, yes. Thanks for listening to my midnight rambles."

"Anytime."

Brooke felt the pause between them, the only sound a slow squeak of a single spring as JJ shifted her weight to get off the bed.

Brooke grabbed her arm. "Wait."

"What?" JJ stopped, turning around.

"It's our last night." Brooke bit her lip, heart picking up speed.

If she couldn't have JJ forever, she could at least have her tonight. One last time.

"It is. And?" JJ didn't move.

Brooke kissed her.

If neat orderly perfection was a scent, this was it—all wrapped up in one big JJ-sized bow: minty-fresh breath, fruity shampoo and clean laundry.

JJ kissed her back, setting into action with a desperation that hadn't been there before. Hands clawed at Brooke's back and dove into her hair. Brooke slipped in her tongue, making them both groan. A low pulse ignited between Brooke's legs.

JJ's hand moved to the side of Brooke's shirt, brushing the edge of her breast, braless and sensitive. Brooke hissed in response. JJ's hand doubled back to brush past again, this time grazing underneath and around. Brooke's stomach swooped low, the sensations between their hot mouths and eager touch driving her crazier than she thought possible in the short amount of time. The build up of all their time spent together.

JJ had never taken things this far before. Was she bending the rules for their last night?

Somehow they'd moved positions, and Brooke found herself straddling JJ, hands either side of her head. This wasn't Brooke's usual position. On top. Hell, women weren't her usual. The last time she'd been with a French girl she'd—*oh*. JJ brushed her breast again, fingers tracing across her nipple. Brooke shuddered.

JJ pulled away, just for a second. "Okay?"

Brooke nodded furiously, launching back into the kiss, happy to follow JJ's lead.

There was nothing delicate about JJ's next pass. This time JJ grabbed, kneaded, tweaked.

"Fuck," Brooke uttered, deepening their kiss in retaliation. Though it only turned her on further too, a double-edged sword. A sound pulled from her, all need and—*god*, JJ was good with her hands. The other one had found her arse, squeezing and clawing. Everything in Brooke wanted to lower her hips, to push and grind against JJ… but that wasn't what this was. And so the space between stayed, a constant reminder of their fragile and brief connection before everything went back to the way it was.

Brooke would enjoy every moment. Every second etched into her brain. Every touch burned into her soul. This wasn't fun and fleeting, the high of travel and riding the vibe of a holiday. This felt like something bigger, like it should mean something more.

Only it didn't, and it wasn't.

It was just for tonight. Right now.

This was all one big dare, and Brooke swallowed down the truth.

But if JJ wanted to touch her tonight, Brooke would be damned if she didn't return the favour.

Balancing on one hand, the other raked its way down JJ's arm and back up to her chest. Braless as well, JJ's shirt left little to the imagination. Brooke cupped her over the fabric, the small breast fitting easily into her palm. She squeezed, then rolled a nipple between her thumb and forefinger, pairing the action with a slide of her tongue into JJ's mouth.

JJ groaned. Brooke smiled and repeated the motion.

JJ's hips lifted off the bed.

Brooke did it again. And again. And again.

Each pinch, each lick in perfect sync, a dizzying harmony that was driving Brooke just as wild having JJ under her like this, writhing and completely under her control.

Control.

This was the furthest they'd explored. This wasn't what JJ wanted.

She stopped, resting her forehead on JJ's. Their breath was harsh. JJ let out a half-whimper.

"We need to stop." It hurt her to say it, but she knew it was time.

"What, no it's fine, we don't have to—"

"No, JJ. I know what this is." Brooke smiled but her chest ached. "I know who you are and what you stand for. Save that for your person."

Not me. I'm just a mess. Just the friend. A bit of fun.

Not dating material.

She felt the lightest of nods against her head, the slow release of a breath.

"Yeah. Okay. You're right."

Brooke dipped down, placing a soft, lingering kiss on JJ's lips, one last time.

If only she was different. The right fit.

Maybe in another lifetime.

TWENTY-EIGHT
Brooke

The sun had only shone long enough this morning to seemingly wave goodbye as they boarded the ferry and left KI behind. By the time they arrived on the shore of Cape Jervis, the sky was dark and low as JJ drove them home.

Brooke sunk further into her seat and toyed with her seatbelt. Every sentence or thought stuttered and died on her lips, at a loss with where to start a conversation let alone talk about what she really wanted to: *them*.

Last night was the end of their fling, yet the urge to reach over and grab JJ's hand was so strong, Brooke's fingers tingled as if they were magnets trying to draw JJ in.

The defiance in Brooke wanted to scream *to hell with the rules* and grab her hand anyway. She wanted JJ's touch and the comfort it brought. It hurt to know that was going away. She wasn't ready to let go... and that... well, she didn't know what to do with that information.

Brooke twisted her bracelets around her wrist. Her chest grew tight with every kilometre they got closer to home.

Home.

She couldn't avoid it any longer. This was Brooke's real test, after all they'd talked about with Hayley, her job and facing everything she'd left behind. It was time, and Brooke had to do this herself.

JJ pulled up to Hayley and Marie's house.

They both sat unmoving, Brooke's hand on the door. "Well." She stopped, smile pulled tight. "Thanks for everything."

JJ rubbed the back of her neck. "Yeah. Cool. Thank *you* for everything." She swallowed. "You were the one who made it happen. Can't believe we're back already."

Brooke glanced at the house and squeezed the door handle. "I guess I better—"

"Yep." JJ turned the car off and launched out of her seat like she'd been bitten.

Brooke frowned, then the back door opened.

JJ grabbed Brooke's bag and looked around the back seat. "Anything else?"

"That's it. Thanks."

Brooke got out of the car as JJ walked around and held out the bag. Brooke took it but set it next to her on the grass by the kerb.

"So." God, this was awkward. "I guess that's it for our holiday fling. That was... fun." Her cheeks flamed. It was so much more than fun.

"Yeah." JJ rubbed her neck again and avoided Brooke's eyes. "Not forgetting that any time soon."

Their eyes met.

"Me either," Brooke whispered.

There was so much to say, and—*fuck.*

But even if she did, what was the point?

JJ had been clear from the start what this was. What Brooke wasn't.

Brooke needed to let this go. Let JJ go.

Brooke's throat felt tight. Goodbyes were a non-event for her, an absolute whatever. What was happening? She blinked. She couldn't stop blinking, and she swallowed trying to ease the ache that had started in her chest.

"I better get inside, check my sister hasn't kicked me out for being an absolute terror." Brooke tried to laugh, but her eyes started to water, so she dove forward onto JJ for a hug instead. Anything to get out of this situation and give her a minute to ease the pressure.

Brooke was so wrapped up in getting inside, she forgot she was hugging JJ. That this was their goodbye. She scrunched JJ's hoodie in her hands and squeezed, inhaling—in a subtle, non-creepy way—as deep as she could. It was like she could still smell the eucalyptus and the smoke from their fire. The memories of their trip flashed past. JJ sunk into the embrace. Brooke may not have the words, but she put everything into the hold.

How could she go back to friends after this? When would she even see JJ next?

They pulled apart and Brooke pressed her lips to JJ's cheek. She lingered for just a moment.

"Bye JJ. Don't go breaking too many hearts."

Brooke aimed for a smirk, but it didn't reach her eyes. Her hand slipped from JJ's arm then she bent down, swung her bag over her shoulder, and walked inside.

She didn't dare look back.

The door clicked shut behind her, and just like that, Brooke was alone again.

She stood. Silence.

At least she had the house to herself—she had work to do. No more mopey Brooke, time to take charge. *Like you did last night,* her brain helpfully supplied.

She headed upstairs. Someone had cleaned her room. Her bed was washed and made, everything put away or tidied up, the window left open to let in the fresh breeze. Hayley was still looking after her, acting like a parent, even after she'd pushed her away.

She grabbed her laptop, flipping it open on the bed.

So many emails.

Junk. Spam. Flight specials. Newsletters from travel bloggers and friends.

Two emails from the airport job application.

One with an offer for an interview the day after she'd left, and another from this morning. *We're sorry to inform you, as we've had no response, your job application has been withdrawn.*

Well, fuck.

She'd forgotten about those missed calls, the notifications. She figured she'd sort it when she was back. Not a great start so far...

She had no updates from the hostel job since her interview, but had a feeling they were looking for someone younger, read: cheaper. Which left the night pick packing position. Still no word.

Take her back on the road already, this was hard.

Her fingers itched to grab her phone and shoot off a

quick text to JJ about it. But that would be weird; they'd only said goodbye fifteen minutes ago.

And now their rulebook was closed. Finished.

Her insides still hurt like she was back on the ferry, churning and swirling—kind of how she assumed a break-up would feel. She'd never been so close to anyone before. Physically, yes. Emotionally... no. These newfound emotions hurt, harder to tamp down or forget about. They stayed with you like a constant reminder: *Oh hey, JJ is on your mind again! Yep, still thinking about JJ. Look outside, that cloud? Looks like JJ, hey?*

She growled, head flopping back onto the pillow.

The rules, the fling—it had all sounded so simple, easy and fun. Now it felt like she was in a nightmare.

Brooke spent the next few hours sorting out her inbox, looking into new job potentials and following up on the pick packing job. When her stomach grumbled, she headed downstairs to make a sandwich and found Hayley in the kitchen putting groceries away.

This was it.

"Hi," she said.

Progress.

Hayley's head snapped up from her current shopping bag. "Oh hey, you're back. How was the trip?"

Brooke stopped at the kitchen island and gripped the end of the benchtop. "It was good. JJ enjoyed it, which was the main thing."

Look at her go, two full sentences. Hayley topped up the fruit bowl with bananas and apples, moving to the fridge next to put the milk away.

"Thanks for cleaning my room. It was nice to come back to."

Hayley faltered halfway to the kitchen cupboard, a tin of beans held in midair for a split second, before she put it away and regarded Brooke. "You're welcome."

The response was cautious, which was unsurprising with how they'd left things.

They were still stepping on eggshells.

Brooke moved around the island to one of the other bags, taking out a few packets and putting them away. Brooke caught Hayley's glances as they moved about, but she remained quiet.

"Thanks," Hayley said once they'd finished, a small smile forming on her lips.

Brooke felt her mouth curve up just a touch in response. JJ was right, Brooke could do this.

"Did you hear back from any jobs?" Hayley asked as she folded the grocery bags and put them away.

Brooke felt the spotlight open back up overhead.

"I missed out on a couple." Brooke kept her gaze on the kitchen sink. When she looked back up, Hayley's frown had returned.

"Did you check up on anything while you were away?"

And here Brooke was, straight back into the firing line. Couldn't she just have five damn minutes?

"No, I was... working." While technically true, they both knew it was a lie. Heat bloomed its way up her chest until her ears burned.

Hayley's hand was on her hip. Exactly like their mum would do when she was disappointed in Brooke. When she'd failed.

"Bee..."

"I'm—I've..." What was the point in explaining herself? Why had she even bothered to come back here? "I gotta go."

Brooke was out the door and down the street, back to the reeds, to her spot.

One. Two. Three—Four.

She flopped down onto the rock and flung a pebble across the water.

How was she here again already?

She snapped a twig in two and huffed.

The water trickled along the river. She closed her eyes, focusing on the sound.

Brooke couldn't keep doing this. Running wasn't getting her anywhere. She inhaled deep. Thoughts settling with the river.

It hadn't all been bad. Chatting to Hayley and doing the groceries together was nice—normal even.

Until Brooke froze. Again. Tongue-tied and unable to explain herself. If she could just spit out her words...

Craft them in a way that—

JJ's letter idea!

Duh, Brooke!

How had she forgotten?

Brooke pulled out her phone to write down her scrambled thoughts, but a new email notification popped up on the screen.

The pick packing job.

It was an offer to proceed, complete with working hours and a start date. Brooke read through their terms. It wasn't perfect, but it was a job. And she'd be earning money again. If only *that* news had come through twenty minutes earlier, she could've had a very different conversation with Hayley.

She opened her notes app again, the cursor blinking. Waiting.

Brooke stared at the water. The app. The trees.

The same blinking cursor.

She squeezed her phone, willing it to tell her what to write. Instead it just brought up the emergency call button.

She swiped it away, back to the blank page.

Taunting her just like her mind when she stood in front of her sister.

Argh. It felt so much easier when she'd spoken to JJ about it in the hot tub.

The pain was back in her chest. Okay, it did *not* help to start thinking about JJ again.

These scribbles didn't need to be perfect, they were just for her.

Just write.

Brooke's fingers flew across the screen, feelings pouring into the note.

An hour later, her phone was filled with half thoughts and fragmented sentences. Memories. Emotions. Anything on her mind, she typed.

At least she had something. The beginnings of a plan.

It would do for now.

Weirdly, just writing it down had made her feel better. Lighter. The tension loosened, not just between her shoulders, but deeper. A shift in her core.

While Brooke couldn't take back the fact she'd run

away again, she could get herself home and maybe offer to help Hayley with dinner instead.

It would be more than she'd done with her sister in a very long time.

TWENTY-NINE

JJ

The weirdest thing about getting back from holiday was smelling her own house. It felt like visiting someone else's place, like it wasn't hers anymore. JJ breathed in again, the scent slightly sweet and fresh, with a touch of sandalwood. "Weird," she muttered, shutting the door behind her.

The house was so quiet. She'd grown used to having Jess around and then having Brooke with her the entire trip. JJ half expected Brooke to walk through the door now *—arms sliding around her from behind, Brooke's smiling face as she leaned back and kissed*—okay, stop. What the hell?

Maybe it was time to tee up a new date? Try to move on. This kind of daydream just made her chest hurt.

Shaking her head, she went straight to the laundry, throwing all her clothes into the wash. The house was exactly how she'd left it, not a single dish left out beside the kitchen sink, and everything tidy, in its place.

Now it was time to get to work. She checked on all her plants, and true to Jess's word, they were all still alive.

Coffee was next. Flicking on the machine, she went to grab two mugs, then shook her head. It was just her.

Tonight was the quarterly tradeswomen's dinner, and it was JJ's turn to speak. She'd jotted down notes before she left but wanted them planned out and memorised before the evening. She'd lined up painting jobs for the day after her return so today she could sort through her stack of emails and messages waiting to be sorted. She brought her mug over to the dining table and set to work.

JJ was exhausted by the time Jess walked through the door that afternoon, her big clomping boots audible down the hallway. JJ still sat at the dining table and was wrapped in a huge hug from behind, the smell of dust and wood thick in the air.

"Hey stranger!" Jess said. "And yes, I'm dirty as all hell, and I don't care. Welcome back."

"Thanks." Words like *it's good to be back* or *I'm so glad to be home* didn't feel right, so JJ just smiled. Usually, she loved her work and her life. But the past couple of weeks had flipped everything on its head. She still loved what she did, but the in-betweens felt empty. She had to stop herself messaging Brooke three separate times today to fill in those gaps. Instead, she'd sent Remi a photo of her inbox yelling at her with over three hundred emails. "You'll have it empty by the end of the day, guaranteed," Remi had said.

She was right.

Jess's eyes narrowed as she came around the other side of the table, looking JJ up and down. "What's going on? You seem down."

Nothing—absolutely *nothing*—got past this woman.

"Post holiday blues?" JJ fiddled with a pen on the table.

Jess stared. "Makes sense."

JJ could tell she didn't believe her.

"Well, how about you tell me all about this trip of yours while I get ready for our dinner tonight, and I'll tell *you* about how awesome your best friend is at—"

"Lalalalala, I don't want to know!" JJ shoved her hands over her ears.

"I was going to say '*at drilling*' JJ, god," Jess said, walking off to the bathroom. "With her fingers!" she yelled at the last minute, shutting the door behind her.

JJ sputtered out a laugh and went back to work on her laptop.

She'd missed her housemate. Maybe it wasn't so bad being back after all.

By Thursday, she took that back.

While the Monday night tradeswomen's dinner and speech had gone well, seeing Jess and Remi so ickily loved up had JJ feeling like a third wheel and incredibly alone, even with a huge table full of women. Tuesday and Wednesday were straight back into painting, her shoulder flaring up with a vengeance after not using it for a couple of weeks. On Wednesday night, her family had showered her with more food and questions than she knew what to do with, over the moon that she was safe and back home. By Thursday night, JJ was on the couch with her feet up, staring at the TV, when Jess emerged from her room.

"I'm off to games night with the girls." Jess stopped halfway to the kitchen and looked at JJ. "You wanna come with? I've finally convinced Remi to join us too."

"Oh. Nah you go, I'm good just... hanging."

"Really? Because you look like the Mayor of Mopesville

to me. Come on, come socialise for a bit. You can admire your handiwork at Marie and Hayley's."

JJ's ears pricked up. Would Brooke be there? While they hadn't agreed to hang out, it also didn't mean they couldn't if Brooke happened to be there tonight... What if she'd been feeling as crap as JJ had without each other's company?

They'd texted on and off since they'd been back, mostly with Brooke's update on job hunting and her initial attempts to spend more time with Hayley. Otherwise, it had been just a few back and forth messages reminiscing about their trip.

"Fine." JJ made a show of shoving off the couch with effort. "Give me a minute to get changed."

Jess drove, picking up Remi on the way. She let them into Marie and Hayley's house like she owned the place. Entering the big open space area, they found the girls were seated on the big blue velvet couch, two other women on a video call streaming through the TV. One had short brown hair and the other was blonde with a high ponytail.

"Hey everyone!" Jess said. "Everyone, this is Remi and JJ. That's Taylor and Sam on video, and you already know the girls."

"Ah, the infamous new housemate and sparkly new girlfriend," Taylor said.

"That's me! I remember seeing you at Jess's birthday, so hi officially." Remi gave them a wave and sat next to Jess on the floor.

"And guilty as charged." JJ raised a hand. "Nice to finally meet you, previous housemate and Sam." She took a seat on the spare couch.

"Likewise." The video on the TV was constantly

moving and JJ realised they were calling from their boat, Manny, that Jess had told her about. It was making her seasick just watching. Thank god she didn't have to ride another ferry for a while.

Brooke was nowhere to be seen. JJ slouched back on the sofa. Damn.

Everyone started talking over each other and JJ couldn't get a word in. The whole group was worse than a pack of hungry seagulls. Jess prattled on about her apprenticeship, Marie about the latest board games she'd tried and wanted to buy, and Sam recounted their latest sea adventures. It was like a tennis match of multiple conversations. No wonder Brooke felt intimidated to join in after so long.

At a rare lull in conversation, Hayley turned to JJ. "So I hear you two had quite the trip. Happy to be back?"

Everyone turned to listen.

"I think Brooke's given me the travel bug because this week's been hard. I think I have a holiday hangover."

The group laughed.

"She did such a great job of the planning though, I couldn't have asked for a better holiday."

"Aww." Brooke appeared with a bag of shopping at the end of the hallway. "Don't stop on my account. Sounds like you were just getting to the good part."

JJ's heart halted. Could it do that? It sure felt like that's what happened. Brooke was effortlessly radiant. No shoes, boyfriend jeans and a slouchy black jumper that looked incredibly soft and huggable. JJ went to move off the couch but remembered where she was. What they were, or... weren't... anymore. It was so confusing. She twitched. Shit.

Should she get up and greet Brooke or not? Friends greeted friends with hugs all the time.

"Did I mention she's incredibly humble too?" JJ said instead, grinning broadly. Everyone looked between them. A mixture of curiosity and maybe caution at Brooke's presence.

"I got the snacks," Brooke said to Hayley, holding up the bag.

"Thanks." The smile on Hayley was new. This was the first time JJ had seen them together since Brooke had begun to make more of an effort. The vibe seemed positive, and the usual wrinkle in Brooke's forehead while around her sister was nowhere to be found.

JJ couldn't sit still any longer. She strode over, meeting Brooke by the kitchen as she unpacked some snacks.

"Thought I better come say hi properly." JJ held out her arms.

Brooke smiled and slipped into them. Why did that feel so bloody good? JJ inhaled. She'd missed Brooke's scent, so girly and spicy and quintessentially Brooke. Could someone smell like sunshine? Because that's what Brooke reminded her of. Pure sunshine. JJ's shoulders relaxed.

Brooke let her go, and everything became overcast.

They caught each other's gaze, then Brooke cut away, busying herself with preparing the food.

What just happened? Everything had seemed okay, yet it felt like Brooke had just put a wall up.

"You want a hand with any of that?" JJ drummed her hands on the benchtop and gestured with her chin to an empty bowl.

"I'm good." Brooke dumped some chips into the bowl, a few falling out onto the benchtop.

"Okay." Everything JJ wanted to say turned to mush. She put her hands in her pockets. Brooke stayed laser focused on the plating up. JJ shuffled from foot to foot.

"Right," she muttered, turning and leaving Brooke to it. JJ's brow furrowed on the way back to the couch. What had she done? Brooke had seemed happy to see her at first, but after that hug... Oh.

Maybe they weren't meant to be touching at all anymore? Even as friends. This limbo business was confusing. As soon as they were alone, JJ was sorting this shit out. They hadn't discussed what things should look like between them when they were back, or come to think of it, what they were telling the others about their fling. Maybe Brooke wanted to keep things professional? She'd follow Brooke's lead tonight.

Jess caught JJ's eye with a questioning look as she sat back down, Remi doing the same. She ignored them both, paying attention to Marie instead, who was setting up their board game of the night—something called *Dice Throne*—and handing out character heroes to each person. They'd dragged another low table over into the lounge so they had room to spread out the boards.

"You and Brooke haven't played this yet, so you can team up and help each other out," Marie said.

JJ peeked over at the kitchen. "Sounds good."

Brooke picked up the plates to bring over, not sparing one glance JJ's way. It was good to see Brooke joining in tonight; JJ had half expected her to escape to her room the way she'd spoken about the last games night.

This must be a big moment for Brooke; to not only be in the middle of making amends with Hayley but now facing all her friends after so many years. Man, she must be terrified. That could explain her behaviour...

Maybe it wasn't JJ, but the whole scenario tonight? JJ noted the stiffness under the surface now as Brooke walked over and arranged all the food on the table. Brooke paused, then sat next to JJ, a wide gap between them. JJ didn't like it one bit. Brooke had said she pushed people away when they tried to help or be close to her... but JJ didn't think that would apply to her.

JJ scratched at the back of her neck. Brooke may have let her close during their fling, but that was over now, yet all JJ wanted to do was be able to make tonight easier for Brooke.

Maybe she still could.

"Brooke, I'm so happy you could make it tonight. Feels like forever since we've seen you!" Taylor's huge smile was so full of warmth and joy it could disarm the sullenest of people.

Brooke tucked a lock of hair behind her ear. "Yeah, looking forward to it."

Lie.

"Are you around for good? Or just stopping over for a bit?"

Oh, too much, too soon.

Brooke scooted the tiniest bit closer to JJ.

"Uh—still making plans in that area but looking into a few options." Her smile was tight.

The answer sounded more confident than JJ knew her to be. Her hand itched to snake across, hold Brooke's hand or rub her back as a way of support. But JJ was also proud that Brooke was sitting there and doing this herself. Facing those fears in the viper pit. Even if said viper pit was just a bunch of really lovely women who Brooke shouldn't be afraid of in the first place.

Marie broke off the conversation, holding up a dice tower and getting everyone to roll to kick off the game. Brooke dumped their die in.

Six.

It looked like they were going first.

"Here are our cards." JJ showed Brooke, who had to slide up next to JJ to get a better look. *Mission accomplished.*

While Brooke didn't say anything personal during the game, she at least seemed to relax once they got into it. She opened up more towards the other girls but still kept all conversation with JJ game-focused. It felt like JJ's hands were tied behind her back, preventing her from fixing what was happening between them.

This was not the night she'd envisioned when Brooke had first walked into the room.

"Sorry guys," Remi said after the first round, eyes pinched. "I'm gonna have to head off. I've got a crazy headache, and I don't think all this concentrating is helping."

Jess rubbed Remi's back with a frown. "I'll take you home then."

"Boo!" Taylor said on screen, her bottom lip pushed out.

"Feel better, Remi!" Sam said.

"All right, I should probably leave too." JJ moved to get off the couch as well.

"Why are you heading off?" Hayley asked JJ.

"Jess brought me."

"You don't have to head off now."

"Oh but—" JJ glanced at Brooke, who was reading the board game's instruction manual like it was a smutty romance novel, cheeks flushed and face wedged between the pages. Interesting...

"One of us can take you home," Marie said.

JJ looked at Jess and Remi. "I mean, only if that's okay?"

Did Brooke want her to stay? She was avoiding eye contact, so JJ had no idea.

"Of course it's fine! You're an adult." Jess helped Remi up and slid an arm around her.

"Okay, looks like I'm staying." JJ flopped back down beside Brooke.

Was that a flicker of a smile on the vexatious blonde?

THIRTY
Brooke

The game night didn't turn out as painful as Brooke had expected. The group hadn't asked her too many questions, she had polite conversation with Hayley, and playing the games had meant more focus on that than on her.

It had also kept Brooke distracted from JJ.

The woman currently sitting next to her on the couch.

The person Brooke hadn't been able to get out of her head all week. The person who, right from their very first meeting, had believed in her.

Brooke sought out her bracelets, thumbing one of the charms between her fingers. Being around JJ, Brooke saw herself reflected back not as a failure, but as someone who had potential, who could be something. JJ didn't see Brooke for her stuff-ups and her mess; she just saw... Brooke. And having that person—that warmth and support—wrenched away when they'd got back had been jarring. The past week Brooke had felt like a fish out of water, and JJ wasn't even there to laugh at her flopping, encouraging her to dive back in and keep swimming.

Brooke missed her; the closeness and connection beyond what any friendship had given her. She and JJ hadn't been just friends though... not that they'd technically been anything more. But maybe Brooke wanted that now? The idea of trying a relationship wouldn't be the worst thing. Especially not with JJ. If only the woman with the stubborn ideals would be open to that, to... dating Brooke.

Brooke grabbed a handful of chips from the snack bowl and shoved them in her mouth. She needed time to think, to allow that maybe she was ready for that kind of support in her life.

Brooke hadn't known JJ would be joining them tonight, hadn't *prepared* herself to see JJ sitting there on the couch looking all cute and... *ugh*. And Brooke certainly wasn't ready for how much her stomach had swooped at the sight. It was... unnerving. At least having Remi and JJ new to the games night crew had taken the pressure off Brooke to try and deal with JJ's sudden presence quietly.

Sam and Taylor had said goodbye a few minutes ago, and everyone was passing pieces to Marie to pack into the box. Without the video call on the TV, it felt much more intimate with only the four of them left in the room. Hayley cleared the dishes on the table and Marie picked up the game boxes to take back upstairs, which left Brooke alone... with JJ.

With everything left on Kangaroo Island between them, now they were in friend zone time. But if that was the case, JJ couldn't just go around giving her hugs like that. They were moreish. Like eating popcorn. Once you started...

Brooke needed space.

Yet here she was, right next to JJ. Thighs an inch apart, begging her to close the gap.

Space. She needed space.

"I can take you home," Brooke said, her mouth betraying her further. She couldn't stop.

JJ's eyes searched Brooke's face. "You sure?"

"Yeah, it's fine." Peachy. She was carefree Brooke. More one-on-one time with JJ? That was *all* good.

Brooke pulled out of the drive in Hayley's car.

"Feels like we're driving off again on another adventure," JJ said.

"You wish."

"I kinda do." JJ chuckled, playing with the hem of her cotton grey shirt. "It's certainly made going back to work a lot harder. Did you accept the job?"

"I did." With the pick packer job the only offer, there wasn't much of a choice, and Brooke didn't want to wait around to start earning money. Income first, happiness later.

"I'm happy for you."

"Thanks."

"So..." JJ scratched at the back of her head. "Did I overstep tonight? Hugging you earlier? Because I'm sorry if I did."

"No?" It came out as a question. Brooke's face heated. It was one thing for her to know the hug had been a lot, but pile on the fact that JJ had noticed? The heat grew stronger.

Who struggled to keep their shit together when a friend *hugged* them?

They stopped at a traffic light and Brooke tried to think of how to explain herself. She let out a long breath.

"You didn't overstep. But—"

Their holiday fling was over, only Brooke felt like her head and her heart hadn't got the memo. Her mind tortured her night and day, a mix of memories and future fantasies, all of them involving the painter sitting next to her. And her body still ached, craving to be close to JJ again. Now, being around JJ again after their time apart, Brooke couldn't deny what was happening to her. What she wanted.

Even if it was impossible.

"Tell me what you need." JJ faced her, head resting against the seat.

That was the million-dollar question.

The light turned green.

"I don't think it's something you can give me."

Houses rushed past, streetlights blurring.

"What do you mean?" JJ's knee bounced.

Brooke's hand twitched and her heart hammered, white noise screaming in her ears.

"Because that would be—you."

Time stopped.

Brooke's entire body flushed, chest burning. She'd admitted it out loud.

To herself.

To JJ.

She refused to look anywhere but the road. A few more turns and they'd be at JJ's house. Estimated arrival time in one minute, according to Hayley's GPS.

It was going to be a long minute.

"Sorry, I—what do you mean?" JJ repeated.

Brooke squeezed the steering wheel. "Ever since getting

back, I've been thinking about our trip. And about you. I know I said I don't date, but I've also never met anyone like you. Someone who's made me consider something else. When we left our trip behind, the weight was crushing knowing we were going back to our regular lives after sharing what we did. I know it was meant to be a bit of fun, and it did start out that way. But it became something more for me."

Brooke swallowed. "And I know I need to deal with that because you're looking for something and someone else. I'm not part of your plan. So I think while what I want is you... what I need is space. Time to get over this." She waved her hand in the air between them. "Then maybe, we could be friends. But right now, it's too hard."

Brooke pulled into JJ's driveway and switched off the car, plunging them into silence. She still refused to look at JJ after her spontaneous speech, but Brooke's eyes were drawn to her anyway. How could they not?

JJ still hadn't said anything. She sat there, nodding. She opened and closed her mouth. More nodding. Brooke had broken her.

"That's... that's a lot to think about. But—thank you. For telling me." More nodding. JJ rubbed at her chin. "Leave it with me, and I'll make sure to respect your boundaries in the meantime." JJ's hand scrambled for the door. She was out of the car and walking up to her front door before Brooke had even let out her breath.

Okay, not the response she'd wanted, but the response she'd expected.

A calm fell over her even as her insides churned and chest ached.

Well, she'd said her piece and spoken up for herself. That had to count for something.

THIRTY-ONE

Brooke

One week later, Brooke scanned her last order of the night and began collecting the required items. Only two days on the job and the work was already mind-numbing. Money or not, there was no way she could accept this as her new life. It was just so... monotonous. And sterile. Rushing around the warehouse all night, a frenzy of scanning, finding the items, scanning again, packing, taping... repeat. How could people do this for a living when there was an entire world outside this massive tin shed?

There had to be something else she could do.

After clocking off, she climbed into Hayley's borrowed car and fished out her phone.

A photo of the Barossa sunrise beamed back.

No notifications. Nothing.

JJ had done exactly what Brooke had asked and given her space. And that damn well hurt. Couldn't that frustrating play-by-the-rules woman skew from the rulebook just this once and say hi? Of course not, because she was too damn perfect and thoughtful for her own good.

"Argh!" Brooke clenched her fists around the steering wheel, then took a huge breath, blowing it out with force.

This wasn't like her.

She started the car.

Now she had a job and she'd started to integrate herself a little more around Hayley and Marie, she'd thought things would be on the up and up—that life would get better. She was fixing things and building things. But over the last week, JJ still took up the majority of her headspace. And for someone she hadn't seen or spoken to during that time, it was too much. She was meant to be using this time to move on so she could at least have a friendship with JJ. She had to get those *feelings* under control. But they were growing like mould on fresh bread, doubling each day.

Brooke let herself into the house, quietly closing the front door.

She checked her phone again. Still nothing. Not that she expected JJ to message at eleven at night. But one could hope. Brooke closed her eyes, chest squeezing. She refused to give up.

"Hey."

Brooke jumped, fumbling with the phone and catching it at the last minute. "Shit, you scared me!"

"Sorry." Hayley's small smile had Brooke's lips tugging up, ever so slightly. Her sister was reading by the dim lamp once again, curled up at the edge of the couch with a blanket draped over her.

Brooke walked around, collapsing next to her with a groan.

"I was gonna ask how work was, but I'm thinking you'll probably want to skip that question?"

"Thank you. Next!" Brooke kicked her feet up on the coffee table and let her head fall back, facing Hayley. "Nah, that place isn't for me. I thought I could do it for the money, but I'd literally do almost anything else if it means not going back there for another shift."

"And there were no other positions at the airport?"

Brooke's jaw twitched. For fu—*stop.* She swallowed down the retort. She could do this. Hayley was only trying to be helpful.

"Nothing," Brooke said. She hadn't snapped. A neutral response was good.

Hayley closed her book and slipped it onto the side table. "Have you thought about what else you'd like to do?"

"Well, I definitely don't want to be a chartered accountant like you. Too many numbers—ew." Brooke's jaw relaxed, and she allowed her shoulders to sink back into the couch.

It felt weird having such a normal conversation with her sister. While there was still work to do, this progress helped. The old memories still ebbed and flowed, but Brooke didn't allow the emotions to take over like they used to. That said, she'd also avoided any serious discussions.

One step at a time.

"I wouldn't expect you to." Hayley chuckled. "What about when you were younger? Any pursuits you considered but never did?"

"Aside from travelling? Nothing that comes to mind."

"And there's nothing else in travel you could do?"

Brooke's mind flashed back to her trip with JJ, when the American—Clark? Cliff? Clive!—commented on her well-thought-out holiday planning. Hmm.

"I mean, I could be a travel agent," Brooke said. "Then again, I wouldn't want to work for an agency. Only having access to certain places or flights..." Her nose wrinkled. "I'd feel like I was handcuffed trying to recommend things to people." She kicked her shoes off and pulled them onto the couch.

Hayley threw the blanket over Brooke's feet. "So work for yourself."

"I couldn't run my own business." Brooke scoffed, eyes down as she traced the edges of her phone.

"Why not?" Hayley sat up, frowning.

"Uhh, because I'm not, like, smart enough to do any of that stuff." Brooke ticked off the reasons. "I have no money, no idea where to start and—"

Hayley caught her hand. "Don't do that."

"Do what?"

"Put yourself down like that. You're Brooke Mayfield."

Brooke rolled her eyes. "Don't remind me." She freed her hand and pulled the blanket up further.

"Brooke, enough." Hayley's mum voice was back.

Brooke forced herself to sit still, inhaling slowly. *Don't run.*

"You're an incredible person, and all I'm hearing tonight are excuses—not facts."

Brooke's eyes shot to Hayley. That was unexpected.

"If you're not smart enough, how the hell did you look after yourself for ten-fucking-years flying and travelling around the globe like it was no big deal?" Hayley didn't wait for an answer, she barely took another breath, voice firm. "And no money? Pretty sure these days you only need something like forty bucks for a business name. Whip up a free website and you could be helping people travel tomorrow."

Hayley smoothed out the blanket. "Actually, I have no idea, but you'd figure it out. You're Brooke. You always do. As for where to start—*hello*? It's called Google. Or Remi and JJ run their own businesses—ask them! What's it going to take for you to start believing in yourself?" Hayley angry-whispered the entire thing, ever so courteous not to wake Marie.

"Yeesh, don't hold back or anything." Brooke tried to smile but it faltered. There was a lump in her throat again.

These words were... everything. Her eyes burned. She blinked, gaze on the kitchen, the lounge. Everywhere but Hayley.

"I'm serious, Brooke."

"No, I know you are." Brooke fiddled with her bracelets, then slid her eyes back to her sister. "You're as bad as JJ with all this pep-talk stuff." Again, she forced a smile but her chin quivered.

"Oh yeah? Well maybe that's because we see something you don't."

Me.

That's what they saw.

Brooke Mayfield. *Just Brooke.*

Hayley and JJ saw straight through her bullshit. It should anger her or have her running straight back down to the river. Instead, for once, Brooke leaned in. Even if there was a frown on her face and arms crossed tight against her chest like a naughty school kid, she wanted to take in Hayley's words.

"I'll sleep on the idea," was all Brooke said, her limit

reached. She slipped off the couch and paused at the bottom of the stairs. "Thank you."

With each step, her mind buzzed.

Maybe there was a way out of this mess after all.

Brooke had tossed and turned all night, finally falling asleep at god-knows-what hour.

She yawned and stretched, the sun streaming through her blinds as she wiped at her eyes and kicked off the covers.

Downstairs was quiet; Marie and Hayley would have left for work ages ago.

Brooke had thought her mind was messy enough with her JJ drama, but last night's conversation with Hayley had thrown a real spanner in the works, and it had nothing to do with the business idea they'd discussed.

This was about Hayley.

This was about them, who they were as sisters. And who Brooke was to her family. She had no intention of reconnecting with her parents, but the thought of Hayley being a bigger part of her life had her thinking of reaching out to Steven too. Maybe not right now—it was still too much, too soon. But she was *considering* it. And that was new.

Baby steps.

Her next one, however, was going to be one giant leap.

Brooke blew out a breath and swung her legs over the side of the bed, heart racing at what she was about to do.

She padded down to Hayley and Marie's study, grabbed a pen and paper, then took up camp at the dining table.

With her notes app open for guidance, words spilled onto the page, an arrangement of thoughts and feelings all wrapped up with a little bit of hope.

An hour later, her wrist ached and the tips of her fingers were numb, but she looked down at the letter before her and smiled.

The words had finally come. JJ had been right. It worked.

Brooke folded it neatly into thirds and placed it onto the bench, Hayley's name in cursive on the front.

Now, she just had to wait, filling her time with internet searches like *ten steps to run your own business* and *how the hell do you work for yourself?*

That afternoon, the door slammed shut downstairs and Brooke froze. Her fingers hovered over her laptop keyboard as she listened. High heeled shoes sounded down the hallway, a bag placed on what must've been the kitchen table. Those long strides had to be Hayley.

Brooke swallowed, hands clammy as she closed the laptop and tossed it beside her on the bed. She strained her ears, but they were met with silence. Only her own heartbeat and someone mowing their lawn down the street. Her stomach growled, and she couldn't remember if she'd eaten anything today.

Brooke closed her eyes, stomach lurching. Hayley would want to talk soon, and this was the part Brooke sucked at.

Fuck.

JJ's brown eyes flashed in her mind. *"If I was Hayley, what would you want to say to her?"*

A knock sounded on the doorframe, and Brooke jumped.

"Sorry." Hayley stood in the doorway, a smart work suit on with bare feet, her hair pulled out of her ponytail and Brooke's letter clutched in one hand.

Brooke gave a hesitant smile.

"Did you write this?" Hayley held it up like something sacred, eyes shining. "I mean, I know you wrote this, but —" She didn't finish, crossing to the bed and flinging her arms around Brooke instead. Brooke stiffened, her body at war with her head.

Relax. Be the sister you want to be.

She wrapped her arms around Hayley and held on. Hayley sniffed into her neck, the paper crumpling at her back.

"I'm sorry," Brooke mumbled, jaw coming unstuck, the words finally spilling free. "I've been such shit person to you. And Marie." Tears spilled down and Brooke bit her lip to stop her chin wobbling. It was unsuccessful.

Hayley pulled back, grabbing Brooke by the shoulders. They had the same eyes. Ice blue and so caring it hurt to look into them, but Brooke didn't turn away.

Not this time.

"It's okay," Hayley said. "Thank you for putting into words what's been going through that head of yours. That's all I've ever wanted. To understand you and just talk to you. I never, ever, ever meant you to feel anything less than. Though, I can't say the same about Mum and Dad—they're arseholes."

Brooke's jaw dropped, and then she laughed. Brooke had *never* heard Hayley speak about their parents like that.

"What! But you never said anything, and they *loved* you. Miss Golden Child. I thought you felt the same way about them."

Hayley looked stung as she reeled back. "Of course not. They were only nice to me because they wanted me to do everything."

"And because you got straight A's." Brooke rolled her eyes. "At least they saw you. Paid attention to you."

"Hey, it's not a competition." Hayley sat back, eyes softening. "And I'm not trying to fight you on this. We got the crap end of the parent straw in different ways. Funnily enough, I thought by helping you more when we were kids, you'd be protected from their shittiness. I never thought about how it would feel from your side *not* getting their attention from them. I'm sorry I didn't see that."

"Me too. I guess there's a lot we didn't know about each other. But—I'd like to try... to get to know you."

"I'd like that a lot."

Brooke was grinning so wide it hurt. At her sister. Who was absolutely beaming back. There was no curl of Brooke's lip. She wasn't trying to vault off the bed and get out of there. Her mind didn't feel like a storm. Just calm.

"Can I give you another hug?" Hayley asked with puppy dog eyes.

"That might be pushing it." Brooke tried to be serious but the edge of her mouth betrayed her.

Hayley leaped on her anyway.

THIRTY-TWO
JJ

JJ cut in along the skirting board with her brush, taking it slow and precise along the edge, no taping required. She hadn't absorbed a word of her audiobook for the past fifteen minutes, every thought captured and fixated on a certain blonde: the one who, apparently, had feelings for her and wanted more.

Not seeing Brooke for the foreseeable future didn't sit right. The last week alone had been hard enough. But when it came to her list, to her ideal, Brooke was right: she wasn't the type of person JJ pictured. But who did she envision? A blurry woman in a pantsuit who, for some reason, always had a briefcase.

Be careful you're not making up this ideal woman who doesn't exist, Jess's voice rang through clearly.

Every single date she'd been on with who JJ *thought* might fit the bill had been an absolute bust. Especially the women who'd said they were one thing and ended up even more chaotic in person than Brooke. JJ loved that at least with Brooke, her feelings came through in every smirk and every scowl. She kept things *real*.

JJ dipped her brush into the paint, methodically wiped off each side, and cut into the next section.

Okay, were there any parts of Brooke that *did* check off her list?

While Brooke didn't have her life together yet, she was actively working on figuring that out. She was also fun to be around and brought unbridled joy into JJ's life that had been missing for so long. Brooke made her laugh and always looked out for her—whether it was remembering her coffee order or giving her a lift up a steep section on a hike. Brooke was exceptionally good at navigating and the kind of person who would sing her a song so she could pee in the bushes. But that was beside the point. She was sexy, in an I'm-not-even-trying type of way. Those tanned shoulders did JJ in. Every. Single. Time.

Still getting distracted.

JJ moved the brush along the edge of the skirting board.

Brooke's values to help other people and better herself as a person really lit a fire within JJ. Not to mention her determination to make things work, no matter what life threw at her. That grittiness was incredibly hot.

JJ eyebrows rose higher with each point. She redipped her brush. Maybe Brooke did meet some of those deeper list items that meant more to JJ, those values that structured who she was as a person.

But what about those cons? Brooke said it herself: she was a walking anti-list.

She could drive JJ up the wall when she spoke her mind. Their disagreements grated, though they usually ended up being valid and helpful conflict. She also made JJ uncomfortable by challenging her to try new things and sway from their plans—oh.

Oh.

She was an idiot.

The brush slipped. JJ gaped at the smear.

She *never* slipped.

She grabbed her rag to wipe it up. Wet paint streaked across her hand. Oh for the love of—

Brooke entered her mind again, burger sauce everywhere, having the absolute best time of her life. Living in the chaos and going with it.

JJ stared at the paint on her hand. The corners of her mouth tugged up.

Maybe Brooke's cons weren't cons after all.

Maybe it was JJ's list that was a con. Something that needed to be pulled back, scribbled on and simplified—stripped down to her most important core life values. Not a long list of rigid requirements. If JJ had been flexible with her list for just a second, maybe she could've listened to her heart: how it thrummed whenever she was near Brooke, the warmth she felt with the persistent need to be near her. It was never enough.

The paint dried on her hand. It stretched and cracked with every movement—a constant reminder JJ wasn't perfect, even when she tried to be.

And neither was Brooke. But none of that mattered.

It was time to pivot.

~

Just over twenty-four hours later, JJ walked up the front path of Hayley and Marie's and pressed the doorbell.

She stood straight, shoulders back, hands clasped in front of her and let out a quick breath. *You got this.* She bounced on her toes, tipping her head back to the sky. The stars twinkled above, and she took a deep breath of the fresh night air.

Brooke opened the door in an oversized shirt tucked into high-waisted jeans. It was perfectly casual, exactly as requested. "Hi."

There was nothing better than those blue eyes and that smile aimed right at her.

"Hey," JJ said. "Thanks for being on board with tonight. You ready?" She held out her arm.

"Yep." Brooke turned in the doorway. "I'm off, see you later!" She stepped into JJ's space and headed to the car.

JJ opened Brooke's door for her, then went around and hopped in the driver's seat.

"Is this really a *date* date?" Brooke asked, clipping her seatbelt on.

"Yes, Brooke, this is really a *date* date."

"What changed?"

It was a fair question.

JJ pulled away from the kerb. "I've done some stupid things in my life, and I think holding onto my list as tightly as I had been was one of them. My plan to find the right woman listed too many things. Things I thought I wanted or that mattered but didn't. As a wise friend once told me, I think it's good to have ideals or want to find someone whose values align with yours, but I'd made up these impossible pre-requisites. It ended up sounding like an AI hallucination by the time I'd added the twentieth must-have trait to my list: a six-fingered, three-eyed woman with a four-handled briefcase."

Brooke laughed. "Well, when you put it that way, maybe it was a little unattainable."

"Yeah. It made me think, who am I to judge someone like that?" JJ kept her eyes on the road ahead. The traffic picked up as houses gave way to businesses and restaurants, and the lights of the Adelaide city skyline blinked into view. "I accidentally brushed paint over a skirting board today."

"No, you?" Brooke replied in mock horror. "Not-a-hair-out-of-place JJ made a mistake?"

"That's just it, isn't it? We're all human. To be human is to be flawed, but I was seeking perfection. Because that's what I wanted and what I strived to be: perfect at life—with my house, my business—and that's what I thought I wanted in someone else. But I forgot about living. Heading away with you flipped everything on its head, and it took me a while to figure that out."

The radio played softly between them. JJ adjusted the car's air vents, trying to dry off her palms. Brooke was patient, head resting on the back of the seat as she waited for JJ to continue.

"When I made that mistake yesterday, it took me right back to that primary school memory I shared." Heat clawed its way up JJ's neck, claiming her cheeks and settling into a low burn. "That time I tried and failed to draw within the lines of the colouring book. It should've been such an insignificant moment. Why have I held onto it for so long?" She glanced at Brooke.

Brooke sat up straight. "Because it meant a lot to you.

Those small moments are when we're trying to learn who we want to be, but there's that dissonance. The difference between who we are in our heads, and what comes out on paper, or in our actions. It's learning and failing, but sometimes we take away the wrong lesson."

Brooke pulled the seatbelt away from her neck. "We should've been encouraged to fail and try over and over again, but we were taught it was a bad thing, in different ways. For me, failure meant losing my parents' attention. For you, failure meant not meeting your own high standards; failing yourself and the expectations of others."

"You know what's worse?" JJ said. "I've been trying to prove that point my whole life. I'm a bloody painter—most of my days are spent colouring within the lines." She laughed, but the sound was empty.

"Oh, wow. I never thought of that connection."

"Me either, until yesterday, when I smeared that paint. I'd been thinking about you and our holiday. It made me realise... everyone is flawed one way or another. I'm always going to be the girl who sometimes paints outside the lines. And just like not expecting perfection in a partner, I need to not expect that of myself. Being me is enough."

They pulled up to the restaurant.

"So long story short, that's what changed."

"I had no idea."

"Yeah, well, I don't exactly go around telling everyone my fatal flaws." JJ shut off the car, rubbing her palms on her jeans. She snuck a peek at Brooke. She was smiling.

"JJ, seeking to better yourself isn't a fatal flaw, as long as it brings you happiness. If you love the challenge of running your business and painting homes, then that's admirable.

Just make sure you're still getting the fun and fulfilment from it."

"I am and I do. Even if some of my expectations are a little high."

"Thank you for sharing all that with me. I think we all try to hold ourselves to a different version of who we aspire to be. Someone smarter, faster, richer—or just better at colouring in." Brooke winked. "Whatever it is. It's nice to talk about it and know we're not alone." She reached across, placing her hand on JJ's knee. It was the first touch instigated by Brooke since they'd got back from the holiday.

The low buzz in JJ's gut settled.

"So, with that somewhat cryptic message from earlier—where are you taking me?"

"To the only place I thought to embrace our flaws and imperfections and have fun while we do it."

They got out of the car and stood in front of the red and black building. A glowing neon prawn opened and closed its claws on the sign.

"A seafood restaurant?"

"You'll see," JJ said, pulling her into the venue. "You got me with so many surprises on our trip, I thought it was only fair I planned a couple for tonight."

The waiter handed them a bib and gloves. Brooke went to put them on, but JJ stopped her. "The gloves are optional, and I say we ignore them tonight."

"Okaaay," she replied, eyes narrowed.

Their waiter was back within minutes, dumping an entire bag of sauced seafood directly onto their table.

"Oh my god!" Brooke exclaimed as lobster, mussels, prawns and vegetables fell to the table in one giant heap.

JJ didn't think twice. She dove into the saucy mess with her bare hands.

Brooke gasped, followed by the most melodic laugh to ever cascade out her mouth.

JJ revelled in her response.

"I wanted to get uncomfortable tonight," JJ said, hot sauce squelching between her fingers, making her want to shudder. "And push outside of those lines I've been living in but have fun doing it!"

She gritted her teeth, smiling through it as she examined the sauce all over her hands. It undid something inside of her, breaking down those rules. It reminded her of being on top of the dunes again on KI and hurtling over the edge into the sandy mess.

"I'm here for all of this," Brooke replied, eyes alight. Her fingers smooshed into the prawn pile. She picked one out, popped it in her mouth and closed her eyes. "Far out—that cajun seasoning."

JJ took a bite of lobster. "So good!"

After five minutes it felt normal to be eating without cutlery. The sensation of touching the food first almost transformed the flavour in a weird way. Somehow it tasted brighter and JJ appreciated the textures more.

"So, what do people talk about on a date?" Brooke asked.

"Whatever we want."

Brooke cracked a mussel open. "We've kinda covered the initial get-to-know-you questions."

"I'm sure there's a lot more to find out about you, Brooke Mayfield. Like who's everyday Brooke when she's not on the road travelling?"

"She's a 'sitting on her laptop in her PJs with a bun' kind-of-girl, probably watching *The White Lotus* or *Gossip Girl* again."

"Same. Though sans-bun." JJ laughed and grabbed the last prawn, using it to mop up extra sauce. "I'm looking forward to discovering these other sides of you."

That pulled a wide grin from Brooke. "Me too." She stole JJ's prawn and popped it in her mouth.

"Hey!"

Brooke licked her lips.

A pull elicited low in JJ's gut. She clamped her legs together. Eating seafood should not be that sensual. She pointed a messy finger. "You're lucky I like you."

Brooke's smile grew, making a sauce smear stretch across her cheek that JJ couldn't wipe off even if she tried. Instead, JJ drew a heart in the leftover sauce on the table and added the letters "B" and "J" inside.

"So lame right?"

Brooke's eyes widened. "Uhh, JJ, that doesn't look like what I think you meant,"

"Sure it does, it's our initial—oh." JJ's cheeks burned as she scrubbed the picture away.

"Here. I've got something better."

Brooke drew a large letter W, then added two dots. Oh. They were boobs.

JJ giggled. Actually giggled, looking around the room and wiping the scribble away before the waiter came past.

"Embarrassed?" Brooke asked, eyes dancing. Oh, she was evil.

And so it went on—Brooke drawing ruder pictures and words, and JJ trying to erase them as fast as possible. She even drew a sneaky penis in a corner JJ had completely overlooked. The waiter saw it and scowled. JJ slid an inch down her chair.

They barrelled out of the restaurant in tears, grins so wide JJ's cheeks hurt.

"You're terrible." JJ wrapped an arm around Brooke and squeezed, her senses bombarded with industrial strength soap. At least they wouldn't stink like seafood all night—that was no way to finish off a date.

Plus, JJ had plans. New, boundary pushing plans.

She hoped Brooke would be on board.

THIRTY-THREE

Brooke

Brooke had no idea where JJ was taking her. They'd left the restaurant and were back in the suburbs near Karkalla Beach.

"I thought we were going swimming!" Brooke said. JJ's text asking her out on a date had been extremely sweet and cryptic. "Your message said to wear bathers."

Brooke's skin prickled at the possibilities.

"I mean, technically?" JJ's voice went up an octave. "But not in water. Well, not—just, you'll see."

They pulled up to a cute red brick house with cream trims. The garden appeared immaculate under the streetlights.

"Is this your place?" Brooke asked as she unclipped her seatbelt.

"Yep."

"Oooh, didn't expect you to take me back here on our first date," Brooke said as they walked up to JJ's front door.

JJ paused, taking Brooke in, hand stilled on the key. "I think you and I both know this isn't our first date."

Brooke cleared her throat, her head still getting around the fact this was a real date. That JJ had asked her—Brooke Mayfield—out on a date, and that she—Brooke Mayfield—wanted said date.

Dinner had been so unexpected, especially because JJ had picked such an out-of-the-box experience for herself. The vulnerability JJ had shown was so sweet and endearing, especially when she'd first shoved her hands into their dinner. Brooke had caught the panic in her eyes, the forced smile, but she also spotted the moment that changed—when JJ let go and started having fun.

"Wait here a minute." JJ placed a kiss on Brooke's forehead and rushed inside, the spot tingling in her wake.

A giddiness swelled inside Brooke. She didn't get doted on like this.

Relax. It was a simple gesture.

JJ returned, grabbed Brooke's hand and guided her through the dimly lit house. Personal spaces were fascinating, no matter which country she was in. There were cookie-cutter homes that felt cold or copy and pasted, like they came straight out of a magazine. Not JJ's house. This was a *home*. Decked out in mid-century furniture, the warm woods of the dining table and kitchen bench were complemented by a mass of indoor plants. There was enough greenery to make a nursery jealous. Still, everything had its place. Considered. Neat. Not a frame or chair out of place. She'd expect nothing less of JJ.

"Whoa."

A few lit candles welcomed them in the lounge, the flickering light bouncing off the greenery. Brooke explored the rear hallway, lined with fancy paintings from a person who clearly had taste. She'd always wanted to be someone with that kind of discernment, though she'd never been in a place long enough to style it.

"So stylish. Though, I'm not surprised," Brooke said, coming back into the lounge.

"Thank you. Also I meant to say earlier—Jess is over at Remi's tonight."

"Cool." Brooke didn't want to think too much into *that* insinuation.

"You want a drink? I have beer, or some of that wine we bought." JJ's hand was paused on the fridge door, fingers tapping the edge.

Brooke thumbed through JJ's record collection. "Let's go beer tonight—something we can both enjoy." Brooke winked.

"Hey—wine's becoming more... tolerable." JJ pulled out a couple of bottles, popping the tops off with her forearm.

"That was very cool," Brooke said, admiring the flexing muscle as she took the beer. "Cheers, to our first *official* date."

"And hopefully—to many more."

"I'd like that." Her stomach swooped low, a smile breaking out as they clinked and sipped their ice-cold drinks.

"So, why bathers?" Brooke asked, flicking the halter strap of her bikini with a snap as she dropped onto the couch.

JJ cleared her throat. "Okay, here me out. I ran with the whole painting outside the lines theme for tonight..."

"I'm listening." Brooke crossed her legs and slung her arm over the back of the soft brown leather lounge.

"And I found a couple's body painting kit." JJ's eyes slid to a discreet box on the coffee table.

"A what?!" Out of all the date ideas... Brooke did *not* expect this from JJ.

JJ's eyes were alight as she shuffled closer to Brooke, barely containing her grin.

"It's art that we paint... with our bodies. And there's a few ways this can go, so I'd love for you to lead with what you're comfortable with—"

"What *we're* comfortable with," Brooke corrected.

JJ smiled. "Right. Well, okay—so there's a canvas, and paints, and... us."

"Uh-huh." Brooke ran a finger along the condensation on her beer bottle.

"And we can create an art piece together. I've already got the spot picked out in the bedroom to hang it."

"I'm sure it'll be so good, we could sell it for millions."

"Right?" JJ placed her beer on the coffee table, swapping it for the large dark box. "So, there's rules." She pulled out the instructions.

"It wouldn't be you if there wasn't." Brooke took a swig of her beer, hiding her grin.

"I hear I'm pretty amazing at breaking them now though... so..."

Brooke's lips pressed together, the edge pulling up ever so slightly, eyes dancing. "Mmhmm."

"Okay, so maybe not *all* the time. But anyway, the rules state that anything goes: swimwear, underwear, or—uh—nothing at all. Put the paint on how you like and, yeah, cool." JJ pulled at her shirt, face going bright red. "Man it's hot in here. Do you want the fan on? And—and some music?"

"JJ?" Brooke placed her bottle on the coffee table.

JJ cleared her throat. "Yeah?"

"Relax." Brooke snatched the instruction booklet and threw it over the side of the couch. It landed on the floor with a papery splat. She held JJ's hands, thumbs making circles in a steady rhythm. "How about we start simple?"

JJ's darting eyes re-focused on their entwined hands, breath slowing. When she looked back up, Brooke leaned forward and claimed JJ's lips.

Fuck, Brooke had missed those lips.

The fact that she'd thought she would never touch them or kiss them again?

Her chest ached just remembering.

This kiss was slow. A beginning. Learning from the start. No rush this time, no *rules*. It was real. Brooke's hands slid up JJ's arms and back again, the touch strangely giving herself tingles all the way to the back of her neck. On the next stroke up, her hand kept going, curling around the back of JJ's head, nails scraping her scalp. JJ deepened the kiss in response, hand gripping onto Brooke's thigh.

Then JJ pulled away, holding up a hand. "Hold this thought"—she gestured vaguely between them—"and let me put that music on." She sprung from the couch, strode over to the wooden record table, and slipped one out of its sleeve, placing it on a turntable. JJ set the needle. A woman began singing in a mix of French and English, the rhythm soulful, the deeper notes thrumming through Brooke's body and making her want to sway to the beat.

"*Charlotte Cardin*," JJ said, swaggering back to the couch, her movements slow, calculated. A grin formed as she walked with the music. Brooke scooted back against the arm of the sofa as JJ climbed on top of her.

"Hi," she said, hands braced either side of Brooke's head. "Sorry for making you wait."

Brooke's eyes dropped to JJ's lips. "I'm sure you can think of a way to make it up to me."

JJ bent down and kissed her, breaking away again almost immediately. "Hang on," she said, sitting back on her heels.

"Wha—" Brooke frowned, her brain still stuck on soft lips and hot breath and—*oh*.

JJ reached for the edge of her shirt, slipping it off in one quick swoop, pausing to fold it, and place it over the back of the couch. Brooke tamped down a grin. JJ was too cute. The amount of JJ's skin now on show though? That wasn't cute—that was hot.

Lean arms and the same swimming top from the hot tub had memories flashing back. Brooke wet her lips and reached up, running a hand from JJ's chest to stomach. Her breath quickened. Brooke sat up next, slinging her shirt off as she did. She threw it onto the floor with the instruction booklet and pulled JJ down on top of her.

How could lips feel this good? This time their kiss was fast, hungry. Brooke wanted more. Her arm wrapped around JJ's back, hand clawing its way down the middle.

JJ lowered herself onto Brooke; it was the first time they'd been this close with bare skin touching while not in a hot tub. JJ's heartbeat thudded against Brooke, the heat from her body like an oven, a reminder of the times Brooke had awoken to JJ spooning her. This was so much better. The press of JJ's weight against her was intoxicating. And not enough. Patience wasn't Brooke's forte. She looped her thumbs into the back of JJ's pants, squeezing her arse and pressing down. More friction. More heat. More JJ.

Lips crushing together over and over, Brooke lost herself in the moment. It took her a second when JJ pulled back, glancing over at the box on the table.

"Ready to paint?" she asked so close, her breath skated over Brooke's lips.

Brooke could only nod.

With a final kiss, JJ jumped up and pushed the coffee table to the edge of the room.

Brooke gave herself a moment to calm down, watching as JJ took out the box's contents and laid out a large waterproof liner. Brooke stood to help. They pulled the edges of the liner tight then unfolded the canvas together.

"I wasn't sure what colours you liked, so I got a mix." JJ started placing the paint tubes in a row, making Brooke smile.

They wouldn't be so neat in a minute.

"We're meant to put the paint on the canvas *then* use our bodies," JJ continued.

JJ slipped off her pants next like it was no big deal, and Brooke broke for a second. Without taking her eyes off JJ, Brooke did the same, slowly sliding them down her legs and discarding them.

Now she had JJ's attention.

Slack-jawed, JJ paused, eyes raking up Brooke's body. They never wavered as she placed the last tube of paint on the floor.

"Bathers off too?" Brooke asked, thumbs hooking into the band.

JJ's eyes rounded, eyebrows sliding up to her hairline. "Uh, we can," she squeaked.

Playing with JJ like this was a tease in itself. JJ needed slow, but it was so fun pulling these reactions from her.

"I'm kidding. Let's keep it slow." Brooke picked up her beer instead, taking a deep pull.

"Good, yeah." JJ's shoulders eased. She set two pairs of slippers at the edge of the waterproof liner. "For when we need to wash this off." JJ's cheeks burned.

Of course. What got dirty... needed to be cleaned. This night just got even better.

"Okay, pick a colour—then share a memory or something you've learned or like about me and squeeze out a dot or squiggle of paint on the canvas."

"Was that in the instructions?" Brooke eyed the tubes, suppressing another smile at how sweet JJ was being.

"Yes," she confessed. "But I thought it was a cool idea."

"So do I." Brooke bent down, arse facing JJ, and picked up a paint tube. She straightened slowly, enjoying this game and showing off her body. JJ followed every move.

"I choose green. I love your appreciation for nature; the way you immerse yourself in it and slow down in those moments to really take it in. It reminds me of the vineyards and the little face you pulled after every sip." She placed three dots of paint sporadically and stood back up. "Your turn."

"Easy." JJ leapt for the yellow. "I pick the brightest colour in the lot, because to me you are absolute sunshine."

Brooke wanted to deny it. To scoff and say *yeah right*

but she held her tongue, hand moving to her arm and rubbing it. People were never this honest with her and being under this spotlight had her heart racing. She forced herself to maintain eye contact, to take the compliments, and accept them. *Don't run away.*

"You're a shining yellow beacon I'd be happy to follow anywhere. You always seem to know what to do and where to go, and it's a rare thing for me to feel that safety in another person. You know what I'm like."

Brooke didn't deny it, lips quirking.

JJ flicked the lid off the yellow tube. "The joy you've brought to my life in the short time we've known each other has been—well..." JJ dropped her head, snapping it back up with bright eyes. "I appreciate it. And I appreciate you."

Warmth flooded Brooke as she broke eye contact. It was too much, too nice. With a final nod, JJ squirted a couple of lines onto the floor.

They went through every colour, one by one.

"I love the confidence you have in your work and your life. What you've built at your age already is nothing short of incredible. I admire those achievements, and hope to one day build something as worthy for myself. Oops, and yeah, I chose gold." Brooke added a dollop to the centre.

"You just like all the sparkly colours."

"Also that."

JJ held the next tube to her chest. "Blue, because you represent the calm when everything around me feels out of control. You know how to ride the chaos wearing a smile the whole time, knowing it will all work out—and it usually does."

"Love the use of your word 'usually'. And don't blame me for the goats again. I had no hand or hoof in those shenanigans." She picked up the next one. "Brown. Because I'm a sucker for your eyes. It also reminds me of autumn, the season of our travels and the warmth and stability I feel when I'm around you."

And so it went on.

The canvas started to remind Brooke of a *Mr. Squiggle* drawing, ready to be finished and turned upside down, or—

Wait.

"This looks like a *Twister* mat."

JJ raised a brow, taking in all the random shapes they'd made. "I'm game if you are?"

"Bring it on." Brooke's grin spread wide as she started planning out positions.

JJ folded her arms, glaring at her in challenge. "I'll start easy. Left foot, purple."

Wow, those muscles. JJ's arms were bulging in that position. Surely she must workout on top of her job?

Brooke, focus. Less drooling, more game planning and domination.

She spied a purple streak near the edge of the mat. Piece of cake. She eased her left toe onto the fabric... and slid straight across. "Whoa!" She wobbled on the spot, catching herself at the last second. She straightened, sending a fake curtsy JJ's way.

What could she say? She was all class.

JJ stifled a laugh. "Well, I thought that was easy."

"Hey! It's slipperier than you think!" Brooke shoved her hands on her hips, smiling. "Yellow, your..." Brooke pretended to think, tapping her chin. "Butt."

JJ laughed out loud this time. "I thought we were going easy?"

"No, *you* said that. I didn't promise anything."

"Fine." JJ flopped her black-bikini-clad behind straight onto a big yellow splotch, carefully placing her heels on some white canvas space. She looked up at Brooke with a shit-eating grin. "Right elbow, red."

Brooke spotted a red line near JJ. Keeping her foot in place, Brooke stretched over JJ's lap, only just managing to put her elbow in the paint. JJ's thighs were at least comfortable to lie on, no complaints there.

"How am I meant to get around this?" JJ complained.

"Not my problem. Left hand... black," Brooke said, blowing hair out of her face. She really should've tied it up. Strands were already dipping themselves in purple and silver paint.

"Easy." JJ barely had to lift a finger to land in the dark patch next to her. Damn. Brooke had completely missed that. Draping herself over the woman really had put her at a disadvantage. Time to up the ante!

"My right hand, beer." JJ laughed and stretched back to grab her beer off the table, sculling it down. All Brooke could focus on were JJ's taut stomach muscles flexing inches from her face. She was more than happy to wait a little longer with this view.

THIRTY-FOUR

JJ

Four more moves and they were a tangle of limbs—but not the sexy kind. JJ had flopped over Brooke's back so she could reach her right hand into white paint on the other side of the canvas, sandwiching Brooke underneath her.

They were at an impasse.

"What now?" Brooke wheezed below JJ, her left hand now wrapped around JJ's back and squished into a dollop of pink.

There was no way either of them were moving another inch.

There was only one thing to do.

"Free for all!" JJ said, sitting up and smacking white and black streaks all over Brooke's back.

Slap!

"Ah!" JJ cried as wet, cold paint slopped onto her own back. Brooke wriggled off JJ, her foot slipping at the last minute. She crashed to her side. Arms flailed in an attempt to get more paint on JJ, the determination on Brooke's face like a wild fox trying to catch a chicken.

Oh, it was on.

Hands and paint flew everywhere, like a mud-wresting slap fight. Why had she set them up right next to the couch? JJ squeezed her eyes shut, arms wildly trying to get more paint on Brooke while avoiding getting slapped herself. They rolled on the canvas, squeals of laughter bouncing off the walls and drowning out the music as they smeared, streaked, and smudged what skin they could touch.

Somewhere among the chaos, mess and scuffle, soft lips found hers.

Like striking a match, JJ's entire body lit up. Brooke smiled against her mouth as she rubbed more colour onto JJ's thighs. What colour? Who knew? Who cared? Not when those lips were on hers. Exploring, nipping, tasting.

Brooke had her pinned down as skin slid over skin, the paint making each movement more sensual, more intense. God, her body was so smooth. Brooke pulled back with heavy breaths, hovering over JJ to take her in.

"We're an absolute mess," Brooke said, a hand pushing into JJ's hair. JJ followed the movement like a kitten.

"We didn't stay in the lines one bit," JJ said as more paint was spread through her hair.

Brooke bit down on a smile, shaking her head. "Not. One. Bit." Her fingertips trailed down to paint a cross-cross of lines on JJ's chest, ending in the shape of a heart. "I drew JB in the heart this time. Looks much better than BJ."

JJ squeezed her eyes shut and groaned. "I can't believe I did that—I blame you. Too distracting. I didn't realise what I was writing down."

"Uh-huh, sure thing."

Brooke's fingers danced over JJ's shoulders next,

dipping down to her swimming top then pulling away. Air hit the space Brooke had touched, the paint pulling at the edges as it dried. It tightened, making her body tingle and itch all over.

Brooke's hand had snuck behind her own back. JJ tracked the movement, head tilting.

"Were there any other specific prints or marks you wanted to make sure we got on our artwork?" Brooke asked.

"I think we've got most of them—"

Brooke's hand moved behind her then grasped at the base of her neck. Her bikini top dropped between them. JJ froze, gaping. A pair of bare, triangle-shaped breasts stared back at her, a crazy contrast against the mishmash of colour smudged across Brooke's tanned body. The sight should have been ridiculous. Absurd. But it was one of the most beautiful things she'd ever seen: Brooke straddling her in a rainbow of colour with two very white, very perky boobs just begging to be touched.

The familiar coiling in JJ's stomach tightened, low and aching. She sat up, reaching for the yellow paint. She clicked off the lid with her thumb and squeezed it over the unpainted skin. Brooke wet her lips.

"Better make sure they're covered properly for, you know, painting purposes," JJ murmured, hands finding Brooke's breasts and kneading the colour over them. Brooke arched her back as JJ pinched her nipples, coating them at the same time. "There," she said, swallowing.

"Your turn," Brooke said breathlessly, head tipping forward and eyes dilating as they found JJ's. She reached over, eyes locked on JJ, and grabbed the green.

JJ could only nod, fingers curling under her top. She pulled it off as fast as possible, folded it in half, and placed it on the liner next to the canvas. She closed her eyes, waiting for the cold paint to hit.

The paint squirted out of the tube, but nothing touched her skin. Opening her eyes, Brooke was smearing it over her—now very yellow and green—breasts.

Oh.

She pushed them up against JJ's chest, sliding up and down, sending JJ's head into overdrive. Brooke's hardened nipples grazed along JJ's skin with each slide. She reached around the back of Brooke's head and crushed their lips together, the desire to touch and be touched becoming a physical pain thrumming through her body. Anything to get them closer together.

It wasn't enough. She pulled Brooke on top of her, lying down on the canvas. Her back slid against the wet paint. Brooke slipped a leg between her, the friction a delicious tease of pressure and sensation. JJ groaned at the contact as Brooke rolled her hips down, thrusting into her further. Tongues danced, their pace speeding up and the heat between her legs growing with each pass of Brooke's thigh. It was so good. Too good. Too smooth. So fucking smooth.

Her body was dynamite and Brooke's thigh was fire, striking her fuse over and over again.

She needed to slow it down, she needed to stop, she needed to—

"Oh god!" she cried into Brooke's mouth, arching completely off the canvas as the orgasm completely took over her body.

Brooke froze on top of her, lips still connected. JJ was clutching Brooke's arms so tight, she let go as if electrocuted, realisation dawning. Her eyes flew open.

Brooke broke off the kiss and pulled back slowly as if gauging JJ's reaction.

JJ's cheeks burned, her body a mess of tingles and flame, the last of the waves still ebbing and flowing.

"Did you just—" Brooke's eyes searched hers, eyebrows flung so high they'd almost disappeared.

JJ folded in her lips, squeezing her eyes shut again for a moment and nodding. "Yep. Mhmm. It's just, you were all..." Words couldn't form quick enough. "And your boobs—then sliding around... was so good. It's just been so long since—"

She was cut off with a kiss. When Brooke pulled back this time, her grin stretched across her face, wide and inviting, lighting up the entire room.

Yellow.

"So, you think I'm sexy?" She battered her eyelashes.

JJ slapped her on the arm, specks of wet paint rebounding and landing on her cheek, making them both laugh.

"You know I do." JJ sobered, clearing her throat. "I clearly wasn't trying to—" She huffed out a breath. "I didn't mean for—"

What did she say to the person who she was so wholly wrapped up in that they'd slithered on top of her for two seconds and made her come? She still had underwear on for god's sake!

"It's nothing to be sorry for or worry about." Brooke gathered JJ's hands in hers. "I'm just honoured you were so in the moment, so turned on by me, that I had that effect on you. From where I'm sitting, I say that's pretty amazing."

Face still burning, JJ let her head fall to the side—straight into a patch of wet paint. She pulled away with a wet cheek and a scowl, refocusing on Brooke.

"That kind of thing is usually hard for me," she confessed. "I know I've mentioned it before, but I meant it. That emotional connection is so important to me, and I'm lying here shocked how that just happened. Usually I take so long... or I don't come at all, but that was so enjoyable for me, it took me by surprise, so thank you."

"You're welcome. As far as dates go, I think this one has shot to the top of my list."

"I thought you said you didn't date," JJ challenged.

"Just because it's my first official date, doesn't mean it can't also be at the top of my list."

JJ chuckled at that, the paint cracking around her face.

"Well, as much as I'd love for us to stay here, I think this is all starting to dry, so we should probably wash up."

"Hang on." Brooke climbed off JJ and pushed her chest into the canvas, forming a swirl of greenish yellow. "There. Now you can have imprints of these babies forever." She jiggled them for emphasis then stuck out a lip. "Feels like I got short-changed though, not sure I even got to touch you yet."

"Not with your hands." JJ attempted to waggle her eyebrows. "We'll have to fix that."

"Please," Brooke said, standing up and stepping off the canvas.

"Give me a hand?"

Brooke pulled her up. They turned, taking in their art piece.

"I mean... it's unique." Brooke examined it, head crooked to the side.

"I love it. As far as paintings go, it'll definitely be the most memorable." JJ picked at the flaking swirl of colour on the back of her hand and slipped on their disposable slippers. "Would you like first shower or do you—want to join me?"

At this rate, JJ wasn't sure separate showers were even an option.

"Yes." Brooke didn't hesitate and shoved her feet in the slippers. "With you," she clarified. JJ grabbed her by the hand and led her to the bathroom.

"This is massive," Brooke said, gawking at the high-ceilinged room. "The windows make it feel like we're almost outdoors."

"I think the previous owners converted a third bedroom into a bathroom. It's abnormally large, but no complaints from me."

"And look at that bathtub." Brooke reached out to touch the edge of the central tub, pausing at the last second and pulling back.

JJ smiled. It was easy to forget they were essentially walking paintings... and semi-wet ones at that.

In more ways than one. JJ's lip quirked to herself as she turned on the shower. Thankfully, she'd had the fore-thought to put clean towels out *before* they started their messy evening.

"Bottoms on or off?" Brooke asked.

In their colourful forms, JJ had momentarily forgotten

they weren't completely naked. It seemed silly to care about taking their underwear off now with everything that had just happened between them, and yet—

"How about we leave them on for now, and save removing them for after?" JJ wasn't ready to call it a night, but she also really wanted this paint off first and freshen up. The longer it dried, the more she itched to scratch it off.

"Yes, please. Looking forward to unwrapping *all* of that." Brooke gestured at JJ's body.

"In the meantime... want to help me wash all this off?" JJ held up a soft scouring sponge as she stepped into the warm stream of water and sighed. Brooke followed her in, chest pushing into JJ's back as she hugged her from behind. They stood like that under the steaming water, holding each other. JJ leaned into Brooke's touch. After a minute, Brooke kissed her neck, took the sponge, and started washing off JJ's back.

The intimacy of the moment was quiet. JJ hadn't experienced this kind of connection with anyone before, one where she was so comfortable in another's space. Someone who didn't make her think. Not in an intellectual sense, but in an I'm-so-here-in-the-present kind of way, where nothing else mattered.

The process of getting the paint on their bodies was easy. The process of getting it off? A somewhat trickier task.

"Ow, ow, ow."

"Hold still," Brooke demanded, scrubbing off a particularly stubborn paint patch on JJ's lower back.

"I'll be rubbed raw by the time you're done with me," JJ said over her shoulder.

"You wish." Brooke slapped her on the arse. "Plus, thought I already did that on the canvas."

"Oh, shut up." But JJ couldn't hold back her grin.

THIRTY-FIVE

Brooke

They were kissing again, unable to keep their hands off each other.

It was JJ's fault.

She'd spent too much time trying to clean Brooke's nipples to perfection with that damn sponge. Every stroke just ended up turning her on and cranking the heat switch directly between her legs. It was a good thing they were in the shower, because she was *dripping*.

Skin thoroughly scrubbed and the last of the shampoo suds rinsed down the drain, Brooke was now up against the cold tiles as JJ kneaded at her breast, her other hand clamped down on her arse. Brooke gripped JJ's arms, revelling in the rippling muscle under her touch as she lost herself in the kiss.

"Do you"—JJ panted between kisses—"want to take this to the bedroom?"

"Thought you'd never ask." Brooke nipped JJ's lower lip.

The water was off in an instant. JJ handed her a towel.

Brooke wiped down her arms as JJ shook her short hair from her face. Brooke flashed back to JJ standing outside their tent after their hike in the storm. The same pang hit her in the chest. She dried off the same arm for a third time and blinked. So distracting. Brooke quickly finished towelling off the rest of her body and bent over to dry her hair.

Crack.

"Ow!"

JJ had whipped Brooke's arse with the towel, the snap reverberating in the large room as lancing pain streaked across her butt... but it was kind of hot.

"Oh shit. Didn't expect that to actually work." JJ's grin said otherwise.

Brooke smirked, wrapping the towel around her torso as JJ tied her own off at the waist, chest out and proud.

"Yeah... I—*really*—like this look for you," Brooke said, taking in every detail now they weren't covered head to toe in paint. She sauntered into JJ's space, fingernails scraping the edge of JJ's breast so lightly, goosebumps sprung up in its wake.

"Before we get distracted, bedroom—now!" JJ commanded.

"Ooo, I like this side of JJ. So sexy. Lead the way."

Diagonally across the hall, JJ opened the door to her bedroom and flicked on a lamp, bathing the room in a warm glow. As expected, the space was full of plants. They covered the dressing table, the nightstand—even the floor. JJ's bed took up the middle, made so neat it would pass an army inspection. Brooke almost didn't want to mess it up.

Almost.

She dove onto the bed, twisting in the air and landing on her back with an *oof*, hair sprawling everywhere.

JJ chuckled, eyes blazing. She undid the towel at her waist, slowly pulling it away and hanging it over her bed frame just so, gaze never leaving Brooke.

"Hurry up," Brooke pleaded, squirming on the quilt.

JJ dipped onto the bed, crawling over Brooke like an animal. Hovering, waiting. The smell of fresh shampoo had Brooke reaching up and plunging her hands into JJ's still-wet hair. But they didn't stay there for long. There were too many other places to explore. JJ watched on, letting Brooke's hands roam. They found her arms next, squeezing at those muscles as they held up JJ's weight. JJ's breaths were steady, her chest moving with the motion and drawing Brooke's eye. The lilting tunes from the lounge had ended while they were washing off, the quiet now accentuating every sound, heightening each murmur, each breath—bringing each other into absolute focus.

For Brooke, past partners were temporary. An enjoyable time to share and move on. But as she took in JJ above her, something new slid into place. This was about staying. Staying in the moment, staying in JJ's space. Giving herself over completely and letting go. Truly letting go, and allowing JJ in.

The steady beat of her heart was like a low bass drum. *Thump, thump, thump.* Brooke's hand ran over JJ's chest then stopped, the same rhythm playing back in complete sync with her own as they held each other's gaze. Her body vibrated, knowing they weren't playing by any rules tonight. Brooke bit her lip, a million choices flashing through her mind for where to take this next.

JJ didn't give her a chance to decide, leaning in. Brooke anticipated a kiss, instead JJ nudged Brooke's head to the side with the cutest button nose, and Brooke could do nothing but oblige. Lips found her neck, hips jerking in response. So sensitive. JJ sucked, hands diving between her towel and ripping it open. Cool air blew across Brooke's chest, the hairs on the back of her neck standing in response. A warm hand covered her breast, pinching the nipple as JJ deepened the kisses on her neck, sucking and licking in time with the pinches. Brooke's nipple was so hard it ached, matching the throbbing that had begun between her legs. She was going to give JJ a run for her money with how quickly she'd ramped Brooke up.

JJ slipped a thigh between Brooke's legs, and Brooke widened them instantly, wanting more. Why had she agreed to keeping their bottoms on? The friction was maddening, her entire body now melting into a pool of need. Suck, tweak, grind. JJ was a fucking machine. What was even happening to her right now? A moan sounded and she realised it was her. Another escaped. Brooke did *not* make noise in the bedroom. But she couldn't stop, each motion encouraged her further, louder. She didn't care anymore.

Let go.

JJ must've been feeding off her energy, groaning into her neck as she sped up her actions.

The familiar build began low in her gut.

Yes, yes, yes.

JJ stopped.

Brooke's eyes flung open. She had no idea when they'd shut. "What are you doing?" She blinked up at JJ who'd pulled away from her neck.

"Making you work for this." JJ bit her lip through the sexiest smile Brooke had ever seen.

Brooke could hardly hear her over the frantic beating of her heart. "Are you serious right now?"

"Tell me you love this. You love people telling you what to do."

JJ pinched a nipple. "Arguing with you."

She rolled her hips down onto Brooke. "Pushing you. Taking control."

JJ's eyes flashed as she sat up, hands splayed on Brooke's stomach.

"Fuck," Brooke breathed out.

"Plus, wouldn't it be better with these off?" JJ hooked a finger under the waistband of Brooke's bikini, running a finger along the inner edge of her thigh.

Brooke could barely nod.

She was done. This was bliss, and she hadn't even come yet. This woman had her on the edge, right on that precipice, and, god, did it feel good. JJ could do whatever she wanted at this point. If JJ was a master, Brooke was her puppet—happy to let JJ play her all night long.

JJ's eyes held as she twisted her finger under the fabric and over Brooke's sensitive skin. Too soft. Brooke needed hard. Pressure. Friction.

JJ kept stroking all the edges, but never where Brooke wanted it most.

Brooke's hips moved again, and JJ stilled, eyes narrowing. "My terms. When *I* say."

That possessive tone wasn't helping. Brooke's core pulsed in response.

"Fine," Brooke gritted out. Her hands grabbed onto her

towel, scrunching it and squeezing it, trying and failing to let out some of the pent-up energy. Anything to lessen the tension.

"Good." JJ grinned, eyes all heat. She hooked her hands into Brooke's waistband this time, pulling down slowly, taking her time. So slow it was painful, the fabric brushing against Brooke's skin in its own tease. Brooke sucked in a breath as JJ dragged them down the rest of the way and onto the floor. JJ's eyes trailed down to Brooke's centre, and Brooke felt the movement like she'd touched her, her skin prickling on her torso.

JJ leaned down, kissing her softly on the lips. "You are so beautiful," she murmured, voice gentle and full of wonder. Her fingers tracked along Brooke's thighs in a light caress.

Still too light. Too soft.

Brooke's heartbeat refused to slow, her breathing uneven as she waited for JJ's next move.

Curling her hands under Brooke's legs, JJ lifted Brooke's knees up, shuffling back as she did so and beginning a trail of kisses down Brooke's leg, biting softly at the edge of her thighs. *So close.* Brooke shut her eyes, the anticipation too much.

A single finger ran down the length of her folds, making her arch off the bed at the sudden touch.

JJ chuckled. "So needy. And so... wet. For me?" Her finger slid up and down.

Maddening.

Next, JJ's thumb started circles over Brooke's clit, and she almost lost it then and there.

Hold on.

"Harder," Brooke whined.

JJ did as she was told, placing wet kisses on Brooke's thighs as she did. Brooke felt her smiling through them, enjoying this way too much.

And then the hand was gone.

How much more could she take?

JJ's hot mouth was on her next, the shock of it eliciting another moan. Whatever the fuck she was doing with her mouth was another level. It felt like licking, but the pressure was fucking ace. *Yes*. The sounds JJ was pulling from her now were obscene. She didn't care.

Then JJ sucked her clit straight in her mouth. A deadly combination of biting and flicking with her tongue that had Brooke thrashing on the bed. Honestly, had JJ grabbed a toy she didn't know about? This woman was definitely a machine. No one could be that insanely accurate with their mouth.

Her body coiled tight. Everything flashed through her mind, from the first time they'd kissed, soaking wet in the hot tub, to earlier in the night when JJ was arching under her with abandon. The pressure built, and she squeezed her eyes shut tighter, breath held. She froze.

Oh.

My.

"God!" Brooke cried out into the room, arching off the bed, again and again and again as her orgasm tore through her body.

"Fucking hell," she said, falling back, an arm flinging over her face. She peered at JJ from beneath. "What the fuck?"

"What?" JJ asked, smile wide, head resting lazily against Brooke's thigh.

"That should be illegal."

The grin got bigger.

"Scratch that, *you* should be illegal. That was too much. How am I meant to handle that?"

Her toes still tingled, and her body said that was only the beginning.

It'd had a taste, and now it wanted more.

She was wrecked.

THIRTY-SIX

JJ

"You're incredible," JJ murmured.

And so was this view. Brooke: completely undone, hair still wet and eyes bright blue as she complained about JJ's apparent mouth talents and the devastation she'd wreaked on Brooke's body.

JJ's cheeks hurt, her jaw burned and so did her chest—so full, it felt like bursting. Being able to do this with Brooke, share this with her and see her react that way was... wow.

Like a fire awakened, all she wanted to do was consume. After the earlier events on the canvas, JJ assumed she was done. Coming once was usually hard enough, yet the pulse between her legs had only grown in fervour with each press of her tongue to Brooke's clit.

Now? Now she was *starving*.

She prowled up Brooke's body, hips pushing down into her, making Brooke hiss at the contact. Want mirrored in Brooke's eyes as JJ kissed her with everything she had. Arms wrapped around her as Brooke deepened the kiss, no doubt tasting herself. Was there anything hotter? JJ groaned at the thought, pressing into Brooke again. It only ramped Brooke up, hands clawing down JJ's back and tugging at the last scrap of fabric between them.

There was nothing slow about the next movements, nothing to savour—her bather bottoms needed to be off, and they needed to be off—*now*. JJ balanced on one shaking arm, not willing to break their kiss. She haphazardly clawed at her own bikini with Brooke's help, wishing her legs weren't so bloody long as she kicked them off somewhere into the void. Thank fuck for that.

She lowered herself either side of Brooke's leg, centres touching for the first time. They were a little off, not *quite* there with the current angle, but the effect was very much real as Brooke whimpered into her mouth. JJ rocked back and forth, shoulders straining under the effort, a fine sheen of sweat starting to form between her shoulder blades.

"Have you ever tried this before?" JJ asked, breaking their kiss.

Brooke shook her head.

"Do you trust me?"

"Do whatever you have in mind."

JJ placed one more kiss on her lips before straightening up. "Try throwing that leg over my shoulder."

"What do you think I am, Barbie?"

"What do you think I did with my dolls when I was little?" JJ's grin was wicked. She held her arm out to give Brooke a hand as she attempted it anyway. Her leg landed on JJ's shoulder with ease.

"Not that hard now, was it?"

Adjusting her position, JJ moved until she was on her

knees and directly over Brooke's centre again. She held onto Brooke's leg for support and lowered herself down, eyes never leaving Brooke.

"Oh." Brooke gasped.

"Now lift your hips," JJ directed as she thrust her own. The timing was perfect, the connection intense as they brushed directly against each other.

"Oh *fuck*."

There was nothing, *nothing* in the world that felt this good, this *personal* and raw as she opened herself up to Brooke. The swell of emotion at their connection was almost too much.

Brooke lifted her hips again as JJ ground down. The delicious friction was wet and rough, making the most obscene sounds between them.

"I didn't think this was real," Brooke uttered in her own haze. She almost sounded delirious as she undulated beneath JJ, a hand reaching out to squeeze her arse—to encourage JJ or to stabilise herself, JJ didn't know.

Their movements sped up, their noises increasing, but she didn't care. It felt too good—again. This was fucking magic. They moved as one, sliding against each other as the sounds grew harsher, their breathing laboured. JJ's thighs burned, her hips edging on a pain that if she pushed further, she'd pull a muscle. She thrust harder anyway, ignoring the pain, ignoring the burn and chasing the internal flame that had built into a roaring fire. All other sounds were drowned out as she felt the wave come out of nowhere, cresting and crashing down as she cried out. Brooke was just as loud as she convulsed underneath her. She felt the pulses between them as they stayed connected, allowing their bodies to calm, for the waves to subside and the warmth and tingles to take over.

Yellow.

Bursts of yellow were all JJ could see in that moment as she took in Brooke's bright eyes staring at her, chest rising and falling, still trying to catch her breath.

JJ eased Brooke's leg down and gingerly collapsed on top of her, thighs stiff and sore, only moments away from having pushed them too far.

No regrets.

They smelled of sweat and sex—the sweet scent lingering in the air between them. Heart beginning to slow, JJ rolled to the side, propping herself up on an elbow. She cupped Brooke's cheek and kissed her, then lazily trailed a hand down her torso. Brooke's skin sported a shimmering glow, and JJ couldn't get enough of it. Couldn't stop touching, even in this post-coital stupor.

"You," Brooke stated, bopping her on the nose, "are something else. I don't even have words for how I'm feeling right now. I've never come like that in such quick succession. You're a literal magician."

"Well, right back at you. I've never come twice in one night. So, we're both in new territory here."

"That angle was heaven." Brooke closed her eyes a moment as if savouring the memory. "I've never felt those sensations or had such a rapid build up. That hit me out of nowhere."

"Me too. I guess we could say that's been building between us for a while," JJ said, eyes fixed on Brooke as she laced their hands together, caressing Brooke's palm with her thumb.

"Yeah, I think you're right." Brooke let out a long, slow breath. "So, do I get a second date?"

"What do you think?"

Brooke grinned, rolling on top of JJ and pinning her down with a kiss.

~

"You didn't tell me you painted as a hobby too!" Jess called out. "Looks great."

JJ blinked. The sun was streaming in the window, Brooke curled up at her side.

Jess appeared in the doorway. "Oop—" she said, skidding to a stop. "Oh." She gawked for a full second like a fish. Enough time for Brooke to wake up and lift her head to see what all the noise was.

Well, shit.

Jess's eyes almost popped out of her head. "Morning. You—I'm—sorry, bye." She squeezed her eyes shut, covering them with her hand for added effect, and walked backwards down the hall until—JJ presumed—her own bedroom door slammed shut. Muffled cackles floated down the hall.

Brooke shared a look with her, still half asleep and ridiculously sexy. "Well, cat's out of the bag now."

"The cats only jumped in the bag last night. We haven't even had a chance to figure this out for ourselves," JJ said.

Brooke gave her a look.

"What?"

"Didn't feel like just last night for me," Brooke confessed.

"No, I know. You know what I mean. I'm happy to tell people if you are. You're not something I want to hide away. How do you feel about that?"

"I'd like that. So, we tell people we're... dating?" Brooke asked, chin resting on JJ's chest.

JJ nodded. "Now I'm going to have to drag you around to meet the family. I'll use you as a shield against all their questions."

Brooke's face was pure horror.

"They're harmless, you'll love 'em. Just make sure to eat all the food Mum serves up, compliment Gran's garden and ask Dad how the footy's going. You'll be a family favourite in no time."

"Got it." Brooke smiled.

"By the way, your sex hair is on point this morning."

"Hey!" Brooke scowled, tweaking JJ's nipple.

"Ow!" JJ ruffled Brooke's hair even further until Brooke swatted her hand away. "So are we getting dressed and spilling the beans?"

This reminded JJ of the time she'd walked in on Jess and Remi almost kissing the weekend Jess moved in. Oh, how the tables had turned!

Fifteen minutes later, they'd neatened themselves up to be presentable and made their way out of the bedroom.

Brooke inhaled. "Is that coffee?"

"And pancakes?" JJ questioned. They found Jess behind the stove, indeed cooking pancakes, while Remi sat at their dining room table with a laptop. Both women froze as the two of them padded out.

Jess kept her eyes down on the frying pan, the tips of her ears pink, while Remi hid behind a mug.

"Morning, ladies," JJ greeted.

"Morning," they replied.

"Before you say anything," Jess added, "sorry about barging in before and bringing Remi over without checking. We had a delay on a part to pick up around the corner, so I figured I'd make us breakfast instead of hanging around —and I thought you'd be at work."

"I booked the morning off." JJ grabbed Brooke's hand, drawing the attention of both other women in the room. "And no need to ask permission for your girlfriend to come over. I'm not your mum—this is your house too, Jess. Now, to the question you both really want to know—yes, Brooke and I are dating. No, we won't be taking questions at this time. We're still figuring that shit out ourselves."

Brooke smiled and squeezed her hand.

Remi lowered her mug, the biggest shit-eating grin on her face. "I'm happy for you two. And you don't need to explain to us." She shared a look with Jess. "We get it."

Jess brought a stack of pancakes over to the table. "We're here to chat over brekkie if you want."

After what they'd got up to last night? Food was necessary.

But first, coffee.

Sitting down to eat with the three of them felt surreal. On the trip, she'd pictured this moment, wondering if she'd be friends with Brooke, or if they'd stay in touch at all—yet here they were, as much, much more.

Of course, there were still many unanswered questions between them. How would they work long term? How would Brooke fit around JJ's current work schedule? For once, JJ didn't have all the answers and didn't have a plan—

and for the first time, she didn't care. They were winging it, one day at a time and figuring it out, together.

She didn't know what the future held, but neither did anyone else. So she sat in the present: Brooke by her side, piping hot spontaneous pancakes on her plate, and some of the best friends she could ask for sitting right across from her with the biggest grins.

Yeah, this was right where she was meant to be, because the best things in life couldn't be planned.

Time to live outside those lines.

THIRTY-SEVEN

Brooke

Brooke set down her knife and fork. *Here goes nothing.*

"So, I'm thinking of starting my own business."

JJ turned to regard her, mouth stuffed full of pancake like a chipmunk. "Whahp?" she said through her food, rounding on her. She swallowed. "Didn't you just start that new job?"

"I can tell you right now, pick packing in a warehouse is not my calling, not even for the money. But I was talking to Hayley and I got this idea. She said to speak to all of you."

"Doing what?" Jess asked, taking a sip of coffee.

"Travel. But not a run-of-the-mill agent. I want to tailor experiences for people. Maybe trial some services to either build their itinerary or organise it and travel with them as a guide. Kind of like what I did for JJ." Brooke's cheeks reddened. Maybe not *exactly* like that. "I'm not a hundred percent sure yet," she added.

With what little research she'd done, Brooke hadn't come across anyone else providing the same type of services. Everything was the same: a cruise through Alaska, go visit the Eiffel Tower or head up to see the hot spring monkeys in Japan.

Once Brooke started, the ideas kept coming. She could team up with local small businesses, have food themed itineraries or make up trips for thrill-seekers. The options were endless, and no two trips would be the same. Each person or group would be catered to exactly. Saying her plans out loud to the girls had the hairs standing on the back of her neck. This is what she was meant to be doing. And surrounding herself with the right people was how she was going to make it happen.

"Seeing as it looks like I'll be sticking around here for the foreseeable future"—she smiled at JJ—"I figured I might as well have a crack at making something of myself, and well, you all know what you're doing."

Remi laughed hard at that. "First rule of business, Brooke: no one knows what the hell they're doing. We all just wing it and keep doing what sticks."

"Noted. Well, maybe you can at least teach me what sticks while I figure out the rest."

Remi eyed Jess with a grin. "Yeah, I'm sure we could teach you a thing or two."

A thing or two turned into an hour-long session of questions, tips, and a rough business plan. Jess was all work, pen at the ready, scribbling down every word like she was taking minutes. For people who Brooke had hardly said a word to since she'd been back, Brooke was filled with gratitude for the lengths Jess and Remi went to in helping to make this dream of hers come true.

For the first time it felt like Brooke was finally building something for herself. A little slice of Brooke that wasn't about getting away; it was about staying put and growing roots—but not too many. Travel was still in her future, part of her life. But now she had more balance, an opportunity for stability, routine, and surrounding herself with good people in her life. Ones who wanted her to stick around, to help her, and accept Brooke for who she was. No judgments.

Later that morning, JJ drove her home.

"Keep driving."

"But your house is right there," JJ said.

"I know."

JJ raised an eyebrow but did as she was told.

Last night was the first time Brooke had slept with someone and *not* kicked them out straight after. No scooping up her clothes and fleeing outside a random house or hostel room barefoot. Her stomach hadn't dropped at her choices and her skin didn't itch to be cleaned. She gazed at the woman driving, still in her space, still *wanting* to be in her space. Brooke smiled.

What a difference a month could make. The streetlights flew past the window, just random metal poles during the day, waiting to be of use once the sun set. Brooke pointed to a car park for JJ to slot into. The bike path was a whir of life. Dog walkers, mums with prams, and cyclists whizzing in between.

"Where are we going?" JJ asked, taking her hand as they strolled across the path and down to the grassy bank. The frogs were quiet, but the reeds still rustled in the morning breeze. "You'll see."

They hit the water's edge. There was no one else around down here. No one took the time to explore and see what was right in front of them—they stuck to the bike paths, the safe paths. Brooke led JJ between the tall reeds, towering a metre above them on both sides. There. The small gap. Blink and you'd miss it.

"Follow me." She parted the reeds.

One. Two. Three—Four.

JJ pulled a face at the rocks, eyebrows furrowing.

"You can do it," Brooke encouraged, arms held out.

JJ leaped, hopped, and jumped into Brooke's arms.

"Got you!"

Brooke sat on the cold surface, running her hand along the rock as JJ took a seat beside her.

Hidden behind the reeds in the middle of the river, even during the daytime, it felt like there was no one else around. JJ looked around in apparent wonder, taking in all the details.

Brooke took a deep breath, her hand finding JJ's thigh. Always touching. Grounding.

The water was still today, reflecting the blue sky, the odd puff of white cloud and all the river gum trees lining the bank. They hung over the water, creating dappled light that made the water sparkle.

"Those times I needed to get away from home, I'd always come here. We grew up a couple of streets away from Hayley's house, down that street over there." She pointed vaguely in the direction of her old home. "So this area has always been home to me. But this spot in particular was always something more. Like if things weren't going well at home or school, I could come here and just be me. Zero expectations."

"This is a pretty amazing spot. I don't even know how

you found it, it's so hidden. And here I was thinking I was cool growing up playing in my backyard between Gran's veggies and fruit trees. Kid-me would've loved this place."

"It's pretty special."

Brooke picked up a pebble, feeling the soft edges worn smooth over time, a tiny chip in the top, not quite perfect. She played with it between her fingers.

"I brought you here because when I first returned, I found myself back here again and again. Not quite fitting in, not knowing where to go or what to do, and wishing I was anywhere but here."

JJ held her gaze, patient.

"Then I met you. My escape. My ticket out of here. I didn't care if the destination wasn't where I wanted, I was away from home. I feel like I have to apologise for using you that way."

"You don't have to—"

"No, I do. While I'm so thankful for how it all turned out, I needed to get that off my chest. To tell you the truth. In the short time we've got to know each other, you've come to mean a lot to me, and you deserve to know everything, even the bits I don't like to talk about. It feels nice that you see me and listen to me anyway," she said with a simple shrug. "That I can just be me."

Brooke threw the pebble in the water as JJ tossed one in at the same time.

Ripples formed, overlapping each other.

Again, and again, and again.

"Trust me when I say—I see you, Brooke Mayfield. And I love what I see."

The buzzy feeling in Brooke's stomach grew until she couldn't contain it anymore.

"Now you're gonna make me cry." Brooke sniffed, wiping under her eyes with her sleeve. "Ugh, god. Between you and Hayley with all your nice words and caring and stuff." She gave a watery laugh. "I don't do deep and emotional."

"No?" JJ checked. "I call bullshit on that."

Brooke side-eyed her.

"I'm pretty sure you're good at nice words and caring and stuff too." JJ grinned broadly. "Especially the stuff though. You're really good at stuff. And things."

Brooke sputtered out a laugh. "You're so stupid."

"You love it."

Brooke nudged into JJ, grabbing her arm at the same time and resting her head on JJ's shoulder. "Can we stay like this forever?"

"I wish. But I gotta get your butt back home soon because this gal needs to get to work."

"When do I get to see you next?"

"Whenever you want," JJ said, kissing her forehead.

"Tonight?"

JJ chuckled. "I think that can be arranged, though we actually have to get some sleep tonight, or I'm not going to be painting between any lines tomorrow."

Brooke screwed up her face. "Mmm, no promises!"

Epilogue - Brooke

Three Months Later...

Brooke heaved another box through the entrance and kicked the heavy wooden and glass doors shut with a bang. She blew her hair out of her face, but her vision was still obscured by the jungle sprouting from the box in her arms. She plonked the plants on the floor beside the makeshift fold-out table-slash-desk in the middle of the office. She straightened and stretched her back. Damn, that one was heavy. And there were three more boxes waiting in the back of Remi's ute.

"By the time we're done decorating, there's gonna be no room to move in here!" Brooke flopped into the seat next to Jess, grabbing her water bottle and guzzling it down. Necessary.

"Stop sookin'. The plants will liven up the space, you know—tropical with a touch of luxe, *and* they improve the air quality." JJ pointed her paint roller at Brooke.

"I guess you tradie ladies are the experts." Brooke pulled her hair up in a high pony to get some air on her neck. How she was overheated in the middle of winter was beyond her. Too much running around, and still so much to do.

"Can you pass me the screwdriver?" Remi asked Jess.

"Which one?" Jess leaned back in her chair, barely looking as she shuffled her hand around in the toolbag.

"Phillips."

Jess held the requested tool out for Remi.

"Thanks." Remi grabbed it, but not before leaning over and kissing Jess on the lips.

"So unprofessional," Brooke joked. They were sickeningly cute together.

"You're just jealous your *girlfriend* is all the way over the other side of the room," Remi countered as she went back to putting the desk together.

JJ was painting the walls of the office a soft pastel yellow. She looked over her shoulder, giving Brooke a wink without stopping. The roller smacked the ceiling, a bright splodge of yellow on the freshly painted white surface.

JJ froze, staring at the obvious mark. Her shoulders shook with laughter. "Well, that's what I get for being distracted."

"Not the first time I've made you go out the lines." Brooke winked back at her, the tips of JJ's ears reddening as she grabbed a cloth to clean it up. Their date night artwork now hung proudly above JJ's bed; marking the true beginning of their journey together, pushing boundaries and pushing each other to be the truest versions of themselves.

Dating JJ these last three months had been nothing short of magic. Because it was easy, like breathing air—

second nature. That wasn't to say it was *easy* easy. Nothing ever is. Only that whenever Brooke was with JJ, everything just made sense. Every obstacle they came across, they worked through together, just like they had when they were travelling. Reflecting back, their trip had been a good look at how well they worked together as a couple, even when the worst came to pass like breaking down in the middle of nowhere. And now that all those silly holiday fling rules were firmly left back on Kangaroo Island, they'd certainly explored new boundaries and new rules in the bedroom, especially when JJ liked to—

"I brought coffees!" Hayley said, nudging the front door open with her butt as Marie rushed in past her.

Brooke's face heated as she turned to the girls barging into the room.

"And I've got croissants!" Marie waved the box around, then dropped them on the table.

"Watch it!" Jess yanked a folder out of the way just in time and placed it in front of Brooke.

It was all systems go at *Mayfield Experiences*.

Because Brooke owned a business now.

Brooke Mayfield: business owner.

How was this real life?

Brooke would've been fine starting up in her bedroom at Hayley's, but Remi and Jess would have none of that. A month later, they'd found a government-led initiative and grant for a small office space that included free rent for a year. The catch being it needed renovating. When Remi had slung the idea past them at dinner one night, the collective tradie ladies had lit up so bright that there was no way Brooke could say no.

So here she was. A little office to call her own, filled with friends and family buzzing about to help make this a reality for her.

"Open the folder!" Jess leaned forward, her chair screeching closer to Brooke on the polished cement floors. Hayley and Marie sat opposite them, waiting, their eyes on the folder too. Weird.

"Okay, jeez. I thought we'd finished all the paperwork for the office. How is there more?"

She opened it, looking for the little yellow "sign here" stickers. Instead, there were a bunch of notes and scribbles on Indonesia.

Brooke frowned, scanning the text. "What's this?"

"Your first clients," Hayley said with a bright smile.

"What?" Brooke repeated. Everyone had eyes on her, waiting. "Who?"

"Us!" everyone called out in unison, throwing up their arms and laughing.

"Hang on, what? What do you mean, 'all of you'?"

"We're going to Indonesia, baby!" JJ said, arms wrapping around her from behind.

"I'm so confused."

Hayley grabbed her hands from across the table. "Listen, Taylor and Sam are eloping in Indonesia—"

"—and there's no way in hell we're missing our bestie's wedding," Jess added.

"Damn straight." Marie nodded, crumbs flying everywhere as she shoved the last piece of a croissant in her mouth.

"When we told the girls about your business plans, we thought who better to organise our travel and make it the best trip ever, than my very own sister?" The way Hayley's eyes sparkled at that statement had a lump forming in Brooke's throat. Everyone was still watching, waiting for her reaction.

She burst into tears.

It was too much, too kind, too nice.

She was surrounded by the most beautiful, thoughtful souls she could ask for. How had it taken her this many years to finally feel like she was home, accepted by everyone around her?

"Aww, Brookie." Jess rubbed her arm.

JJ held her tight.

Hayley squeezed her hands.

Brooke Mayfield wasn't alone anymore. No more *Just Brooke*.

She was Brooke Mayfield: friend, sister, partner.

She'd found her place in the world.

And it had nothing to do with Adelaide—though, that wasn't so bad after all.

Acknowledgments

I can't believe this is book three of The Tradie Lady series already!

As I write these words, I wasn't even a published author this time last year, but I think it's safe to say that writing has well and truly sunk its claws into my soul.

I didn't think it was possible to have this much love for the sapphic community as much as I loved it as a reader, but my love for this community has grown exponentially. I love being a part of something that's so magical, and fun, and such a beautiful space that I'm so thankful to be a part of each and every day.

You are why I write.

So that's where I want to start: with my gratitude. I wouldn't be here writing these love stories if it wasn't from the community that came before me. The authors, the readers, the reviewers and everyone in between that grew this space to what it is today for sapphic books to have an audience and a space that is more necessary than ever before.

Anywhere But Here was such a wild ride. I had an absolute ball taking Brooke and JJ on their journey, and I hope you also fell a little bit in love with Adelaide by the end of it too. My home state will always have a special spot in my heart, and being able to show that on one very epic road trip adventure meant a lot. On the writing side of things, wow, that was a hard one. Some stories come easier than others, and it took me a long time to work out where Brooke and JJ would end up. Maybe I secretly never wanted their road trip to end? But I'm so glad they finished up where they did.

Thanks to all my readers, I can't tell you enough how much you're all absolute legends. Thanks for reading, for talking about my books, sharing them, and most importantly, reviewing. It makes such a difference as an indie author! Special shout out to Luiza for her support.

Thanks to my beta team for your time, your thoughts and your hilarious reactions to my words. You certainly know how to bring a smile to my face!

Thanks to my editors. To Kathryn, I've never had so much fun and hard work rolled into one very tight manuscript. What a collab. I honestly can't wait to write more just for the chance to work together again. Just don't get too booked out in the meantime (kidding, please do, because you're bloody awesome). Thank you for pushing me with this one, I appreciate you. To Chloe, thanks for absolutely smashing through the proofreading and putting in all those necessary commas. PS. I still want to spell it woah instead of whoa.

Finally, to my wife, Laura. The bestest alpha reader in the world, and now my official cover designer too. (She's over on IG as @drawnbybls if you wanna be nosy!) Is there anything you can't do? Bloody love you to bits, and yes, I'll take you on that road trip now!

Rian xx

About the Author

Rian Birch writes fun and witty sapphic rom-coms for fans of low-angst romance who love a splash of emotional growth with their happily ever after. The perfect balance of sweet and spicy with a good dash of Aussie humour.

She lives in Adelaide with her wife where she likes to potter in her backyard food forest and cycle to new cafes around the city. Every one of her childhood stories ended with her characters coming home and having a cup of tea. She promises to write new endings for her adult novels.

Also by Rian Pirch

Swept Up In You

Tradie Lady Series Book 1

Swept Up In You is a fun and spicy lesbian romance that will have you laughing, crying and craving puppy cuddles.

Perfect for fans of low angst romance, who love a splash of emotional growth with their happily ever after.

Samantha Garner dreams of sailing away. If only her family business didn't have her completely anchored down. A conversation has her plotting new paths that may just get her out to sea, *if* she can avoid hurting the people she loves most.

Taylor Scott knows what she wants. To build up her maintenance business, forget about her ex, and to not—*definitely not*—get into another relationship. Discovering a new boat shop by accident lands her a client she didn't expect and can't take her eyes off.

As their friendship grows, a games night leads to a spark they can't ignore. While Sam questions everything she knows, Taylor must decide whether to keep her heart safe... or dive into the unknown.

Will they find common ground and sail off into the sunset, or will their relationship sink to the bottom before it even begins?

—

On The Right Path

Tradie Lady Series Book 2

Get ready for a sweet and sexy sapphic workplace romance full of new beginnings, witty banter and delicious tension.

Things have been heading downhill for Jessica Reaves. Underpaid and overworked, her waitressing job has her at her limits. Top that with feeling abandoned by her best friend and a boyfriend who's more like a man-child than a partner, and she's in *no* mood to celebrate her 30th birthday.

Remi Pearce is about to land the biggest building contract of her life, except she's down an apprentice and desperate to find another tradie lady to join her team. When Jess serves Remi one night, Remi offers her the chance to escape her job and start an apprenticeship.

For Jess, shaking up her life completely could have more flow on effects than she realises. As her new career builds, so do her feelings for her boss. So when a worksite injury threatens to bring Remi's dreams crashing down—it brings them closer than they can handle.

When professional boundaries slip into dangerous desire, embers flame and lines blur. Will Remi and Jess lead each other onto the right path? Or will they lose themselves even further?

Pick up a power tool and embark on a journey of learning to trust yourself—from the ground up—in this next instalment of the Tradie Lady Series, an interconnected set of standalones from sapphic author Rian Birch.

www.ingramcontent.com/pod-product-compliance
Lightning Source LLC
LaVergne TN
LVHW091019080826
845145LV00002B/300